Praise for *The Journey*

"As soon as I began reading, I couldn't put it down and read it in one sitting. Rasmussen has a talent for pulling the reader in from the very first page. I can't wait to see what he comes up with next. 5-stars!"
— AMY LOUISE HILL,
Readers' Favorite

"Stunning! One of the most provocative and engaging books I've read in years. The Journey takes you on a wild ride that becomes increasingly more riveting with every turn of the page. Rasmussen is a tour de force, weaving literary magic with beautiful music in a format unlike any other I've seen. A must read!"
— JENNIFER JUVENELLE,
author of *Daughter of Belial*

"An ultimately upbeat novel with an engaging hero. Our verdict: Get it!"
— *Kirkus Reviews*

"It's a rollicking road adventure… and those seeking a character who undertakes a life-changing journey, will find *The Journey* epic on a psychological level that draws all ages."
— D. DONOVAN, Senior Reviewer,
Midwest Book Review

"Excellently penned and emotionally accomplished, in this dark, intense, and deeply interesting novel, Mark T. Rasmussen rewards readers with a fascinating tale of transformation. *The Journey* is a novel that I enjoyed a lot. 5-stars!"

– K.C. FINN,
Readers' Favorite

"An engaging, satisfying journey with a number of distinctive moments arising throughout, Rasmussen delivers an impactful story!" – *BookLife*

"I was not expecting to enjoy this novel as much as I did. Once I started reading, I just couldn't put it down. Mark T. Rasmussen did a great job of conveying the main character's emotions purely and evocatively. While the ending was not predictable at all. I thoroughly enjoyed it!"

– RABIA TANVEER,
Readers' Favorite

THE JOURNEY

MARK T. RASMUSSEN

BY THE PURE SEA BOOKS
Written From The Heart, Made With Love

For permissions contact: Mark Rasmussen at mark.rasmussen72@gmail.com

www.marktrasmussen.com
Published by, *By the Pure Sea Books*
Los Angeles, CA

The publisher is not responsible for websites (or their content) that are not owned by the publisher.

ISBN 979-8-9867231-5-0 (paperback)
ISBN 979-8-9867231-8-1 (hardcover)
ISBN 979-8-9867231-9-8 (ebook)

Publisher's Cataloging-in-Publication Data
provided by Five Rainbows Cataloging Services

Names: Rasmussen, Mark T., 1972- author.
Title: The journey : no matter how far you run, your demons always follow /
    Mark T. Rasmussen.
Description: Los Angeles : By The Pure Sea Books, 2022.
Identifiers: LCCN 2022916680 (print) | ISBN 979-8-9867231-5-0 (paperback) |
    ISBN 979-8-9867231-8-1 (hardcover) | ISBN 979-8-9867231-3-6 (ebook)
Subjects: LCSH: Men--Fiction. | Voyages and travels--Fiction. | Midlife crisis--Fiction. |
    Family life--Fiction. | Rape--Fiction. | Redemption--Fiction. | BISAC: FICTION /
    Literary. | FICTION / Romance / Action & Adventure. | FICTION / Family Life /
    General. | GSAFD: Road fiction.
Classification: LCC PS3618.U86 J68 2022 (print) | LCC PS3618.U86 (ebook) | DDC
    813/.6--dc23.

Cover design by Richard Ljoenes
Cover artwork by Jean-Marie Gitard
Interior design by Stewart A. Williams

Printed in Australia and The United States of America

First Edition Paperback 2022

Dedicated to my beautiful, happy, always smiling son, Kailan.
Long may your adventurous spirit and loving energy shine.
I hope I make you proud.
Para Siempre,
Dada.
xoxo

AUTHOR'S NOTE

This book does things a bit differently, insomuch that it's semi-interactive. By interactive, I mean that there are featured songs, sprinkled throughout the novel. In the e-book version, you have the ability to click directly onto the song title itself and listen instantly to that same song. This is deliberate on my part, because I wanted my readers to be able to hear and listen to that exact song, to feel the mood of the main character, setting and moment. I also included this option for anyone unfamiliar with any particular song who likes to put a book down and seek out that song. Now you can do it right here!

Of course, you can completely ignore the song link and continue to read like you normally would, free of any musical distractions and sounds in the background. For those readers who prefer this method, I have created a page at the end, where I list 'The Journey's entire playlist. I did this to save any interested readers the time to go back through the book and find a specific song (or songs), that they wanted to hear, didn't know, or were simply curious by.

If you are a reader who can listen to music as you read, and are excited by the prospect of this fun little feature, then know that as I was writing this story, more often than not, that exact song was playing in the background while I wrote.

As a genuine lover of almost all forms of music, this was my way to give those interested, a look into my writing process.

I hope you derive as much pleasure from my music choices, as you do from my novel. Rock on!

"The journey of a 1000 miles begins with a single step."
~ Lao Tzu

1

The Hardest Decision

It's 3:17am, Tuesday morning. I sit with a cooling cup of tea staring at the freshly written letter. It's sealed, the envelope carefully placed next to her phone where I know she will see it.

I take a deep breath. This is the hardest decision I've ever had to make and having made it doesn't offer me any comfort. I've decided to not only leave my relationship, but one containing an unborn child–I'm the father.

But I'm not just leaving her... them, but this city. A city I've never warmed to. One that is so frigid and uninviting, I've often wondered if it reflects my own state of mind or a mirror for the relationship I have endured.

I take one last sip of tea. The liquid now tastes bitter. I move from where I've been sitting with guilt reflecting on the gravity of my decision, and as quietly as I can, I place my cup in the sink and wash it. Ironic, given that after all these months I would leave it in the sink until there were a few more things to wash, but today is different. Today I am breaking the heart of the woman I love.

I place the cup in the dish rack to dry. I gaze one last time through the expansive windows that stare out into a part of Toronto that I'll never miss with its endless concrete, steel and glass. It's one tall, soulless building after another. They're all devoid of any imagination or creative design.

I gather up the only bag I was able to secretly conceal the night before, with what things I could all packed tight inside. It won't be enough but it will have to do.

With a heaviness in my heart, my hand rests upon the cold metal handle of the front door and lingers, unable to move, before my fingers slowly wrap around it. With a slight twist I step into the open corridor, where the rush of air from the building's heating system hits me. It takes me a second to catch my breath. I close the door as quietly as I can behind me and lock it. I then gently open the mail slot and slip the key back inside. The clang as it hits the tiled floor below, reverberates around my head long after the key comes to a quiet rest.

Despite the early hour, the elevator takes much longer to arrive than usual. Perhaps it's a sign. Maybe it's not too late to turn around, knock on the door, ask for forgiveness. Is it possible I can make it work? Or that she can be less reproving?

The elevator dings, then opens. I stand immobilised.

Right before it closes I slink forward. It swallows me with a thud. The sudden descent makes me stumble and I reach for the side rail to brace myself. I catch my sad reflection in the surrounding mirrors, knowing this decision will haunt me for a long time to come, possibly the rest of my life.

When I arrive at the ground floor, the doors slide open and cool air rushes in towards me, though the coldness I feel isn't from the outside. I take one last look back at myself. My eyes can't hide the anguish.

I walk out of it into the foyer before I'm faced with the last door and the final thing between me and… I can't find the words. It's not fear, nor is it even remorse. It feels more like cowardice, yet it's deeper than that.

I take a beat. A lone tear stains my cheek. I don't wipe it away as I step outside, preferring instead to feel the sting. The freezing winter wind whips up around my face, a temperature that seems fitting.

I turn up my collar, zip the winter jacket up as high as it will go. I take a look back at the place I've called a home for the past three years. Other than fleeting moments, there are few happy memories here. I reach into my pocket, fumble inside, then press play on my iPod. Moby's haunting 'Memory Gospel' sears through me while its deep pipe-organs seem to echo throughout the still sleeping city.

I take a single step, and just like that, I've begun a new journey. One where I hope to rediscover myself, seek some sort of absolution, or at the very least, an uneasy peace. It may be little consolation but it's all I have.

2

Hollow Plan

I'm scared of failing. Scared I'm not ready for fatherhood. Scared of scarring my child without even knowing it. Mostly though, I'm scared of turning my kid into someone like me.

But then, how could I leave behind the only woman who accepted me, flaws, fluctuating moods, depression, frustrations and all, for an uncertain path? A path that I'm sure will provoke more questions than offer solace or provide answers.

I'm no good to them until I can find myself, and so believe that my girlfriend, Clea and our unborn child, will be better off without me. Maybe I'll be better off without her. I mean, we all have our breaking point.

While I am questioning my decision, everything feels like it's moving in slow motion, like one tiny grain of sand after another is slipping through my fingers, and the tighter I grip, the more the sand slips through them. I'm reminded of Oliver Tank's delicate song, 'Grain Of Sand' that scalds deep and reiterates the pain in my heart.

Honestly, I am unequipped to face up to the biggest responsibility of my life–that of being a father. How can I be? My own dad cast me aside when I was six, leaving the onus resting on my mum's already overburdened shoulders. A load she attempted to do her best with but in truth failed. Although, I couldn't have done any worse than my own often absent, abusive dad.

While the scars have faded and the memories are hazy, I still carry the baggage that comes with years of verbal, physical and emotional abuse. Like everyone else, I have a breaking point. Seems it came right when I was about to undertake the biggest, most radical change in my entire life. A change that involved raising a child.

I've had no father figure to look up to or mentor to guide me, let alone a male figure of any note. None ever stuck around long enough to make an impression or leave a meaningful impact.

There's also the unexplained impulse to seek out a past flame. Someone I had an intense, passionate and deep love affair with back in Los Angeles, and a connection that's been gnawing at me for months now. While I know it's feeble and feels incidental, I'd be lying if I said it hasn't played a small part in my leaving.

But ultimately, I'm scared.

That's the best answer I can give right now.

While I am aiming to chart my way southwest down to Mexico and maybe end up on a beach to write if it doesn't go the way I hope in Los Angeles, I know I'm directionless. There is no real plan here. While this hasn't been made on a whim, the fact I have a quasi-destination in mind offers little consolation.

As the wind howls up the empty streets, with no cars, blaring sirens, endless construction noise, or cold people, this city feels peaceful, nearly liveable. Nearly that is.

I know I won't be walking the whole way but this inconspicuous, discreet start feels right. Despite the freezing cold,

I find that with every step I take I undergo a sense of relief. While I feel terrible about walking out on Clea and leaving her to bear our baby alone, I know in my heart it's the right thing to do.

The constant arguments and disagreements, the lack of physical touch or any real affection, all of it has driven a wedge between us, which will only grow with the addition of another more demanding little human who'll need full attention.

Sure, that sounds selfish, and perhaps I could have pushed through, tried to work out our differences, even endured this city, but with every conversation we had, the sooner we neared yet another heated argument or worse, stone cold silence. We'd tried couples counselling but I always found them more draining than helpful. I knew they were designed to bring us closer, but it all felt like a ruse, a false dawn... a lie!

It was beginning to seem like we were only with each other out of obligation. I convinced myself that if there were no baby in the picture, she would have ended it months ago. She had told me many times, she felt let down by what I promised versus what I did. I knew I wasn't pulling my weight or contributing equally–financially and emotionally–so was I salvaging pride or just being selfish? Probably both, but in all honesty, I was struggling with the weight of expectations being placed upon me from her, and from myself on me.

I was unable to keep up with all these new demands and pressures associated with parenting and fatherhood. I was constantly being asked to study this book, look at that website, listen to this podcast, read that blog. The books, websites, blogs and podcasts weren't helping. I simply felt overwhelmed and despite my best efforts to appease her, I resisted even learning about parenting. Why?

That was a question I hadn't been able to answer. I had gone through so many changes in an attempt to continually better myself for this relationship, that I simply drowned under the expectations of it all. I no longer felt like changing. I had no desire, no will, to yet again undergo another transformation.

Surely there's an end point, a reason for all this constant growth. Maybe I'm wrong. Perhaps we change just to adapt to a current situation to fit in better with our environment. I'm sick of fitting in. I'm fucking tired of change. I want easy. I want peace. I just want to fucking be.

Yet here I was always being reminded at every moment by those who felt the need to share their unwelcome opinions, how a baby changes you, how it's "the making of a man". To me, it seemed like they had resigned themselves to their own pitiful fate and were simply trying to convince the rest of us that parenting was pure bliss. I knew firsthand by the hands and fists of my own dad, that that was not always the case.

If that wasn't enough to convince me, any parents I saw always looked exhausted. They'd do their best to smile and talk up the benefits of raising a child but underneath it all, I knew it was bullshit. You could feel their struggles and their own self-doubts or worse, the lingering 'what if' had they chosen a different path. I could always see the envy in their eyes when I, or their other childfree friends, talked about their latest overseas adventure or the kickarse band they got to see at one of those late-night gigs or my favourite, sleeping in late on weekends. I wasn't about to fall into the trap or succumb to their miserable fate.

So I made a decision to leave, taking all my personal problems and inner demons, and fled. Sure, I had my issues, namely my sex starved, hungry demons (which were always present), instructing me to tap any female who caught my eye. An eye that has wandered more than once in the past. While I had never done so in my current relationship–something I might add I had worked at and was proud of–I knew it was only a matter of time before I caved into them. Once born, I knew I couldn't bear to look my child in the eyes, knowing I'd succumbed and strayed behind the back of the woman who gave birth to my child.

Even though I loved Clea, I knew full well I couldn't outrun my demons. They'd always haunt me no matter whether I ran thousands of miles away, or whether I confronted them head on. Even if I did manage to cut any down, a new one always rose up in more menacing form. So rather than have them plod about the small apartment and scare my baby, perhaps shadowing my youngster for the rest of my life, I had to escape. In a way, I was doing this for my child and shielding them from my own personal nightmares, battles and mental scars.

My mind wasn't convinced. The debate in my head knew that it was a flawed, fragile logic full of holes, so I took the easy road and opted out.

I hear the sound of a car approach, then slow behind me. By now it has started snowing and the wind is a brutal Arctic howl. I know I won't last too long out here.

I'm about to try to thumb a lift, hoping someone will take sympathy on my desperation. However, I don't have to when the car slows, then comes to a complete stop. The driver cracks the passenger side window open a smidgen.

"Where you headed?" the male voice inside asks.

I bend down to speak into the tiny interstice, where I am hit with the instant heat inside the vehicle that escapes outward through the small opening. Even through the narrow gap, it warms my bones.

"Buffalo," comes my meek response.

"Buffalo, eh?"

I'm too cold to reply.

"Got no idea why anyone in their right mind would be out in the middle of the night in this weather, but you're in luck. I'm heading there myself. Got some *business* to take care of."

Even if he did put extra emphasis on the word, making sure to enunciate it for me, I feign interest in the business he has. After a brief moment the door lock clicks open.

If he knew just how tormented my mind was, he'd have kept going. I hesitate for a moment. This is it, I think to myself. Once I step inside the car, my decision to leave is real. I suck in a long, cold breath as an icy wind whips my legs. It's all the motivation I need to step inside.

As I plop down, the car's heater suddenly makes me feel nauseous. This wasn't only goodbye to a city, it was a sad farewell to the only woman who not only put up with me, but verily seemed to care about me. And here I was abandoning her in her greatest moment of need. It's such an arsehole act. I sigh.

"Everything all right?", the driver asks.

"Just getting nostalgic."

Thankfully, he doesn't push me to further explain. It's not entirely accurate, yet it is. I know I will miss her.

When the car drives away, I turn toward the passenger window and let the tears roll. No amount of justification for my selfish decision will ever hide the enormity of what I've done.

3

Think Fast, Act Faster

The drive was done in silence, save for small talk. I found out Steve, my driver and saviour, worked in insurance banking. He had a wife, two young kids, with a third on the way, and that was it. To his credit, he never pushed me to reveal anything about myself. Maybe he sensed my unrest.

The short one hour drive didn't give me any comfort. If anything, it only brought up more questions and self-doubt. I wouldn't have to think about them for now because the US-Canada border approached.

It was still dark when Steve pulled over to the side of the road. The sun wouldn't be up for at least another two hours.

"I think it's best if we both go to the border separately. We wouldn't want to arouse suspicion."

Arouse suspicion? What the hell was he talking about? If anything, pulling off to the side of the road just shy of the check point would be much more suspicious but I didn't have the energy to argue the point. I thanked him for the ride, got out into the crisp morning air and eyed the border ahead.

In relation to other US entry points I'd made before, the Canada-US Buffalo border crossing was smaller than I expected. As a result, things seemed less hectic here. It could also be the hour of the morning I find myself here.

I throw my bag up onto my back and walk the two hundred metres or so to the entrance. Even at five in the morning, there are still a few cars, trucks, and buses wanting to cross. I am the sole pedestrian. As soon as I open the heavy doors to enter the building, all eyes are on me. Suspicious or not, I am a drifter, a misfit, and out of place.

I watch the car I had sat in just minutes earlier, be waved through and over the border. Just like that, Steve is in America... I on the other hand, was more nervous than usual. While my Australian passport was valid, my US work visa had expired during the year. I don't think it will present a problem but it might.

I wasn't yet able to legally work in Canada because I was still waiting and waiting for Canadian bureaucracy to grant me that opportunity. It had been a major hurdle in my relationship with Clea, given it put most of the financial burden on her, although ironically it now seemed like I was mere months away from finally being granted a work permit and thus, would be able to contribute much more than I had.

But I felt more a freeloader, and less a man as a result. It always gnawed at me. And it's ironic, given that although my US work visa had expired, I not only had a valid ESTA travel visa, but stamped right across the front of my US Social Security card were the words, 'Valid to Work'.

I could, if I wanted to, work here and contribute to my child's upbringing but that would mean living apart. Something I had raised with Clea as a short-term fix until I was granted a work permit, but she never went for it. Regardless, that is not my modus operandi here.

Every time you enter the United States, there's always this overzealous approach, like everyone is a terrorist suspect or fugitive. For all their hoopla about being the land of the free, this country more than any of the 50+ others I have travelled through, was the least welcoming and most oppressed of all.

I force a smile at the guard who doesn't return it.

"Passport," he says in an authoritative tone.

He checks it over, asks the obligatory questions, '*What brings you to the United States? Where are you headed?*' I've learned over the years the best answers are the shortest, most honest ones.

"A woman."

"In Buffalo?"

"L.A."

Immediately I regret this as it piques his interest.

"It's a long way to Los Angeles by foot," he retorts.

I felt like going the slow way, I want to reply, but I know this will just rile him, so I say the most honest thing I can.

"I'll be bussing the rest of the way."

"Where will you be staying?"

"Hotels and a couple of friends' places in between."

He senses a weak spot, so drills further.

"What friends? Where?"

I revert back to my short, direct responses. "Detroit, Memphis, Dallas." Two of the places I have actual friends in.

"How long do you plan to stay in the United States?"

"Only a few weeks before I fly home," I say hoping the interrogation will ease up.

"You already have an onward ticket?"

If I lie here, I know he'll want proof.

"No," I resign.

"So how do I know you won't stay longer? Do you have money to fly home?"

I feel cornered, unsure of what he's looking for, so I keep

the half-truths going.

"I've got three bank accounts, one here in the U.S, two back home in Australia. There are more than enough funds, sir." I add the sir to let him know I know he's in charge.

"And what do you do for work?"

Man, is this guy ever going to let up? He's clearly looking for a chink in my armour so he can deny me entry. I don't give him one, even though I begin to shift my weight slowly from one foot to the other.

"I'm a freelance journalist and writer. Here's my International Journalism card," I say and begin to fumble for it from inside its small, red wallet. When I pull it out, I cover the recently expired date with a well placed thumb. Thankfully, he doesn't take it from my grasp.

Seeing the card seems to satisfy him, however, as he enters a few details into his computer. I smile. Bad mistake.

"Do you also have bank statements?"

This throws me. If I falter here, he'll deny me entry. I have to think fast.

"Of course. I don't travel without them. If you just give me a minute, I'll dig them out of my bag."

Before he can answer, I start placing one thing after another on the small desk. First other documentation, which are really former itineraries, old airline ticket stubs, boarding passes, and so on. While I'm doing this, the door opens and a horde of Chinese tourists file through.

At first I'm perplexed, until I see the coach nearby. I keep digging into my bag, though I can tell he's frustrated knowing he now has to go through about 40 foreign passports and ask questions to people where English is not their first language.

"Place your fingers on the pad," he barks.

I do as I'm told.

"Look into the camera."

I follow his orders.

He stamps my passport with force and tosses it back on the counter. Just like that, I'm in the United States. I hurriedly scoop up my passport and snatch up my belongings, haphazardly throwing them into my bag. I exit before he can change his mind.

I know I got lucky and dodged a bullet. If not for the busload of Chinese holiday makers, I'm not sure whether he would have approved my entry. I had no bank statements, nor enough cash in any of my accounts to support this undertaking. Perhaps the biggest invention of all, that I'm a "writer", couldn't be further from the truth.

I haven't written anything in over six months. I feel like a fraud. I start to get despondent as that thought sinks in. I try not to dwell on it and make a small promise to myself to eat Chinese tonight, thankful for their intrusion.

I place my passport back into its pouch and breathe a sigh of relief. I look at the cover of it, its gold coat of arms catches the first rays of morning light. It's then that it hits me. It's my Australian passport that saved me, that, and being a white male. Two things I've learned on my many sojourns abroad are the safest, nonthreatening elements to gain entry, as long as you don't count the crazed, white gunmen within U.S borders. But I'm neither crazy, as debatable as that might seem at present, nor have I ever owned a gun. There's no denying though, that as a white, Australian male, I'm given preferential treatment.

I don't like admitting that where you come from affects how you're viewed or treated, but I know better. Clea is living proof. Being Colombian has always been a hindrance when travelling. Even though it's been 20 plus years since Pablo

Escobar was killed, the world still believes every Colombian is either a drug lord or drug mule. Blame sensationalist American news media or television drama. Being Australian, however, well, we're practically treated like royalty or distant cousins. It's a blessing, I'll admit.

While I'm not some beer swilling, flag waving, patriotic Aussie who bellows out that cringeworthy catch cry, 'Aussie Aussie Aussie, Oi Oi Oi,' today I'm grateful for being one. I even whistle a few lines from 'Waltzing Matilda' as I walk.

My mind soon gets drawn back to Clea and the problems she has as a Colombian flying in and out of most countries. When I think about her alone and with a baby, needing to travel back home for family support, I cease whistling.

Even though the early morning sun begins to poke out from the low-slung clouds, my mood becomes dark. It's knowing that she'll be awake and up by now, will have read the letter, and no doubt in tears. She's probably called my phone a hundred times and left a thousand texts. It sits in my pocket, turned off while I sit on the roadside barrier feeling like shit.

A small slither of morning sunlight reflects off a nearby vehicle's window and catches my eye. I look up to notice the bus the Chinese tourists came in on, waiting there off to the side for them to return. A sign above its windscreen reads, Pittsburgh. Could be worse.

I ponder it a moment, then pick myself up and march over. When I reach the bus, I notice the door is open with the driver nowhere to be seen. I look around, seize my moment and slip inside. I walk the narrow aisle where I spy tourist guidebooks, ostentatious handbags and other items, littered over the seats. I look for an empty seat and find one towards the back. I plop down and place my bag on the seat next to me.

Once comfortable, I make a second promise to myself to tip a Chinese waiter tonight to make up for it. Just a little something to show my appreciation.

I'm startled from my thoughts when I hear another passenger clamber up the steps. I sink a little lower into my seat so as not to be seen. However, I needn't worry because he doesn't notice me. Instead, he plonks down somewhere near the middle and huffs impatiently while he waits for the others to return. It'll take some time before the bus fills up, so I place the hood of my jacket up over my head, zip it up as high it will go, and lean against the window. It's not long before I've drifted off to sleep.

4

Waitress From Hell

It's the sound of the air brakes that stir me from my slumber. A slew of passengers chatter animatedly about our current stop as they gather up their possessions in an excited state and cram the aisle, eager to file out. It makes me wonder if Pittsburgh is some hidden new tourist wonderland I don't know about.

I wipe the sleep from my eyes and peer out the window. It's a grey, overcast day at the Pittsburgh bus station, in what is very much a modern architect's vision of the "future" for bus terminals. To me, it's just a failed attempt to reclaim the existing space and modernise it.

I get up and join the last remaining passengers and file my way out. The bus driver gives me a quizzical look when I walk by. I just bow my head and smile before I exit the bus. A big clock face indicates it's 12:07pm. My stomach growls in desperation to remind me it's long overdue for a feed.

I realise I haven't eaten since I ate dinner with Clea last night, a delicious home cooked stew she lovingly slaved over. Despite the uncomfortable silence as we ate, I could never fault Clea for her cooking. The culinary dishes she made were always scrumptious. I'll miss them.

I shake it off and let my feet carry me to the nearest diner, which is teeming with other lonely souls all chewing down on life's disappointments. As soon as I sit down I'm greeted by an overweight, late 50's woman, who looks like she's been in the job far too long. She grunts when I enter, seeing me as nothing more than a disruption to her day.

"Whattya want?", she spits.

"Can I see a menu?"

She swipes one from a customer at the counter and slaps it down in front of me.

"Better?"

"Much."

"Coffee," she asserts, not waiting for my response.

She proceeds to pour a thick, black, sludge into a cup. Normally I find these types amusing but for whatever reason I am intimidated. That, and I don't even drink coffee.

"Err, can I have a cup of tea instead?"

"Whatever you say, Your Majesty," she snaps.

She seizes up the cup, tosses the black liquid into the nearby sink. Rather than give me a clean cup, she pours a pale, watery grey tea back into the same cup and slams it down on the counter in front of me. A quarter of its contents splash onto the counter.

"Happy, Your Highness?" she remarks.

"Yes. Thank you."

"Should have guessed you were one of *those* types," she mutters under her breath but loud enough for me to hear.

One of what? I want to ask. I decide not to push it, instead I try to soften her by giving her a warm smile.

Just like the spilled tea, she ignores it.

"I'll be back, so hurry up and make up your mind," she barks before she tramps off to harangue the chef.

I stare into the dishwater before me, then dip my finger into the tepid, almost cool liquid. I want to ask for a hot, fresh cup but know I'll be pushing my luck.

I wait until she has her back turned and slide the cold cup of tea away from me. In doing so, however, I simply spread the spilled tea further across the counter. I grab the nearest napkin and do a quick mop up to avoid her wrath. Satisfied, I fling the napkin into the cup and watch it disappear under the surface. I sigh.

The waitress returns, proceeds to tap her pen impatiently on the pad. I give the greasy menu a quick once over and opt for the closest thing to healthy there is.

"Pancakes," I stammer.

"Maple syrup, jam or honey, princess?"

I want to ask for all of them but that'll just rile her.

"Jam's fine."

She rips the menu from my hands and storms her way back to the kitchen. Despite her brusque persona, she'd make one hell of a character I think to myself. Inspired, I pull out my journal from my bag and open to one of the many blank pages inside. However, instead of writing I simply stare at the last journal entry. 'Feb 10, She Arrives Today!'

I don't have to read it to know this was the moment Clea first came down to visit, when I was still living in Los Angeles. It was a happier, more exciting time. The headline reminder turns me away from the loose thought I had of writing and back to her. It catches me off guard.

While the thoughts torment the inside of my head, I hear Roxy Music's beautiful cover of 'Jealous Guy', play on the diner jukebox in the background. While I wasn't the jealous type, I wondered if I did feel some kind of envy or resentment about having a baby, which I knew would shift the dynamics of the relationship away from just us.

I was nervous about being a first-time father. I was worried about not being much of a provider. I was unsure about the baby. I wondered if I should care more for it than I did. But if I'm being candid, I felt detached from the baby. Stunned by the unexpected revelation, I shut the journal, and waited for the food to arrive.

5

Love Motel

After eating what were better than expected pancakes, my stomach is full and I feel satisfied. I sit to ponder my next move. It's funny, but without a plan I don't feel as free as I thought. With no real direction, let alone having a map on hand, the loose plans to make my way back to L.A. now seem misguided.

Despite only being after 2pm, I'm too tired to think. I'm also mentally exhausted. I stare out the window in despair when right there, across the lot opposite the diner, a small, discreet hotel advertising "low rates". Not only could I use a nap, but a place to formulate some kind of plan, perhaps even find a map to plot my next move.

I go to get up, when the waitress eyes me with a scowl. I had planned not to leave a tip, not because I wanted to save a few bucks but because the service was sub-par. Her cold glare puts the fear of God in me and makes me change my mind. I reach into my pocket, grab a couple of dollars and some change, and drop it on the counter. She gives me a wry grin, which catches me off guard and I almost walk into the sliding glass door on my way out.

I take the few steps across the road and as I get closer, I

can see it's not much of a hotel. It's not much of anything. Cigarette butts, spat out gum which has blackened, and empty beer cans litter the front entrance. Despite my reluctance (and best judgement), I need sleep so trudge in regardless. The small bell on the top of the door announces my entry.

Behind protective glass sits a smug attendant counting out a wad of fifty-dollar bills. The badge on his tight polyester shirt reads 'Manager'. He draws hard on his cigarette and through whitened, glossy teeth, gives me a smarmy smile.

"What can I do for ya?" he drawls, puffing smoke out towards me.

"A room," I say brushing away the smoke cloud.

"One or two hours?"

It takes me a minute to realise exactly what this *fine* establishment is. I almost leave but my eyes are heavy and I'm not sure they'll stay open much longer.

"How much for a whole night?"

He almost chokes on his cigarette. I'm guessing he doesn't get this request often.

"Six hours minimum, loss of rentals during that time... that's $150!"

"Why so much?"

"You're taking up my best business hours."

"Surely you have an overnight rate?"

"No."

"I'm tired. I just need a cheap room for the night. Can you do any better?" I say, hopeful.

"Just you?"

"Yes."

"No crooked business?"

"No!"

"No private entertaining?"

"No."

"Will you be drinking?"

"No."

"Smoking?"

"No."

"Drugs?"

"Definitely not," I say agitated, not realising I'd have to answer 20 questions.

"$65 then," he replies.

"Fine, $65."

"But no dirty business, no bringing a working girl back to your room, no drugs (hard or soft), no outside alcohol, nothing. If you do, it'll cost you more than triple. Understood?" he says, eyeing me with a dubious raised eyebrow.

"Understood," I begrudge.

"Oh, and you change your own sheets. No maid or cleaning services either," he retorts.

"Fine," I sigh.

"ID and credit card."

I already have it out and fling it under the glass. It makes a clatter on the silver tray. Licking at his cigarette-stained fingers, he grabs at the cards, studies the licence, then me, then back at the licence before he figures I'm legit. I'm almost tempted to pay more so the maid can clean my cards after he's done.

He gets up off his seat, which has a permanent indention shaped to his arse, and takes five steps to the photocopy machine. I watch him huff and puff as he lifts the flap, places the cards down onto it, then bends low to flick the power switch on. He's red faced by the time he hits the copy button.

The copier splutters to life before the familiar green light grinds and whirs its way from one side to the next. He repeats the struggle from before as he lifts the flap, takes out my ID and credit card, closes the lid, turns off the power button and in a forced exertion, pulls the power cord out. I look on as sweat beads pool, then fall from his forehead, and I wonder why he bothers to go through all this effort when he'd be doing it on a regular basis. I get my answer when the photocopier hisses in agony before it spews out a noxious cloud of some unknown matter into the air. He switches on the nearby desk fan, directs it at the smoke, which proceeds to blow away the dark mass until it disperses, then clicks the fan off.

He hands over my cards and slides across a piece of paperwork for me to sign. There's no pen on hand, so he just points to the coffee table opposite. When I finally spy one, I wonder why he doesn't provide a pen in the first place but it seems like everything is an effort for this guy. I sign my name and slide the paper and pen back across. He takes the paper but points back to the coffee table. Confused, it takes me a minute to realise before I pick up the pen and drop it back on top of the table.

Satisfied, he hands back a key that comes attached to a big, red, glittery love heart with the number '12' scrawled on its side in black marker. I have to suppress a chuckle at its tackiness. I wait for directions but when none come I make my way towards the door before I'm stopped by a disturbing, hacked cough.

I look back towards him and instantly regret it because when I do, he hocks up some phlegm and spits it straight into a glass that's half full of god knows what. I'm not sure if I feel sick, disgusted or both. I cannot exit fast enough when under a strained, forced breath I hear.

"Outside, down the far side of the parking lot on your right."

"And clean sheets?"

"The maid will be along soon enough," he squeezes out before another smoker's coughing fit takes over.

The stale stench of discarded cigarettes and dry, warm beer hits me on my way out. I walk quickly through the parking lot, where the air feels a little cleaner.

With the jangle of the love heart key in hand, I look up and spot room number 12. It's on the lower right, near a flight of stairs. Most of the rooms are partially curtained off, though even in the bright glare of day, there's the unmissable low glow of dimmed lights. Most seem occupied, which surprises me given the time of day.

I reach my room, enter the key in the door and unlock it. I'm immediately hit with a barrage of foul smells. I recognise the unmistakable linger of musky sex in the air but the rest, I don't even want to take a guess at. I rip apart the curtains to unlatch a window, which is tricky given it's on a twisted rail track. I manage to get it partially ajar as best I can. I decide to leave the door wide open to air out the room and wait until the maid comes to drop off my sheets.

I grab the nearest chair and place it outside my room and sit. Despite my tired state, I'm not putting my head or body anywhere near those pillows or the bed. At least not until I'm given a fresh set of sheets and the room has been deodorised.

While I wait, I try to imagine what Clea is up to. Being a weekday, rather than face the prospect of work with a broken heart, I am sure she called in sick to stay home and try to make sense of my leaving. She's probably not eaten, even though putting on weight is crucial to the development and health of the baby. I am sure she's drafted, crafted and re-written an email she wants me to read. Something she used to do regularly whenever we had problems that remained unresolved. And knowing how fragile Cancerian's are, no doubt there have been tears.

My heart also feels the void. While it may not seem like it, I'm a sensitive soul too, and being a Libran, I am way off balance. I really could use a hug, though not as much as Clea.

Before I can get too emotional, an early 20s Mexican girl, in that typical pastel blue and white maid's outfit they all universally seem to wear, looks at me with confusion. At least I think it's confusion. It could be pity given where I am staying. She does her best to wheel along a trolley full of fresh linen and cleaning products. I say best, because the trolley has a wonky wheel that she constantly has to fight against to keep it pointed straight.

When she reaches my room, her eyes look to the ground in that shy, timid way Mexican women seem to do when they think they're disturbing you. She hands me some sheets and pillowcases, then moves onto the next room.

"Hola," I call out. "Limpio, por favor!"

She turns, wags her finger and shakes her head, no. Instead, she bends over and pulls out a deodoriser can and tosses it at me. Despite my dismay, she carries on with her duties and leaves me with a can of, "Sweet Comfort"–'A soft, sweet fragrance with a touch of the South!', it proclaims on the front. Before I can protest, she disappears into the next room.

I spray the fragrance in the air to test it and immediately repel in disgust. South where? I wonder. Before I hazard a guess, a door opens to my right and a pudgy, middle-aged business man, his shirt flaps untucked, fly half unzipped, steps out. When he sees me, he smiles in that secret 'boy's club' kind of way men do when sharing unspoken, common knowledge. I don't return it. He lowers his head, doing his best to tuck and zip everything in and can't seem to get into his car quick enough.

A minute later, a long pair of fishnet legs in red stilettos exits. My eyes move slowly upwards and meet the owner. A mid-30s, maybe older, exotic, mixed race female, readjusts herself and gives that fake, confident, always-on-the-clock smile all hookers wear. For some reason, I return her smile with a genuine one, which disarms her when I see her body relax. She seems to contemplate coming over to say hello, but she opts to head to the manager's office instead. Clearly, he gets a cut of whatever she just made.

I re-enter my room, where the smell seems less repulsive than the 'Sweet Comfort' air freshener. I strip the sheets and pillowcases off and replace them with the clean set. Once in place, I'm not overly convinced they're that clean. There's a few marks and faded stains, which no amount of heavy cleaning will ever remove. I wonder how thoroughly they get laundered. I contemplate whether to ask for a better, cleaner set but my head needs a pillow, my body needs sleep. I close the door behind me and as soon as I hit horizontal, I'm out.

6

The Whore

It's after 11pm when I wake, or more aptly, get woken up. The sound of a squeaky mattress and a woman's over-the-top moans in the room above, bring me out of my sleep. While I'm not one to listen in on other people having sex, the paper-thin walls and flooring make me a spectator whether I like it or not.

As I have no choice other than to listen in, I can't help but laugh out loud. Not at the constant 'squeak squeak' of the mattress, or of a woman clearly faking to appease her lover, but at the man's choice of words to her.

"You like that, don't cha baby?"

"You love smoking papa's big pipe," among other cringe-worthy comments I can make out.

First, if you have to ask her if she likes "that", then you're not paying close enough attention. Second, any man that has to throw in 'big pipe', is usually always under-endowed. It's just a fact!

As much as I'm getting a giggle out of it, I can't bear to listen anymore. I also don't want to be there to hear his grand "finale". I get up off the bed, wash my face in the bathroom sink, then pat it dry. When I walk back into the room to get dressed, it happens.

"Oh Gawd, Oh Gawd, Oh Gawd, I'm comin', I'm comin', I'm..." followed by the obligatory, and quite frankly, disturbing groans that follow as he does.

Whether I wanted to or not, I'm forced to be a part of the moment. While I didn't need to hear it, I can't help but laugh out loud. In between bursts of laughter, I yell back, "Way to go, Papa."

I hear the woman chuckle before the man storms off towards the bathroom to regather what's left of his dignity. I change out of my dirty t-shirt and into a clean, long-sleeved shirt. I snatch up a jacket, grab my wallet, slip it inside my jean pocket and make for the door, but something's missing. I pat myself down when I spy the ostentatious love heart key on the desk. I scoop it up and walk out.

The hotel's parking lot is a mix of vehicles, some parked, others just cruising through. There's a few people milling about between a couple of them, and even from my vantage point, I can tell most are in the middle of some kind of transaction. It's impossible to tell these days between a pimp and a pusher. It's not impossible, however, to tell I stand out like a sore thumb. I sense many eyes follow me, while I see money put back in pockets as I saunter through the motel's carpark.

It's enough to make most people feel uncomfortable but I've been in enough countries with higher crime rates, and more desperate miscreants, to care. That doesn't mean I'm not cautious, just not so uptight or vigilant about it.

A wolf whistle rings out from the edge of an unseen doorway, which I ignore, but it's quickly followed by a female's voice.

"Want some company, handsome?"

Before I can decline her invitation, I hear the slam of a door and a woman's high heels catch up to me on the asphalt.

"You must be the quiet, sensitive type," she announces.

When I turn to face the voice, I'm surprised to see it belongs to the long-legged, exotic female I saw earlier. Now that's she's in front of me, however, and even with the ageing signs of her profession on her face, she's way more attractive than I'd first realised.

"More observant than quiet, and sensitive only when needed," I retort.

"With just the right amount of sarcasm," she quips. "Looks like I've found my date for dinner," she says with a chuckle.

"Sorry, I'm not buying."

"Relax honey, I'm not on the take. Just seeking some decent company to eat with."

"No offence but isn't this rush hour," I say looking out over the carpark.

"Every hour's rush hour around here. Besides, I could use the break, my back's killing me."

I'm not sure how to respond but then she bumps into me and says, "Though, I'd actually have to be on my back for it to hurt," she taunts, laughing again.

It's a warm, loveable laugh. The kind you can't help but get swept up in, which I now find myself doing.

"So how about that dinner date then? On me," she adds.

I stand a moment, mulling the offer in my head. I'm trying to determine if she's setting me up or actually genuine. She can tell I'm weighing up those exact thoughts.

"I don't bite… not unless you want me to," she grins before she snaps her teeth at me in jest. "What harm can come from a free dinner with a beautiful woman?"

A lot, I want to say. Only when the cheekiness disappears, replaced with a more sincere smile, do I relent.

"Okay, but just one drink," I respond, giving her a nudge,

which comes off more awkward than playful.

"Good, for a minute there I thought I was going to have set my pimp on you."

I hesitate, my body tensing up.

"Relax darlin', I'm just messing with you. I'd actually have to have one before I could do that," she jokes.

I breathe a sigh of relief and let my body slacken.

"Brianna," she adds, extending her hand.

"Raiden," I reply, shaking her soft, chestnut coloured hand.

"Ooh, cool name. Wonder if you're as fun to play as the old arcade game of the same name."

"I get that a lot, but it's pronounced Ry-den, not Ray-den."

"Sure it is. Let's see if I can be your top score. Come on, let's run," she grins, before she tugs my arm and sprints off.

This woman has spirit. I like that. I'd forgotten how to have fun, so without thinking, I give chase.

Even in heels she's got grace and poise. I find myself in a small trance as I jog after her. My eyes unable to take their gaze off her toned, firm behind, which entices with every move it makes from inside her tight, electric blue short dress.

When she stops suddenly, I almost bump into her. Brianna knows I've been staring, and rather than act all coy and de mure, opts instead, to give her butt a shake all for my benefit.

"Pilates and Zumba three times a week, and a tonne of squats," she beams.

I'm embarrassed I got caught out. I don't know what to say, so I go with the first thing that comes to mind.

"Whatever it is, it's working."

"In my line of business, you're only as good as your ass."

With that, she grabs my hand in an almost intimate gesture. For a split second I think she's about to place it upon her derrière, but rather, she leads me into a restaurant I hadn't noticed we were standing in front of.

"Best butternut squash and pumpkin ravioli," she mouths.

Brianna opens the front doors and leads me through the main entrance where we wait to be greeted. While we stand, I notice many eyes are on her, with men sneaking glances when their wives or girlfriends aren't looking. When our host approaches, she smiles at me before she notices my companion. The smile disappears. She plucks two menus from the stand and without a word, leads us towards a table near the back. I catch almost every man's gaze while I walk behind Brianna, some envious, others almost congratulating me. I also see the women and their apparent revulsion or jealousy upon seeing her revealing, figure-hugging dress, but Brianna walks on by either oblivious or not seeming to care.

We plonk down on opposite sides of the table in a small booth. I'm about to say something when she beats me to it.

"You get used to it. It comes with the territory of my job. But how much fun is it to see all the dirty looks women give?" she smirks.

I smile and nod in agreement, amazed she knew my question.

"You want to know the ironic thing? If these women spent half as much time on their bedroom techniques and bodies as they do on clothes and makeup, their men wouldn't have any need for my services. I'll never understand their petty insecurities and jealousy."

Before I can respond, a waitress is at our table.

"Can I get you both a drink?"

"We'll have a bottle of your finest red please. We're celebrating," Brianna says in a triumphant tone.

"We are?" I enquire.

"Of course. I'm quitting the industry and you look like you

could use a travel companion, not to mention a drink to loosen up. Why so stiff?" she asks.

I'm astounded by her boldness and caught off guard.

The young waitress suppresses a chuckle before she walks away to fetch the wine.

"Call it intuition, honey," she exclaims before lighting up a cigarillo.

I can already see a few customers get uncomfortable when the smoke plume rises from her lips and floats out over towards them. Sexy, sassy, unfazed… I like her.

Our waitress returns with a bottle of 2007 vintage shiraz, and presents it to us.

"Great year," I smile.

"Why's that?" asks Brianna.

"The year my beloved Geelong Cats football club finally broke their drought and won the AFL premiership," I smirk.

"No idea what that means but here's to felines," she purrs.

Confident we're happy with her selection, the waitress opens the shiraz, pours it into our glasses and places the bottle on the table.

Brianna clinks my glass and exhales another cloud of smoke.

"Err… Miss, you're not supposed to smoke in here," the waitress says in an unconvincing, non-plussed way.

"If you get any grief, tell Antonio, Be-Be says hello," before she winks at the girl.

The waitress shrugs her shoulders while admiring Brianna's assuredness. She already knows it won't matter whether the other customers complain.

"Can I take your order?"

"Yes, two butternut squash and pumpkin raviolis, with a side dish of sautéed veggies for me, a mixed salad for him,"

Brianna replies, flicking her eyes at my paunch.

The waitress removes the unopened menus, then hurries off to attend another table.

"Tony and I go way back," she says, answering before I ask.

"So, tell me your story, Mr. Australia. What brings you to this landfill of the world?"

"Most Americans always think I'm British."

"Most Americans are ignorant."

I feel my head dip forward in agreement.

"I've gotten to know my fair share of Aussies *downunder*. While a little rough around the edges, they tend to treat a woman with more respect than their US counterparts. They've also got great stamina and love going south," she giggles out loud.

While it's not directed at me, I can't help thinking she's testing me, feeling me out, and flirting in that professional way they do to lure you in. I know that I don't buy she's quitting the industry.

The food arrives part way through our conversation and as soon as I take my first bite, I can see why she ordered it. It's good, seriously bloody good. In between talking and the food, the wine is going down a little too easy. Aware I'm with a hooker who's always on the take, I try to watch my intake. But the more I drink, the more I open up, and the more I open up, the more I reveal.

Over the next couple of hours I proceed to tell her my story, albeit a truncated version, though I do tell her how I came to be here. If there's one hard lesson I've learned over the years, it's to be upfront and honest, no matter what.

To her credit she doesn't judge, just listens. As I prattle on, she nods in places, sympathises in others, while at one point she places a warm, caring hand atop mine. I convince myself it's more in reassurance than anything else but the gesture could be construed to mean something else if my mind lets it.

When we drink from a second bottle of wine, I feel relaxed enough to tell her of my loose plans to head as far south as I can, hoping to land in Mexico. When I'm done speaking, there's a long pause. Brianna cocks her head ever so slightly to one side and studies me before centring it again.

"What are you *really* doing?"

I hesitate for a moment, not sure what to say. My eyes avert her stare while I muse. Lying doesn't seem a choice, given she sees straight through any crap. I take a deep breath and exhale the air slowly out.

"Running away... mostly to give myself some time and space to think things through.

"I don't buy it."

"You don't need to," I say defensively.

"There's more to your story."

I stay silent, wanting the questioning to end.

"Call it women's intuition but there's something you're holding back and not telling me."

"Let's just drop it, okay?" I beg.

"Why? What do I care?"

"Can we move on?"

"Not until you tell me why you really left," she presses.

"Forget it. There's no other reason."

"Yes there is."

"No, there isn't."

"You're just like every other man out there. Too much of a coward to speak your truth," she spits out.

I don't believe there's any real malice in her rebuke, but it strikes a chord nonetheless. Forced to think about her comment, I ponder what I have to lose. I'm not one to open myself up all that easily, especially with someone I just met.

"Honey, if you really had anything to hide, you'd have hidden it already. I just know bullshit when I hear it."

"That so?"

"Quit the delay tactics."

"You're unrelenting," I reply.

There's a tense pause between us. It's clear if I don't speak up, she won't talk and the night comes to a premature end. I'm not ready to call it a night just yet, so I take a deep breath and give a reluctant sigh. When I exhale, I open up.

"When I hit 40, I figured fatherhood had just passed me by, and so I made peace with it. But then at 44, my girlfriend got pregnant and my world got flipped on its head. I thought I'd be really happy, and for a time I was, getting swept up in her excitement. However, when reality finally dawned on me, I discovered I didn't share her joy. So like any major problem I've ever had to face, the only way I knew how to deal with it was to run! And so, rightly or wrongly, here I am."

She examines me, says nothing. I carry on to fill the silence.

"On top of that, I'm carrying around this foolish notion of believing I can rekindle something with a former flame back in L.A. Although that relationship now feels disingenuous, given I haven't heard a thing from her in over 12 months, so the likelihood of anything happening there seems absurd."

I breathe in deep when I'm finally done.

"Happy?"

"Only if you are."

I mull her response over in my mind for a moment. Am I happy with that? I'd be lying if I said I was. While I'm not looking to justify my decision, I don't find a suitable answer. What comes up instead though, is that sitting opposite someone free of judgement and opinion, means I'm better able to ponder my actions. I may not like the process or her line of direct questioning when she pushes back on me, however, it forces me to think about my choices, and why I took them.

While Brianna provides a tough, yet attentive audience, maybe now's as good a time as any to hear her take on it. Even though I may not like the response, I swallow my pride and just flat out ask her what she honestly thinks.

"A lesser person would judge and condemn your perceived spinelessness for running out on her, but I can tell you're genuine and think it's the best thing to do for you. I can also see you're hurting by your decision, so don't be too hard on yourself. There are a lot worse things out there in the world than leaving a pregnant partner, believe me. You're a saint compared to the sinners I've run with."

"What do you mean?"

"Look honey, I've been spat on, shat on, had too many cum facials and been called a whore more times than I can remember. I've been beaten, kicked, raped, shot at, had two abortions, and done a short stint in jail for false drug possession charges, all while getting harassed on a daily basis. In short, I've experienced the worst of men where my best days with them have been dreaming of the afterlife. Your mind is a mix of emotions and while you don't need lip service from the likes of me, be gentler on yourself."

Her honest responses floor me. Whether it's what I need to hear or not, I want to reach over and give her a hug, yet I don't want to blur the lines or give off the wrong signal. I'm feeling a little vulnerable after opening up, but also lightheaded after drinking way more wine than usual. It might explain why my eyes feel as if they're about to well up.

"Maybe we both need a breath of fresh air to clear our foggy heads," she says catching my forlorn expression.

I shake my head in agreement. Brianna reaches into her purse and places some money on the table. I offer to contribute but she won't hear it.

"Tonight's on me, remember? We're meant to be celebrating, not commiserating. The least you can do is hold my hand like a gentleman on the walk back," she suggests.

It's a slow, silent walk back to the hotel. When we arrive, I'm surprised that there's very little activity given it should be prime time for action.

"Most men can explain staying back late at the office for a couple of hours, but not coming home at one or two in the morning on a weekday," she says, reading my mind.

She walks with me to my room because after the wine, I'm a little more unsteady on my feet. When we get there, I'm not sure whether she will want a kiss or expects to come in. I fumble with my keys to delay any decision I might regret but then drop them. Brianna bends down and picks them up. In one swift movement, she grabs my nervous hand, holds it steady, then uses the key to open the door, before she hands them back.

Since I'm not thinking straight, I'm also anxious. There's a long pause before she leans in and my body tenses up as a result. This is the moment, I think to myself, the moment a kiss is about to come. I get nervous and freeze but she does something unexpected. She wraps both her arms around me in a tight, warm hug and simply holds me.

A sigh escapes my body before it relaxes into her soft embrace. It's the most unanticipated thing I could have imagined, yet it's perfect. I draw my arms up and enfold her. We stand, holding one another for what feels longer than normal. I'm not sure if I need it more or she does.

When Brianna eventually lets go, she smiles, then gives

me a quick peck on the cheek.

"Thanks for an *intriguing* evening," she says. Brianna then turns and leaves.

My eyes follow her shapely form, that glittering, electric blue dress of hers seeming to shimmer even brighter in the blackness of the night. It's an image that lingers long in my mind, even after she's disappeared from view. While I'm grateful the night ended where it did, I'm unsure what I would have done had it possibly gone any further. I ponder that thought as I enter my room and close the door behind me. Once inside, I emit a long, deep, audible sigh of relief, thankful I didn't have to find out.

7

Wild Ride

Sometime around 3am, I hear a loud argument outside. There's lots of yelling, swearing, and what sounds like a scuffle, followed by a punch or three. I also hear glass being smashed onto the ground followed by more verbal threats. It's hard to place exactly where it's coming from because it sounds like there are a few people involved, with their voices echoing through the thinness of the night air. I don't bother getting up. Whatever it is, it's none of my business. It all simmers down almost as quick as it began. While I'm able to drift back to sleep, it's a fitful slumber.

Around 8am or so, I hear a knock on the door. At first, it's a light tap but because it's so gentle, I think it's for next door. But the rap gets louder on my door. I get out of bed, still tired from a disrupted night's sleep and groggy from the amount of wine I consumed last night. It makes it feel like my brain's two sizes too big for my head. In short, I feel worse for wear.

I scramble around for my boxer briefs, and as I slide them on I lose my balance. I crash sideways onto the floor and whack the side of my head on the desk for my troubles. I gingerly get back to my feet feeling a little dazed and rub my sore head as I open the door.

"And I thought I had a rough night," half jokes Brianna.

It takes a moment for my eyes to adjust to the harsh glare of the bright morning light outside. When I'm able to focus, I see that she sports a black eye, and a fist sized bruise on the right side of her face.

"Let's blow this dump. Be ready in 20 minutes," Brianna orders before she marches off.

It takes me 40 minutes, but I can tell she's not happy about the delay. She stands by the side of her car, tapping impatiently on the roof of an immaculate, mid '60s Pontiac GTO. I give her a sheepish apology and throw my bag into the open boot of her car. When I close it and look up, Brianna's already in the driver's seat. I hear the click of the ignition key, then with agitated frustration, she revs the motor hard to hurry me up. The engine roars to life as if it's got 100 angry tigers caged underneath its hood.

I clamber into the passenger seat and before I can even pull the seatbelt over myself, Brianna smokes up the tyres and spills out onto the road sideways. Two cars have to take evasive action and swerve out the way in order to miss us. They honk their horns in fury, which only agitates Brianna further. In one swift motion, she extends her arm out of the open window, raises her middle finger in the air and gives them a what for as we thunder down the road.

She pushes a cassette into the old school tape deck and before I know it, I'm clobbered around the ears by Motley Crue's 'Kickstart My Heart' that blares at full volume. I manage to buckle my seatbelt into the slot and look over at her. Brianna's got big, black sunglasses on but even behind the wide lenses, I notice the single tear roll down her cheek. I opt to say nothing, instead just look out the window and watch as buildings, shops, and the city pass by in a hurried blur.

It's been a good hour or more since we left the hotel, yet we've remained silent throughout the whole drive. My stomach's been rumbling for the last 30 minutes and while it's not as loud as the big cats under the bonnet of this classic beast, it's roaring in defiance nonetheless. I take my chances and decide to break the silence.

"Hungry?" I enquire, quickly adding, "Brekkie's on me."

She's stone cold silent. I decide not to push it.

A couple of minutes tick by and then from out of nowhere, she turns the steering wheel hard left, my face slamming into the passenger window. Before I know what's going on, we slice across four lanes of traffic and beeline straight for a diner. We approach way too fast, and for a split second I think she wants to crash into it. I brace myself as best I can, while people scramble out the way. All of a sudden she hits the brakes hard, and the car comes to a screeching halt in a big, thick cloud of black smoke.

When the rubber haze dissipates, I notice a guy cower in front of us. The takeout food he had rests by his feet in a clump on the ground, and a spilled drink spreads its wet mark outward in his lap... or at least I think it's a drink, I just don't see a cup. He staggers to his feet, salvages what remains of his food, and shakily ambles off. Brianna's hands remain clenched on the wheel.

I just stare straight ahead and say nothing. Inside the diner, I observe a table of people clean up a mess I can't fully make out, their nerves no doubt frayed. After a moment, Brianna's hands unclench themselves from the wheel and rise up to her face. It looks like she's about to burst out crying.

"WHOOOA FUCK YEAH! That was fun," she bellows before exploding into a wild, raucous laugh.

I don't see the humour and yet, while I'm concerned,

somehow her manic laughter overtakes me, and I find myself inexplicably laughing along. We must look like a couple of deranged lunatics, sitting in her car cackling like hyenas. I'm sure everyone who was petrified for their lives, in and out of the diner, also don't see the funny side. They're probably more terrified now than before.

Forced to eat our food inside the car, something about *'not being welcome inside'*, gives us time to refuel and both relax. While Brianna continues to wear those dark shades of hers, her body language is calmer. Despite her facial bruises, she appears in pretty good spirits, even if she sits in a quietude in her thoughts.

"The fight didn't involve you, but it was about you," Brianna says breaking the silence.

I'm not sure if I'm meant to respond, so don't.

"I was supposed to get you drunk using my powers of persuasion, wait until you passed out, then steal your valuables. But you turned out to be an authentic, genuine guy. After you opened up the way you did last night, I couldn't bring myself to do it, to take advantage of you."

I take another bite of my veggie burger to process the information, although it's now harder to swallow.

"Some things you revealed last night resonated with me. I really felt your hurt and torment. You showed a vulnerability I've not seen from a man before. It also reopened my own wounds, wounds that have never fully healed."

I sit conflicted yet thankful for her frank admission.

"After we stood and hugged, I went back to my room and cried hard for the first time in a long time. When the tears stopped, I made a decision to alter my path and try to resolve my biggest regret. While I can't change what I did, I'm hoping my daughter will forgive me after all these years and want her mom back in her life. Now that she's 12, I don't know if she will, but I don't want to end up another haggard hooker still turning tricks at 50 to get by, so I have to try. I just hope my parents will be receptive to see me, after I dumped her with them when she was barely two years old."

While I'm listening to her revelation, I make out the familiar sounds of Mondo Cozmo's beautiful, and perhaps apt, 'Hold On To Me', playing from an open window of a nearby car's radio. I'm touched by Brianna's open statement but now I'm also wary and unsure how to respond. Last night I opened myself up to this woman a little too easily. If not for her change of heart, I would have been fleeced of all my possessions.

"You don't have to say anything, and I wouldn't blame you if you just got out and continued your journey alone. I know that's what I'd do. But I'm hoping that while I work on a plan to see my daughter again and get my life back on track, you can forgive me and allow me some more time to hopefully get to know the frightened little boy I see inside the man."

The last comment of hers hits its intended target. I do feel scared. I've so many thoughts swirling around my mind: anger, hurt, disappointment, confusion, empathy, that I take my time to mull over the most suitable response.

"Take all the time you want, just so long as you promise not to roll me," I jest as I place my hand on Brianna's arm.

She says nothing, just simply smiles at me. She then leans across, gives me a hug, and whispers, "thank you."

8

The Road Trip

We take turns driving until we're just too exhausted from the emotional whirlwind of the past 24 hours. We pull off the interstate and crawl into a place called Shady Springs, a tiny town in the middle of West Virginia. A town whose only claim to fame was when the future 19th president, Rutherford Hayes, passed through during the Civil War, the welcome sign read when we drove past it.

Shady Springs is a sleepy hollow of a village, with a population of just over 2300. It abuts the George Washington National Forest, which explains all the greenery we found ourselves in for the last two hours. We're on the lookout for a cheap dig to stay the night but we come up well short. The only place we find is Glade Springs Resort. The name alone makes it sound pricey. Given I've got limited funds, I baulk at it, but with no other options we're left with no choice other than to drive the extra mile or so to reach it.

As we pull into the long, sweeping driveway, we're greeted by a big holiday resort, which looks way out of place in such a small town. We pull up close to the entrance and park the car. We wait a moment, half expecting a valet to run out, but the place looks deserted. Brianna switches off the engine, and we both step out into the brisk night air.

When we enter the main foyer, we're instantly swallowed up by its capacious space. We give each other a look, aware this will be way out of our price range. Rather than waste our time, we start back towards the car but before we get more than two steps, a man appears from a side passageway and greets us.

"Welcome to Glade Springs Resort! I'm Gershwin, the hotel manager here," he says in that formal official way they do.

He extends his hand outward, which we feel obliged to shake. I'm surprised at the softness of his skin. For a man who looks to be in his late fifties, he's either a big fan of anti-ageing, rejuvenation creams or the springs that run through here are the fountain of youth.

"I'm sorry, I didn't know we were expecting any guests tonight. I could have vowed we had no reservations listed but let me double check. It is possible it's just an online booking glitch," he says with a look of consternation on his face.

Before we can stop him to say we won't be staying, he's gone back behind the front desk and scans the computer's register.

I catch Brianna's eye and it seems it'll be up to me to explain we won't be staying.

"I want to say hello Mr. & Mrs. Benedict, but they're not due until tomorrow, and looking at their registration details, you both look far too sprightly to be 83 and 81," he quips.

"Gershwin, is it?" I ask.

"That's right, named after the famous composer. My mom never liked the name George, so Gershwin it was," he says with a shrug of resignation.

"I think there's been a misunderstanding. We just drove down from Pittsburgh and were simply looking for a cheap place to crash for the night."

The expression on his face changes when he hears the word cheap. To his credit, he bounces straight back into that fake, warm smile and offers a suggestion he thinks is a "win-win".

"This is the last week we'll be open. Glade Springs shuts down for the winter season as things get real quiet in these parts this time of year. If you like, I could work out an agreeable deal, just don't tell anyone," he says with a serious tone.

He's got our attention, especially given Brianna mentioned on the drive that she was owed money. Money she will no longer see thanks to storming out of the hotel this morning.

"I can give you the Manager's 'end of season, one-night-only special' of $369. It's normally $549," he says in a hushed voice, even though we're the only ones here.

I give Brianna a 'what do you think look?'. She shakes her head no, letting me know it's out of her budget range too.

"I know it's a good deal but right now it's a little more than we'd like to spend. Are there any other places you can recommend that are a little less pricey?" I ask in hope.

His expression changes.

"Well, there's the Sleep-Inn Beaver back north in Bexley or the Knight's Inn further down south. Both are a good hour or more by car, but you get what you pay for," he says tersely.

"Can you give us a minute to chat?" I ask.

"Take all the time you need," Gershwin says, knowing he holds the balance of power given our predicament.

We move off to the side to discuss our options.

"What do you think?" I ask.

"It's too expensive," she says flatly. "But going back north is a waste of time and I'm too beat to head any further south."

Brianna takes off her sunglasses and I see the weariness in

her eyes. Even though the swelling around her eye has subsided, the blackness is still noticeable. As we speak softly among ourselves, I observe Gershwin scrutinise the markings on her face. He glances at me with a serious sternness.

Before we can make up our minds, Gershwin, who's been tapping away at the computer screen in front of him, interrupts in a voice loud enough for us to hear.

"Well, that's unexpected. There's a last minute, one night deal that went unclaimed," he announces tapping away on the computer. "It's $248 but doesn't include breakfast, mud-pack facial, or a complimentary bottle of champagne. However, the room comes with free access to the hot springs. I'll even turn on the outside gas heaters."

Brianna and I both look at each other. I know she's being given the 'I'm sorry for your arsehole boyfriend' treatment, but so be it. She nods.

"We'll take it," I exclaim.

Once we've provided all the necessary ID's and credit card information to satisfy the check in policy, he hands over the swipe card to our room.

"Is there anywhere we can possibly get a bite to eat at this time of night?" Brianna asks in desperation.

"Bunkers Sports Bar & Restaurant, but I think they've closed down for the winter. We usually have an on-duty, late night chef, but given we had no bookings for this evening, I sent him home two hours ago. If you like, I can whip you up a box of mac 'n cheese? It's the best I can do," he says apologetically.

"That sounds great," our tired voices say in unison.

"I'll bring it to your room once it's done."

I scoop up the swipe card, then proceed to follow his directions by taking the stairs up one level, before we walk down the long hall until we eventually find our room near the end. We step into the large, lavish room, and as soon as I close the door behind us, we both breathe a tired sigh of relief.

9

Too Hot Springs

Once we have demolished the mac 'n cheese, Brianna and I decide to head out to the hot springs. We change into the thick and luxurious, towelling hotel robes provided, and while I'm tempted to sneak a peek, I do the gentlemanly thing and keep my back to her as we do. Once we're both changed, we walk outside and follow the softly lit path to the rejuvenating springs.

The chilly air from the encroaching winter, dances and tingles over the exposed parts of our skin. Thankfully, with the fired up outdoor gas heaters lining the pathway, it's fleeting but as we near the water of the hot springs, the temperature becomes cooler. While the warmth provided is very welcome, the sharp variation between the cold is an unusual sensation.

The springs have been dug out and shaped to resemble a small, West Virginia State shaped pool. It's both kitsch and cute. I slide off my robe and stand there a moment in my board shorts, allowing the fluctuating air temperature to swirl around me. Eventually I succumb and jump into the inviting warm waters.

I notice there are small, bench-like seats that run along the side of the pool, hidden under the surface of the water. I position myself on one of them and look back up at Brianna, who has yet to take the plunge. Her eyes are closed, and she seems to be inviting the light breeze to flow all about her. I study her a moment, taking in her beauty, elegance and grace while she's in this semi-meditative state.

Even though Brianna's still dressed in the robe and not doing anything other than standing still, I can't help but appreciate the calmness that exudes from her pores. Despite her past and troubled life, she seems at peace with where she is in the world. Maybe it's a sign of the decision she made to go see her daughter that brings her serenity. When she opens her eyes, I give her a reassuring smile.

"Come on in. The water's incredible," I say, even though I'm content taking in the view.

Brianna gives me a wry smile before she slips out of the lush, white robe. To my amazement, she is completely naked. No bikini, bra, panties, nothing. She makes no attempt to cover up her nudity either, instead she just stands there in all her intoxicating glory as the cool breeze snakes its way across her skin until her goosebumps come alive.

Even in the low light, her figure is astonishing. She's toned and well-defined in all the right areas, yet has all the sumptuous lines and curves females are blessed with. Brianna catches my admiring eye, and rather than avert her gaze, she simply holds my stare. As a result, I don't know where to look without coming across as some lowlife perv. I'm left with no alternative than to give a sheepish smile and lower my eyes.

To avoid me any further embarrassment, in one fluid motion, Brianna dives gracefully into the water and ends the free peep show. While she is swimming under the water, I can't help but wonder if she's testing me or she's simply one of those women who's confident in their own skin and thinks nothing of being naked, regardless of the company they're in.

When her head breaks the surface of the water just a few feet away from me, my thoughts become diluted. While I watch the water trickle down the side of her face, I feel my pulse quicken. I'm aware my body has responded to her physical beauty, yet instinctively my mind races ahead with a myriad of possibilities. I desperately want to pull her in close and touch every inch of that exquisite physique. However, I also want her to keep her distance because I'm not sure I need, want, nor am ready to complicate my situation any further. But my god, that Goddess-like beauty!

When Brianna edges closer with a mischievous look in her eyes, I sense I'm about to find out. I attempt to keep my composure, or whatever's left of it, but inside, my heart and mind are racing. She creeps closer until she is directly in front of me. That sly, confident grin on her face is a total contrast to mine. As soon as I feel her hands on either side of my upper thighs, I start to quiver. But only when her expert fingers find the waistband of my shorts then rest inside it, do I really tremble. My heart's almost pounding out of my chest, while I can feel the nervous sweat beads that pool on my forehead fall down over my face. She licks her lips seductively, then leans in real close to me so that there's less than an inch which separates her mouth from mine.

I'm caught somewhere between her beguiling allure of the spell she's now cast over me, and that of total helplessness. Fleeing to the sanctuary of the room now no longer feels possible. I'm transfixed as I stare into her deep, dark liquid eyes… eyes which feel like they're boring straight into my soul. I've become so lost in them that whatever she wanted to do, I'd surrender. There's a deliberate pause and I feel the fever of anticipation soar, until Brianna presses her lips softly against mine.

My mind fights to keep my mouth closed and just when I think it will win, once I feel the slow heat of her breath, my lips begin to part ever so slightly to allow her in. What Brianna does next totally catches me off guard. The deep, passionate kiss I was expecting, doesn't come. Instead, she bites down hard on my lower lip then whips my board shorts down over my legs until they've been completely removed. Vulnerable, exposed... nervous, all I can do is watch my shorts float away in the gentle current of the pool. All the while, she never takes her eyes off me, just smiles. She's in full control.

"That's cheating," she says in a provocative whisper, referring to my shorts. She bursts out laughing and duck dives back under the water, where I get a quick glimpse of her delightful, exposed derrière before it disappears.

I sit there with flushed cheeks, embarrassed. What was I thinking? I'm not sure if I'm being played with, teased or she wants me to pursue her. When she resurfaces, the cheeky grin returns, but it's softer, less exploitative.

"Why the face, Raiden?"

"I... I don't know," I utter.

"You really think I was going to screw you–in here?"

"I thought we... that maybe..." I say trailing off, deflated.

"Oh honey, I'm a woman of the night. I don't ride bareback. You never know what nasties someone might have. If I want you, you'll know it, trust me. But it won't ever be in here, in these bacteria carrying waters," she chuckles.

In my mind, I keep hearing Whiskey Go-Go's '2 Cent Girl'. Some of the lyrics which are now echoing my own thoughts, in so much as I really feel taken for a ride. I must admit, even though I now know she was just playing, I feel a little rejected. Brianna picks up on it.

"I couldn't have you enjoy the sacred, healing waters while

wearing board shorts," she smiles. "Warm springs like these are *always* best enjoyed naked," she purrs.

Dejected, I shrug my shoulders.

"If you want to play and have fun with me, Raiden, you really have to loosen up. Do that, and who knows what might unfold," she simpers.

Oh, I think to myself, before concluding she's right. Ever since I left Clea, I've been tense, uptight and on edge. Maybe even long prior to that, before I made the decision to leave. While I may not be all that comfortable with what I've done, or at ease with it, I've known for a while I had to relax. Even my doctor advised it at my last check-up, after my physical (and mental health) had suffered.

"That so?" I retort. I then proceed to stand up on the seat fully out of the water, let go of my dignity as it all hangs out, and beat my chest Tarzan style. AHHH AAAAHHH AAAAHHH AAHH!

Brianna applauds before calling out, "Help me, Tarzan!" as she thrashes about in the water pretending to be in trouble. I beat my chest again then dive into the pool. When I emerge in front of her, now it's me wearing the mischievous grin. I pick her up and hoist her over my shoulder, giving her firm arse a playful smack. She giggles at my silliness before we both fall back underneath the water. We must make for a crazy pair.

When we surface, we come up laughing. The sexual heat I felt before disperses, replaced with a more chilled, relaxed and manageable vibe. The laughter soon gives way to a gentle silence save for the water, which laps delicately against the pool's edges. We spend the next two hours in the soothing waters, having one honest conversation after another.

"I chose Brianna because it means strong, virtuous and

honourable. And before you say it, yeah, I realise the irony given the profession I am in," she says with a grin. "Some days I really do feel like a Brianna, but in truth, my real name, Rachel, is probably more apt."

"Why's that?" I ask.

"Because I am a kind, caring, sweet person," she replies. "Rachel is meant to be a great person to have fun with, though sarcastic at times, but not in a mean way, or so says Urban Dictionary," she laughs.

We both do. From what I know of her, I feel like Rachel is the better, more beautiful, and more appropriate of her names.

The more she speaks, the more I listen. The more I listen, the more I want to know the woman behind the names.

"I'm originally from Portland, Oregon but left after I was wrongly convicted of drug possession. I found my way to Las Vegas, where one thing led to another and before I knew it, I turned to prostitution. Somewhere along the way I fell pregnant to an addict of a man I thought I'd end up with. But I split when I found he had been cheating on me with two other women. I hit it hard and was in no state to handle a baby, let alone raise a child, so I gave her up, leaving Sofia with my parents one night. At the time, I thought it made sense and was the right decision to make. In hindsight, it's the choice I've regretted the most in my life," she confides.

For the first time since we met, I really feel like I'm discovering the real woman behind the makeup and persona. It makes me appreciate Brianna... Rachel, even more. As I listen to her speak, my mind begins to drift. Before I know it, it's wandered and attached itself to the thought of what it would be like to be together as a couple. I begin to imagine the carefree, vagabond lifestyle we'd lead as we traipse across America and beyond. The lazy sleep-ins wrapped up in one another's arms. The hot, passionate sex and intimate lovemaking. The endless, deep conversations we'd have. The thoughts don't so much catch me off guard as creep up on me. And as crazy as they are, it sits comfortably with me even though I do have to tell myself to keep it all in check. Thankfully, there's also plenty of laughs to distract me, so my mind doesn't get to meander too far beyond an, *'I wonder'*.

Brianna also regales me with a few stories of past clients. There was the time she was with this super hairy man who was so fat, not only could she not even see his erection, but she had to literally use her shoulder and arm to lift his huge stomach upwards just to be able to get to it. To the "stud" who was built like a Greek Adonis, and kept telling her how he was going to make her cum hard and often, that she was never going to forget him, then prematurely ejaculated inside a minute.

"It's always the ones with the loudest mouths that orgasm the fastest," she chuckles.

There are other tales she tells me, the ones which aren't so funny. The ones that make me genuinely cringe. And then there's the stories that are far worse, the ones which would bring most to tears when she retells the more painful, horrid and darker side of her profession.

Somehow, despite the pain and anguish Brianna's suffered, she chooses to see only the good that came from the experiences. I'm not sure if she chooses to mask those moments or if there are deeper wounds she bears. Wounds she won't face up to. Either way, despite her hardships and struggles, the thing I like most about Brianna, is her optimistic positivity. No matter how many times she's been knocked down, she chooses to get back up.

At any other point in time, I could find myself falling in love with this woman, but right now I'm just a means for her to communicate and express in a very raw, honest way. Something she probably has not done in a considerably long time. It also offers a great escape valve for me, allowing me to get out of my head for a change and not have to reflect on the gravity of my own tough decision.

When we finally make our way back to the room in total silence, there's a quiet understanding between us, like a calm that has washed over us. I'm not sure if it's the soothing hot springs or the fact the dynamic between us now seems more real, after having opened up in ways we could never have expected when she first invited me for dinner. I could easily ponder the wheres and whys of it all, and normally I would, but this time I don't. Instead, I prefer to just be as present as possible when I am in her company tonight, choosing to appreciate every single moment as best as I can. It would be easy to get swept up in my earlier thoughts, allowing myself to fall for her beauty and charms, but as of this moment, right now, I savour this time. I won't know how grateful I'll be for this encounter or the time we spent together.

10

Night Demons

The night is a restless one. Beside me, I have this naked, near perfect female form, that even as she sleeps, captivates me. While in my head, I hear the shrieks from my demons, all who cast their long, dark shadows, screaming for me to reach out and touch her.

My demons take on many forms. There are the ones who are howling the loudest right now, the deviant, sexually charged, always-on-for-sex regardless of the repercussions or damage they inflict. There's the selfish ones, the self-fulfilling prophecy ones, the downright mean and negative ones. I also have the subtler, though much more dangerous, tormenting ones. They are the demons who are all too willing to point out my weaknesses and flaws, then exploit them, forever reminding me just how weak and defective I am.

They've been the hardest to gain control of, let alone even slay. For now, they relentlessly remind me about the pregnant female body I lay up against only a few nights before.

Even though I behaved impeccably and managed to keep my hands to myself–and my demons and their sexual urges at bay–I'm at constant war with myself. As I lie here dead still, on the furthest edge of the bed I share with Brianna, for most of the night, I've been besieged by their battle cries and screams.

'*Reach out, touch her, taste her, kiss her... have her*'. It is unrelenting. Despite the growing chorus, I'm also being sounded out by the lone, barely audible, soft voice of the woman I left behind. It's much fainter and harder to hear, drowned out by the ravenous choir of the dark demons and their carnal desires for their hunger to be fed.

It all becomes too much and I have to get up out of bed. I look over at the illuminated, digital green clock. The time 2:41am blinks back at me. I slink into the bathroom to splash water on my face. The restless sleep evident in my eyes. I sit on the toilet and stare back at my own reflection to ponder. 'What the hell are you doing?' I don't get any answers, not that I was expecting to, and definitely none that make any discernible sense. Discounting the devil voices that just want me to jump Brianna and have my wicked way with her, I'm haunted by far deeper thoughts than those of where I have failed as a partner... a father. No, the thought that tortures me the most in these long, slow hours before dawn–I am nothing more than a shitty man.

I leave the claustrophobic confines of the bathroom and rustle through my bag looking for my phone. There's an unnerving desire to call home to say, 'I'm sorry,'... or just to know Clea is okay. Once I've located it, I ease the balcony door ajar ever so silently so as not to wake Brianna. I step out into the biting chill of the night air, where the thin veil of the inner curtain billows behind me in small flutters.

Once I turn on the phone it seems to take an eternity to come to life. As soon as the Apple icon disappears from the screen, I thumb through my contacts to find Clea. My finger hovers over the call button waiting for the mental order to press it, but it doesn't come. I get too scared and nervous to call. I'm also unsure of what I would say if she did pick up and answer. I exit that screen and head to my messages but nothing comes. Zip, nada, naught.

Not one text from her, nor are there any missed calls or voicemails either. It rattles me. If my mind taunted me while I tried to sleep, being upright and awake is far worse.

My brain races through all the worst-case scenarios, as I start to wonder if something serious has happened. Is she in hospital? Is there a problem with the pregnancy? Is the baby all right? Did something happen to them? I'd never forgive myself if I brought about some kind of irreversible damage on account of fleeing, leaving her to fend on her own. The first descent of a tear makes its way down my cheek. I hope everything is okay… that they both are.

Desperate for news, my finger hovers over the green call button again. My sobs dissipate while my mind disappears into the cover of darkness. I'm cold, I'm sad, and despite the great, fun company in the hotel room behind me, I feel alone. But what's more disconcerting, I now find myself concerned that I care.

I want to ring, my finger poised to press the call button, but right before I am about to, a warm hand lands on my shoulder. I jump in fright and almost drop the phone over the rail. I hurriedly wipe any tears from my eyes as Brianna steps out from behind the curtain to join me on the balcony. She's wrapped herself up in a warm blanket and without even asking, she opens it up and envelopes me inside it. Her arms hold me close to her, while she stands uncomfortably behind me.

She doesn't say anything, she doesn't need to. She knows where my heart and mind were. The bright, luminescent phone screen against the morning darkness tells her everything she needs to know. Even though she won't say it, I can tell that's confronting for her.

"Why don't you come back to bed with me to warm up and get some rest," she whispers into my ear, though there's a sadness in her tone.

I know it's not an invitation for anything more, and while my mind is currently elsewhere, I allow her to lead me back inside where I slip back into the bed. Even though the press of her warm body provides some comfort, the care and affection she gave me earlier in the night is missing. It's enough to make me lament, for I know this is the last time we'll ever get to be this close to one another again. We lay like this a moment until somehow, exhaustion takes over, and I drift off to sleep.

11

A Long Goodbye

When I wake, Brianna is already up and dressed. She looks resplendent as the morning sun filters through and catches her face. Her bruises are now much less obvious, but there's an emptiness behind her eyes. She offers me a listless smile when she sees me awake, but it's a half smile, the kind people give you when everything is not all right and they don't want to talk about it.

"I can take you as far as Nashville but after that, I'm heading north-west," she affirms.

The revelation is not a total shock, but it still stings.

"Okay," is all I can muster despite wanting to plead with her to stay on a little longer.

"I need to reconcile with my daughter while I am in this mind frame, and I need to take care of it," Brianna says. There's a long pause before she adds, "Raiden, I'm a hooker, call girl, pro, ho, harlot, streetwalker, whore… however you want to label it. It's all I have and all I know. To be blunt, I don't think you're ready to share me with other men. And I get very possessive. I won't share you with anyone else. It's a no-win situation," she states.

Before I can respond, she gets up and pads off to the

bathroom, closing the door behind her. End of discussion. Not that there's much to discuss because she's right. Despite my mental and emotional state, to be with a woman I realise I have genuine feelings for only to see her sleep with men for money, would be a bitter pill to swallow. And to just forget about Clea and jump into something so soon after walking out on her would be a low act, even for me.

I get up out of bed, throw on some clothes and wait. Maybe there's something I can say, something I can do, to tell her or show her that I care, but after she saw me early this morning on my phone, it would feel hypocritical and insincere. Besides, she's too smart to see through my hollow words and false actions. When she comes back into the room, I can tell she's been crying. Despite her best efforts to mask them, there's a small streak of mascara that's left its mark below one of her eyes.

I desperately want to hold her, let her know everything is all right but she avoids me as she keeps herself busy while she packs, never staying still long enough. It's simply her coping mechanism not to allow herself to get close anymore. I wish she'd let me hold her the way she did with me on the balcony this morning.

We make our way out of the room and down the hallway in a tense silence. Even though we walk side by side, there's a distance between us that can't be filled with expression. There's no one at the check-in desk, so I drop the key on the counter. I follow Brianna outside and that typical, confident, alluring walk of hers that makes heads turn and minds spin, is absent. I can't help but feel responsible.

We throw our bags into the car and climb inside. She starts up the GTO and instead of a roar from the engine, there's just a gentle mewl as we idle down the drive, away from Glade

Springs Resort. You could cut the air with a knife, and while I make attempts to start a conversation, it's futile, so I reach for the radio and flick it on. The lilting harmonies and forlorn words of Jeff Buckley's 'Last Goodbye' ring out. I immediately regret it and go to turn it off but Brianna scolds me, so I leave it on.

As his tender song plays out, I sense the music work its way into our subconscious. There's aggravation on one side, sorrow on the other, for as much as it torments us, we both know this will be the last time we are together.

It's about a six hour drive to Nashville, and while we pass by some picturesque green scenery, surrounded by rolling hills and small mountains, we might as well be on Mars. We barely speak to each other, and when we do, it's small, worthless, inane talk. Nothing like the long, in-depth conversations of before that we had while on the road. I think it's those raw, honest discussions that I will miss the most once we part ways.

We stop just once to fuel up, both on food and gas, and while the mild, outside air is a welcome relief, as soon we get back into the car, the same stuffy fog smothers us once again.

When we near the outskirts of Nashville, the greenery we were surrounded by is replaced at first by the outer suburbs, then the inner city sprawl of a dense city. I never made it to Tennessee on my one and only overland trip across the States, some twenty years prior, as a wide-eyed 22 year old. On one hand, I'm glad to be discovering a new place but underneath, there's a heaviness that fills my head with dread and my heart with sorrow. It's a melancholy that no matter what wonders Nashville may hold, won't replace what I am about to part with.

As we enter into the city's centre, it's ironic to think that this is the home of country music. The epicentre for aching ballads of loneliness, heartbreak and hurt.

Brianna pulls up to the side of a cheap motel that backs onto a small family restaurant which is attached, and parks the Pontiac, letting the engine idle. This is it; this is the moment I know will be our last time together. I've been mulling over something poignant or memorable to say for the last hour but nothing feels right, and anything that I think remotely sounds good, I'll probably stuff up or miscommunicate it somehow. I go with the only thing I can.

"Rachel," I say in desperation to delay the inevitable.

It lands. She switches off the engine and turns to face me, making no attempt to cover up the mixed emotions she's also fighting, which flit across her face, then vanish just as quick.

My own emotions simmer to the surface and rather than quell or ignore them, I do the only thing that feels right. I impulsively reach out to place my arms around her with one last hug, determined to give her everything I've got. She swats them away. This isn't the lasting impression I want to end on. I only want one last embrace in the hopes of attempting to end our time together on a beautiful moment.

We sit in silence under the strain and tension for a good ten minutes, neither of us saying anything before I break.

"Rachel, I'm sorry you saw me on my phone this morning."

"Don't be," she cuts in. "It's exactly what I needed."

I shake my head in disbelief.

"While I had hoped you might actually want to get to know the real me, this morning confirmed that's not possible if you're still thinking about your ex. The ex that you walked out on!"

Her comment lands hard. I want to reply, let her know I had hoped for more or at least to spend some extra time with her but no words come. I'm clearly affected by her remarks, and while I'm hurt and left reeling by the sting of them, I can't end our time on this note. Out of desperation, I do the only other thing that feels authentic. I grab my iPod and headphones, furiously scroll until I find what I'm looking for. Despite her protests, I put the headphones over her ears and press play.

The powerful, sublime, near perfect emotive song, 'My Love' from Until The Ribbon Breaks, pulsates out. I watch the song weave its magic across her face, a face that becomes more relaxed courtesy of the song's lyrics, as they sear their way, into what I hope, will be a beautiful, lasting memory. The words have always cut me deep, so when I look at Brianna, I see they appear to be having the same affect on her. When it's over, rather than take off the headphones, she surprises me and hits repeat.

When the poignant tune finishes its second play, she eases the headphones off of her head and sits a moment.

I know the song has hit the mark and disarmed her because she now turns to face me, not attempting to hide the disappointment and sadness she feels. I linger, expecting her to say something, but nothing comes. I'm not sure anything else needs to be said now, so I grab the door handle and open it. I step one foot out onto the gravel and right before I lift myself out, she grabs my hand. I look one last time into those beautiful, jet black eyes of hers, and wait.

"I'm sorry about my callous, cold mood this morning, Raiden. It's just that… well, you've given me more in these past few days than any man has in the last ten years. You made me realise what matters and what's truly meaningful to me, but more importantly, what I'm worth, so I will always be thankful for that. And now I have my very own song to remember you… us by," she smiles.

My mood lifts, and I know the moment that I wanted to end on is something like this. It may not be perfect but it's raw and it's real.

I smile back at her, knowing that she will hold a small place in my heart and a bigger one in my memory. I exit the car closing the door behind me. She loiters a moment, her mind reaching for something.

"I hope you find what you're searching for," she says with a sincere warmness, before she turns on the ignition and slips the car into gear.

I watch the Pontiac GTO one last time as it begins to creep across the asphalt, and then merge with traffic until she slips away. Like me, I know she has her own demons to vanquish, her own personal quest to make peace with. I hope she succeeds at both. I whisper a 'good luck' after her before she finally disappears from view forever.

For the first time since undertaking this journey, and despite the difficulty of this moment in saying goodbye, I find a certain calmness within me.

12

God Awful Country Song

Once I check in to a room of the motel and dump my bags, I head straight to the quaint family restaurant attached. I take up a small table at the back, away from the other patrons. Tonight I want to be alone. It may not be the best thing for me, but it's what I feel I need.

When my meal comes each bite is difficult to swallow but it has nothing to do with the food. Everywhere I look I see Brianna, be it the dark-skinned female sitting at the counter or the constant laugh from a vivacious woman tucked in a booth. But it's her words that are the biggest reminder, which continually swim around in my mind.

"It's the woman that rocks your head not your bed, that makes all the difference in the end," she once said describing relationships and why most men fail to grasp this basic principle. Even though I knew I wasn't in the right head space, I'll admit I found myself falling for her. I'm still coming to grips with the mess I made of my relationship with Clea, which I'm now deeply concerned by given she hasn't reached out once to call or message. Now I find both women circle around inside my head which gives me twice as much to worry about. For tonight, however, it's Brianna's company I miss.

It takes much effort to eat more than a few bites before I push the plate aside. I leave some money on the table and head straight back to my room. As soon as I close the door behind me, an overwhelming need to bring up my meal takes hold. I grip the nearby desk for support in an attempt to keep it at bay but I need more, so I down a glass of water, hopeful that it will settle my stomach. It seems to do the trick. After waiting a few minutes until the nausea recedes, the motion to dry retch passes but that uneasy feeling remains.

I do my best to distract myself with mindless TV but after too many commercials, it's more noise than diversion, so I switch it off. I pace about the tiny room like a caged tiger. It all gets too much and knowing I won't get any sleep if I lie down, I exit the room and head outside for some fresh air. I then begin to walk, to where, I have no idea but I find once I'm outside I feel marginally better, so I just keep walking.

In spite of the evening nip, the cool air penetrates my head and while it won't clear my thoughts, it offers me some relief. There are a few people milling about the streets, though I pay them scant attention as I stroll past. When I catch the sounds of music from a nearby venue, I know where I am going.

I cross the street and beeline for the bar. As I get closer, I realise it sounds a lot like country music. I let out a small groan. I'm too tired to walk any further and find another place more suitable, so I enter the barn-like doors of the bar. I'm now craving a drink to drown my loneliness, so I do my best to ignore the amplified country sounds which qualify as music in these parts.

I pull up a seat by the bar and look around. Everyone inside is either wearing cowboy boots and a hat or they have the hat placed on the table or bar in front of them. It's clear I don't belong here. I contemplate leaving but because the alternative of leaving and going back to the cramped, lonely room, is even less welcoming, I order myself a beer instead.

While I've been the lone foreigner in many cities and countries before, tonight it feels like I have more sets of eyes sizing me up than I care for. At least in those other far off places where they didn't speak English, I always had a certain degree of anonymity. But here, among the cowboy folk that surround me with their God-awful country music ways, it feels unnerving. I normally wouldn't let the blatant stares get to me, but tonight they do.

To shake it off, I down the first beer way too easily. I order a second and that gets polished off almost as quickly. I'm not much of a drinker, bit of a lightweight actually, though tonight I feel like getting on a bender. I know it's not wise given my mixed emotions, nor helped with the unease I feel in the bar, but I figure I deserve to let loose and forget… to forget about Brianna, to forget about the lack of reach out from Clea, and if possible, to forget about the pregnancy, even if it gnaws at the back of my mind day and night.

The bartender returns back my way, and this time I order a whiskey with a shot of tequila because the beer's going down way too fast for my liking. I sense the hesitancy on his face when he hears my order, though I'm hoping the whiskey will slow the drinking and quell the fuzziness which has crept into my head. While the tequila is designed to take the edge off and numb my overthinking mind.

The country songs don't help my mood any, so I close my eyes for a brief moment and do my best to tune it out, however, what I hear instead is not good. The dark soundtrack sounds from the film 'Sicario', that I rewatched only a week earlier with Clea. It's now those foreboding tones, which drip with dread and reverberate around inside my brain.

In an almost ominous fashion, instead of the happy, smiling drunk I normally am after I've had one too many drinks, I feel a scowl form across my forehead.

What am I angry about? Brianna challenged me right when I needed it most. Sure, she had a smoking hot body that emanated heat from every pore, along with a brain and wit I found even hotter, but I wasn't equipped to handle it so soon after leaving Clea pregnant back in Canada, that's for sure. I think that's what pains me the most. I got close with someone I really enjoyed hanging out with and also desired, yet the guilt of what I did hung heavy.

I order another whiskey along with another tequila for good measure. Did I really drink it down like water? I can tell the barman is now a little wary. He's seen this pattern before. I spill a few coins onto the ground when I go to pay and then teeter off my stool to pick them up. On my way back up, I knock into the guy next to me. I give him a bit of macho lip, he tells me to pipe down, so I tell him to mind his fucking business. We glare at each other as my fists clench ready to rumble before his friend intervenes and pulls him back, telling him to let it go. I showed him, I stupidly think to myself.

After four drinks and the two shots, I need to take a leak. I stagger my way towards the back, bump into the jukebox that churns out the ridiculous, sap filled country drivel I so despise, and make my way into the loo. I do my best not to pee all over my shoes, which is made a lot more difficult as I sway from side to side. Somehow, I manage not to piss on myself, though I have to wash my hands because I dripped all over them during an extended, vigorous shake.

After running them under water, I go to take paper towel from the machine but it's empty or stuck, or I don't bloody know, but it doesn't work. This is my breaking point. I punch it only to hurt my hand on the hard, plastic exterior instead. I cry out in frustration and grab it with both hands and attempt to rip it off the wall. I try once too often and tumble backwards where I slip on my arse. Now I'm really pissed off because the floor is wet.

I get to my feet, take a run up to kick the thing and somehow, miraculously, I connect. It tilts to one side and now looks beaten and forlorn. There's still no paper towels inside, only the cardboard cylinder but I feel like I've won. I attempt to tear it out in triumph only to cut my hand on the dispenser's serrated edges. I punch at it one last time in anger, defeated.

My hand shakes when I run it under the water once more as I watch my own blood drip into the sink. I catch my angry, frustrated reflection in the stained mirror above. I'm frazzled, my hair mussed up, while my face is flushed from the exertion. I need another drink to calm down, I think to myself.

When I'm satisfied the small trickle of blood has clotted, I wipe my wet hands on the side of my jeans, exit, then make straight for the bar. In my rush to get another drink, I carry too much momentum and fail to maintain my drunken balance and slam into the jukebox again. I half crumple, half collapse onto the front of it, making the record inside skip. Now I'm just an irate, intoxicated mess of a man. I get to my feet and without evening thinking, I take my good hand and slam a hole right through the perspex screen. Instead of pulling my hand out, I reach further in and rip the record straight off the turntable inside before I pull it back out and smash it on the floor.

I want to do it to all the crappy songs in this shitty jukebox but before I can, I'm grabbed from behind and being frogmarched out by both the bartender and the guy I bumped into earlier. I try to punch and kick out at them, swearing as

I do, but nothing connects. Instead, I just get politely walked through the doors to outside, like an old buddy of theirs. I go to take a swing at the guy I was ready to fight earlier but he's sober, faster, and more agile, so he ducks and weaves to avoid all my punches. In my drunken exuberance to brawl, I slip and lose my balance, which sets me on my arse. Both he and the barman stand me upright, make sure I can stay vertical long enough, before wishing me safe travels, then close the door behind them.

I go to shoulder barge the door but I just bounce straight off it like an upended pogo stick. I lay on the ground, crumpled, beaten, and in a complete daze. It takes me a few moments to regain my composure and dignity, or what's left of it. I rise to my feet and stumble my way back slowly in the direction of my hotel. I must make for a great sight because people clear a wide path as I trip and totter along.

Although I think I'm headed in the right direction, I'm not sure which way my hotel is in to be honest, so I pause on the side of a park bench nearby and draw in some long, much needed deep breaths. I get to my feet again and stagger a little further before I now feel hopelessly lost. I look about for any recognisable landmarks but just catch unfamiliar store fronts. The only thing I do identify, is my bloodied face staring back at me from the window I now face. I stand there a long while feeling miserable for myself.

Before I get a chance to find my bearings, a flash of blue and red lights illuminates the darkness in the reflection behind me. I straighten up and do my best to look sober, while I pretend to ignore them, but then the unequivocal short blast of a police siren breaks the silence.

One minute I'm standing in the front of a shop, the next I'm in the back of a cop car. It's a sad way to end my first night alone without Brianna. She'd be disappointed in me. Ashamed by my actions, I lean my head back on the seat and peer out through the rear window and watch the lights and stars shine above me.

Without now needing to decide which direction to go in, the enforced drive back gives me a moment to think. I start to worry about being fined, jailed, or both. When one of the cops finds out that I'm an Aussie, he mentions he's married to one.

'I'm sorry' I joke, before they both laugh out loud.

However, because I am, I catch a lucky break. Rather than run me in, they take pity on me and before I know it, I'm being chauffeured back to my motel, albeit in handcuffs.

When we get there, they remove the cuffs from my wrists and the one that's married to the Australian, gives me a bit of stern advice.

"Clean yourself up, stay off the booze, get some rest, and don't let me see you again." With that, they get back into their squad car and drive away.

I bumble and fumble my way down the hallway until I find my room. It takes me a little longer to insert the plastic card into the slot but once it's in, I kick off my shoes, ignore most of his advice and crash face down on the bed, where I stay for the next few hours. At least here, I can't do any more harm.

13

Memphis or Bust!

The next morning is a rough one, so I do what I can to clean myself up as best as possible. Sometime during the sorry process I decide to get out of Nashville, but where? I catch the sublime 'River' by Leon Bridges, which plays on the TV video hits show I have playing in the background, and just like that, I have my answer. Memphis it is! The more soulful rhythm & blues will be much more my style. While Bridges is not from Memphis, his stirring music most definitely is, with his song conjuring up images of the Mississippi River that runs right by Memphis.

Even though it's only three to four hours away, it takes me much longer to reach. I have to hitch the whole way, where it requires a couple of cars and a truck, and plenty of waiting on the side of the road, until I finally make it here. Once I reach the Mississippi and see the river flow past me when I stroll its banks, I know I've made the right decision. I feel my mind and body relax and come down from the night before.

Memphis is most famous for its influential strains of blues, soul, and rock 'n' roll music that originated here, with luminaries such as: Elvis Presley, B.B. King, and Johnny Cash, all of whom recorded albums at the legendary Sun Studios–a place that's high on my must-see checklist. However, before I get too excited, first port of call is food. I haven't eaten since the meagre portions of the hotel continental breakfast, that I only just made in time. I'm not even sure I'd class what I ate as food. A bowl of stale Cornflakes, burnt toast, swallowed down by sour orange juice, and a bitter black tea, doesn't cut it in my world. Though at least it staved off the hunger and subdued a raging hangover.

The Arcade Diner, which has occupied the corner on South Main Street since 1918, with its buzzing neon sign, is known for its hearty breakfast and lunch fare. It's exactly what my head and stomach had in mind. As soon as I enter the oldest diner in town, I know this is more my pace and taste than the country twang of Nashville. While the building has been refurbished a few times, the old-time charm and nostalgia still exist.

I'm greeted with the warmest smile I've seen in two days and shown a seat at one of the cool 1950s styled booths. I'm handed a hefty, mouth-watering menu which is enticing enough, but it's all the incredible photos that hang behind the main counter, then run on down the hall into a larger back room, that has my mouth agape. There's the King of course, and plenty of other well known musicians and beat poets. It's a veritable who's who of Americana during key periods.

I opt for an old style burger and a ginger ale to wash down the taste of alcohol from the night before. Once the amiable waitress walks away, I take myself on a little tour. Besides the obligatory souvenirs they offer, the charm of the diner is not lost on me. It'd be easy for me to close my eyes and imagine Elvis or Cash, enter the main doors to refuel here. I'm sure one or two of their famous choruses were written on the back of napkins as they ate here.

While not as vibrant as its heyday, the energy of the place can still be felt. I find my spirits lift as a result, and I even notice a smile edge its way onto my face. I resume my seat back at the booth where a big, fat, juicy burger awaits me. From the first bite to the last, I decide to stay in Memphis for a couple of days and play tourist, something I've not done for a long time.

I was recommended 'The Peabody' as a place to stay but as grand and stately as she is, it's way out of my price range. I make a promise to myself to at least head back there and have a pot of tea from their restaurant. I settle on a cheap room on the outskirts of town that's much more within my modest budget. While it's a bit of a walk back into town, it's not far from the main action and is close to the river, without burning a hole in my pocket.

I dump my bag on the bed, which groans under the weight. I don't hold much hope when it'll be time to put my body down on it to sleep, though for the small amount I'm paying, I can't complain. I head straight back into town along the river and that's all I plan to do... walk, ponder... wonder.

I saunter down a couple of back streets, where I spot a few signs alluding to some historic point of significance or importance. I notice beautiful old buildings and quaint homes being squeezed out by bigger, newer ones. I continue on until I find myself on the famous Beale Street, where I take in the more recognisable, well known Memphis landmarks. I don't stop, though, I just keep walking on, soaking up the town's atmosphere which seems to give my mind a much needed break.

It doesn't take me long to realise that as amazing as this town is, steeped in so much history, it's somewhat of a lonely discovery. I'm sure Brianna and I would have had a blast, but she's not here. My mind then wanders further, and I think of Clea back in Toronto. While she wasn't much of an Elvis fan, she definitely dug some of his music, even getting me to play some of his songs to the baby via headphones placed on her stomach.

It's easy to cast my mind forward to when they would be older, and where I could play them any amount of the endless, cool old music I have. Even better, to bring them here on a trip myself, showing the rich musical history of this place.

That very thought stops me dead in my tracks. While the idea is not at all unwelcome, it totally catches me off guard. It's fair to say, it leaves me reeling somewhat. Up until now, I'd been selfishly thinking of myself, my goals and my own plans. To now imagine plans involving a family and introducing my little one to things their daddy loves, isn't something I had given much thought to. While it's probably not possible now after I walked out on them, I find it fills me with a sense of warmth that I never expected.

When the thought drifts away into the back recesses of my subconscious, I look around and find myself now standing out front of the Memphis Rock'n'Soul museum. Being a lover of all things rock and soul, I decide I can spare the $12 admission fee to wander aimlessly about the rooms and allow my mind to sit with the unexpected revelation.

While I was in a contemplative mood before I made my way inside, once I enter the doors I'm like a kid in a candy store, only I'm a middle-aged man geeking out. There's photos, memorabilia, old musical equipment, videos, and the like, along with the music of course. One of Elvis's earlier, and lesser known tracks, 'Mystery Train' (and one I absolutely love), echoes out through the old style 1960s speakers.

It's impossible for me not to get swept up in the euphoria of the place, knowing the idols all around me created arguably the most iconic and memorable music scene of last century! Pretty soon I find myself singing to the celebrated tunes which continue to play out. While they don't invade my earlier thought, it's definitely a welcome distraction from thinking about Brianna or how Clea and my unborn child are doing.

An announcement comes over the museum's speaker system declaring the museum is closing in 15 minutes. I rush to take the last few things in and when I'm done, check the time and find it's almost 7pm. Did I really spend 4-5 hours traipsing through here? On my way out, I catch a sign I missed on entering that reads:

'The Mission of the Memphis Rock 'n' Soul Museum is to preserve and tell the story of Memphis music to maintain its legacy and keep it alive'.

After what I just took in, they achieved their aim.

"Long live rock 'n' roll," the ageing museum attendant says to me on my way out.

While I don't reply, a wide grin forms across my face knowing for this patron at least, it will.

Before entering, my mind was filled with a sense of loss. After exiting, it's now filled with hope.

I don't remember the last time I got so absorbed in a museum. I make a vow with myself to discover other equally memorable places of interest for the remainder of this journey, in the optimism they may yield similar surprising revelations. At the very least, they'll offer a welcome distraction.

With extra purpose, I head into town and back down along Beale Street, which is now full of life and neon colour. The semi-quiet street from earlier in the day has come alive. I catch snippets of conversation and excitement from a flock of tourists who retell old stories about memories they have when a particular song came out on the radio, or when a popular band came to town to play, to hearing the news of Elvis's sudden death, or other famous pop and rock musicians who passed away. It's compulsive listening and despite the subject matter and recollections of dead singers, their spirits are high, and I find myself being swept up in their jubilation.

While I was too young to experience the Elvis craze, the words I know, the tunes I can hum. Even though I was heading back to my hotel, I inexplicably get caught up among a group of about 20 people who head into B.B. King's 'Blues Club', where for a short moment, I find myself included as part of their large entourage. I extricate myself and watch them enter in high spirits, then it dawns on me, *join them*. I rush in after them, and before the ticket attendant can speak a word, hunched over, I overplay the panting, breathless card and say I'm with them, uttering an excuse that I forgot my wallet. I expect to be questioned but when it doesn't come, she waves me through, where I waltz in to catch up to the group who have disappeared inside.

I'm soon seated alongside them and do my best to go with the flow and remain as inconspicuous as possible yet fit in, though it seems no one either cares or notices they've got an interloper among them. The food and drink which follows, is fit for a king. I help myself to the generous portions being served and chat quietly with an older couple next to me, who are both from Holland and here to recapture their "glory days" they tell me. There's an older aged guy opposite me from Russia, who remembers being stationed in Siberia and recalls being instantly hooked when he first heard 'Heartbreak Hotel' on the little transistor radio he'd smuggle into his security booth every night.

There's also two young Japanese girls farther along, and barely twenty, who giggle their way through dinner like overexcited teenagers. They seem out of place among the mature age group, but pronounce "Elvis king," in unison when I catch their eye. Even though they're young enough to almost be any of the group's grandchildren, no one seems to care. In fact, their exuberance reminds one or two group members of their own feverish teenage days during the Elvis rock 'n' roll hysteria.

Our plates get taken away by a slew of wait staff, and then the lights go down. There's a hush over the crowd before the stage curtains open up and the irrepressible and recognisable blues music of the man the club is named after, rumbles out. While B.B. King is long dead, like Elvis, his legend lives on with the house band, B.B King's Blues Club All Star Band, who sound every inch like the man and his music.

It doesn't take long before people from the group get up to make their way out to the dance floor. From my vantage point, I watch them jive and have fun. The more timid members in the group stay seated, preferring to clap and encourage their peers on.

I know I caught a lucky break tonight, and while it would be easy to stay on and enjoy the free alcohol, food, music, even the company after last night's antics, I think better of it. Besides, I'm still a little sore and beat. I slink away into the dark of night, where the music follows me out the door and carries me all the way back to my hotel.

Once in my room, as expected, the bed creaks under my weight but it doesn't matter, because tonight there's a happy and relaxed disposition to my sleep. I'm not sure if it's the buoyant mood I find myself in, or if it was the late afternoon revelation I had, which seems to have me wondering. Either way, it makes for a sound sleep because tonight, tonight my mind doesn't think.

14

"Deluxe" Star Tours

When the next day comes around, I feel refreshed, revived and ready to renew my tour of this town. I've already mapped out my day. First, a visit to Sun Studios, to soak up the history and mystique of the little studio that changed the face of music forever, then a tour of Graceland. Both will be welcome distractions from yesterday's introspection, though overnight the thought has gained a foothold in my brain and growing.

My parents provided me with my earliest childhood musical memories, back when they were civil to one another and still together that is. Elvis Presley records had always been playing on the old turntable stereo at home. Ever since then, and for as long as I can remember, thanks to those early recollections, my own desires of wanting to travel here to Memphis and visit the home Elvis graced, will become a reality, although I always pictured it under better circumstances.

I know it would be sacrilege not to visit the King's spiritual heartland while I'm right here on his doorstep. Mum may never talk to me again if she knew I'd come here and had bypassed his hallowed turf. I'd never forgive myself either. But that's not going to happen. I'm arguably more a fan of the King than either of my parents were at the peak of his career, so there's no question of me not taking in Graceland. However, if my mum knew I was here, leaving Clea to carry the term of pregnancy and her grandchild hopes all on her own, then she might disown me all together.

First things first though, I have to figure out a way to get there, and on the cheaper side. It's already going to cost me anything between $38.75-$47.50 just to enter the revered gates, and that's at the lower end. If you want to tour the King's private jets or walk the grounds, then the price goes up significantly. While I wish I could make my way out there by foot, it's simply too far to walk, even from Beale Street. I've also got to take into account the added cost of a Sun Studio tour, but at least I can walk to it from here.

I speak with the hotel's attendant, a mid-fifties woman, who upon hearing my Australian accent, immediately stops typing on the desk computer and gives me her flirtiest smile and fullest attention.

For as long as I have been in North America, my Aussie accent has been both loved and misunderstood. Loved for the cool ocker twang of it, and misunderstood because it seems American's ears are only attuned to their own American voices. Give them an accent or voice from outside the U.S, and their understanding of basic English language collapses. I mean, I can't even get the hotel desk clerk to understand I want to go to *Graceland*, probably the single most repeated phrase in the establishment.

"Oh, a Graceland tour," she perks up, when I slow to pronounce and enunciate the words more. "Well, why didn't you say so?"

She pulls at the drawer under her counter but it sticks. With a hard whack from above, the drawer opens. She rifles around inside until she finds a scrap piece of paper with a scribbled phone number written on it.

"Uncle Louie is your man," she says, in her slow Southern drawl. "He's the unofficial tour guide in these parts. He's got connections," she winks at me.

I'm already concerned by "uncle", "unofficial", and "connections". Despite an uneasy feeling, I take the piece of crumpled paper from her and find out her name is Grace. Her parents were huge Presley fans and were overjoyed when she was a girl. I'm left to wonder what they would've called her if she had been born a boy.

"This *Uncle* Louie, is he legit?"

Grace takes one look at me like I must be crazy or slow, or both, and hesitates a moment.

"Uncle Louie is to tours as a fly is on shit."

I've no idea what the metaphor means and I don't dare try to decipher it. I just give her a thankful smile and back away from the counter. I begin to question if I'm better off to hang the expense and pay the extra to do the more official tour.

"There's a phone in the corner. Tell 'em Gracie sent ya," she barks from behind her booth when I walk away to go and find it.

I locate the phone, notice oily fingerprint marks all over it, so hold the phone away from my ear to dial up the number.

It rings a number of times and I'm just about to hang up when I hear a weary, heavy smoker's voice of a man answer. He then proceeds to go through a throaty cough that makes me feel ill upon hearing it. In the background, I hear the clatter of bottles being displaced before rolling their way over a wooden floor.

"Ello, Louie's tires, computer repairs, and drugstore delivery service," the voice says groggily.

"Um, is this Louie, Graceland Tour guide?" I ask hesitantly.

"Tour, aye? Geez, I've not done one of those in, well, not since the last time I was told to…" but he trails off.

The last time what, I wonder. I look over at Grace who gives me a droll smile. I turn back and carry on, hopeful.

"Grace told me you're the 'best' guide there is," I chime, wondering whether they are even related or not.

"Grace… Grace," he mulls, over and over.

I can feel him burrow his brow, hard in thought, pondering who the hell Grace is.

"Possibly your *niece*," I utter with scepticism.

"GRACIE," Louie screams into the phone before he hacks away once again sounding like he's coughing up a lung in the process.

"How is she?"

I look back over at her and see she's now got her head arched back, snoring loudly.

"She's doing great," I reply.

"Haven't seen that young scamp since she was out rousing an' trouble makin', getting 'dem boys all crazy and hard everywhere she went."

It's a little more information than I care to know about Grace's past.

"She still with that Reggie fella… or is it Louis? Maybe it was Alessandro. She's always had so much interest.

I wonder how long it's been since he's seen her? I decide to humour him.

"You know her, stunning and popular as ever."

I hear a hearty laugh, followed by a long, two-pack a day, smoker's cough. I cringe, holding the phone even further away from my ear than before.

"So that Graceland tour," I soldier on. "You still do them?"

"Uncle Louie will get you into Graceland, no problemo,

kiddo. The King and I were practically best buds. I'll give you the special King deluxe star tour. Only a few lucky folks ever got that, you know?" he bellows with pride.

While I've a few doubts, starting with *special* and *deluxe*, and questioning how "legitimate" he is, I know it will be a lot cheaper than the more expensive, VIP tours on offer, and who knows, maybe a lot more interesting if he did truly know Elvis like he claims to. Though I have way more doubts about that than all the above together.

"To hell with past indiscretions," he jokes.

Did I say a few doubts?

"I want to visit Sun Studios first," I say.

"What do you wanna visit those shysters for? You're better off keeping your money safe in your pocket. Screw those assholes," he snaps.

"It's just something I'd like to do while I'm here. Perhaps you can pick me up after I'm done?"

"Complete waste of time and money, but suit yourself. I can show you plenty of other, better sights than that dump."

"Maybe after Graceland," I reply, wanting to quickly move on.

"Sun Studios. Pfft! See you out front at 11 sharp," he commands before he slams the phone down.

I place the receiver onto its cradle and check my watch. It's already 9:17. If I'm lucky, I'll get about an hour or so to tour the studio. It'll have to do.

By the time I get to Sun Studios it's almost 10. Fortunately, there's no line, though I'm not sure I was expecting one. I guess it helps that I'm here midweek and possibly out of season, though I'm not even sure if there is a 'season' for Memphis.

The Studios open from 10am, however, just my luck, public

tours are only given at the bottom half of every hour starting, so it'll be a whistle-stop visit. I'm hoping that because it's a small space, that'll be enough time.

For the twenty minutes or so I have to wait, I fill in my time peering through the windows at the photos and memorabilia planted around the walls. I spy the souvenir shop tucked up in a corner, which thankfully doesn't look too out of place. I also do a little self-reflecting on exiting the way I did. I know we had our problems, what couple doesn't? But the constant badgering and belittling, the incessant emotional, mental, and verbal abuse by Clea, had taken its toll. I was genuinely concerned that it would only get worse once a baby was in the picture. I wasn't looking to bring up a child in the middle of a constant sparring match, one where I always had to be on guard. What sort of example would that set?

My doubts are cut off mid-thought when I hear the lock on the front doors being opened. While I know the history—a recording studio opened by rock-and-roll pioneer, Sam Phillips, back in 1950, hosting luminaries like: Howlin' Wolf, B.B. King, Johnny Cash, Elvis Presley, Roy Orbison, Jerry Lee Lewis, etc–what I don't know is that it was fairly dormant in the years that followed.

While it must have been a crazy, wild, insane time during its heady, rock'n'roll glory days, when the music scene moved on, Sun Studios became a shadow of itself. You could feel it, too, from the worn, wood panelling and tattered upholstery, to the outdated recording equipment. Its best was past it.

However, as luck would have it, that old school charm appealed to one of my all time favourite artists, U2, who recorded a handful of songs here, three of which subsequently ended up on their successful album, 'Rattle & Hum'. Other artists also took advantage of the history, with former Beatle,

Ringo Starr, the most famous among them. As a result, they brought back some of Sun Studios' former fame and energy.

Sure, it's nothing more than a pit stop for me on my way to Graceland, but it's still somewhat of a surreal feeling for me to stand here in the same space as all of the incredible music artists who once came through its doors to record here.

When 10:30 rolls around, I, along with five others, are itching to walk through the rest of the studios. By the ages of most of us, I'm guessing we are all aware of who has recorded here, so when we're met by the current owner, Knox Phillips, son of Sam, who proceeds to tell everyone the long list of household names, we're not really that surprised. Although a couple of names raise my eyebrows. Def Leppard, really? He has an agreeable charm and along with his personal experiences, it's absorbing to get his local take on what it was like to be here in its heyday, surrounded by so many famous musicians during, what I believe, is one of the greatest periods in musical history!

Eventually we're lead through another set of doors into the heart of the studios. There are more photos and a swag of gold records on the hallway walls. One or two take photos on their smartphones for posterity. How times have changed I think to myself. We're then led one at a time through a small entry when all of a sudden, the lights go out and a mash of voices music rings out. Then a small projector lights up one wall flashing the accompanying musicians we are hearing. Sure, it's kitsch but I catch myself mouth the words to some of the songs all the same.

When the little show ends and the lights come on, Knox has left us. He's now on the other side of the recording booth, behind the glass, in front of the sound mixing desk. We're not sure if we're meant to follow and join him but as we start to make a move, his voice booms out from the speaker system in the room.

"Okay, now it's your turn. Let's see if I have the next Elvis, B.B. or Cash in there," he chuckles.

There are a few confused looks from each of us because we've no idea what he wants. But he's a pro and just asks each of us to sing a line or two from a selection of Elvis songs, which appear up on a screen in front of us. It's just like karaoke, only without the stench of beer or the hooting and hollering from a drunken crowd, except we're in Sun Studios!

To everyone's credit we all play along, and we have a few laughs as a result. While none of us will score a record deal courtesy of our amateurish singing voices, it's a fun little extra component tacked on to the tour. I'm glad I came.

We're shown back down the hallway, and out into the foyer again, and asked to make a donation or purchase merchandise to help keep the studio afloat. No one hesitates. I'm about to reach into my pocket and drop a note and some small change into the donation box, when from out of nowhere, a loud, blaring air horn rings out.

When I turn my head to see what's causing it, true to form and unbelievably, right on time, appears what I can only guess is Uncle Louie, hand on his car horn, yelling out, "Hurry up, time's a wastin', kid."

"What the?" Knox vents.

I drop my head in embarrassment. I'm about to leave when I hear Knox curse under his breath.

"I don't know how many times I have to tell this parasite, he's not welcome here. Sorry everyone, that's a previous disgruntled "business partner" from my dad's era. He's still pissed about a supposed deal they agreed to decades earlier. He thinks he's the one who discovered Elvis," Knox recounts to the fascinated group, who all laugh.

When Louie notices I'm the only one who's not laughing, he waves way too enthusiastically in my direction. Knox turns to me with a 'You're with him?' look. I drop my money into the donation box, mouth a small apology, and make for the exit as fast as I can.

When the doors open to the outside, at the top of his voice, Louie gives Knox a verbal spray and yells, "I want my fucking money, Knox, ya swindler. Give me what I'm owed, cunt."

A passerby is forced to cover the ears of her young child. I attempt to open the door of some clapped out, rust bucket of a whale of a car, which looks like it should have been buried in the scrapyard 30 years ago, but it doesn't open.

"Gotta open it from inside," Louie berates me like I should know.

I reach inside the already opened window and turn the handle, where the door proceeds to drop open. I can't get in fast enough. Louie plants his foot flat to the floor as the old V8 engine does its best to make the tyres squeal behind us, before it lurches and splutters. He gives the dashboard a hard whack and the car pitches then shrieks its disapproval.

In full view of everyone, including those inside Sun Studios, he squeezes himself half out the car and with his arm outstretched, crosses one arm up behind the other by the elbow and forearm in a 'fuck you' fist skywards.

I don't bother to look back because I can only imagine Knox has seen this behaviour countless times before.

"Double crossing, lying sacks of shits," Louie bellows when he finally squeezes back inside the car. "So who's ready for Graceland?" he beams at me through a yellow, teeth-stained grin.

Is it too late to cancel the tour, I think?

When we've returned to a more comfortable speed for the car, I look over at Louie, who reminds me of an older, balder, fatter, and if possible, surlier version of Paulie from Rocky. Even his shirt is stained with God knows what. What the hell have I got myself in for, I wonder?

"Beer?" Louie chirps.

Before I can answer no, he's reached back around behind the seat, grabs two cans from a cooler and hurls one at me.

"Let's rock'n'roll," he says as he cracks open his can and guzzles it down in almost a complete, single gulp.

It's an inauspicious way to start a tour to say the least. I can only hope it picks up from here but when he immediately reaches for a second beer, my doubts just increase.

On the short 15 minute drive towards Graceland, Louie makes sure to fill me in on every detail of his version of the "deal". The one he was supposed to have had with Knox's dad, Sam Phillips, back when Elvis was about to breakout. To say it's a shaky argument is a massive understatement. That didn't stop him from taking legal action and while he lost, several times, appealing the verdict or finding yet a new angle to pursue as he continued to represent himself, he still feels aggrieved and thinks he's owed millions.

I'm grateful when we hit Elvis Presley Boulevard and I see the signs pointing out 'Graceland: The Home of Elvis', so I don't have to hear his bitter and sour take much longer. Louie keeps on talking, however, this time about how he used to burn Elvis up and down this road when they were younger. Something about underage, illegal drag street racing, he chuckles.

As we approach the mansion's gated entrance, I spot several coaches ahead of us near the toll booth, waiting entry to park. Just when I think we'll slow down and wait our turn,

Louie takes a hard left and we end up down a side street, driving away from the entrance.

"Short cut," Louie assures me when I look back over my shoulder, astonished to find we don't join the queue.

From the big, wide boulevard of before, we're now on a much smaller street, set among the residential homes that occupy it on either side. The road continues to narrow until we hit the dead end of a cul-de-sac where we come to an abrupt stop. I'm starting to question whether his memory has faded, or if he started on the beers long before he picked me up and it's simply become foggy as a result.

"Okay, let's go," he says.

"Where?"

"Graceland," Louie says, bewildered.

He gets out of the car and doesn't wait for me to follow. I stare into the quiet, empty street, and all the doubts I had before about this tour being remotely legit, have all but faded.

"Come on," he says, forcing the door open, which hangs limp as he yanks me out of the car.

Before I have a chance to argue, he scurries through a nearby backyard and disappears behind some shrubs. I take a deep breath and despite my reservations, follow the path he's just carved out with his bulk. When I catch up to him, he's trying to hoist himself up and over a fence but failing miserably.

"A little hand," he gestures.

I amble over with serious concerns about whether jumping over the fence to break into Graceland to save a few dollars, is really worth the risk. I'm convinced we'll either get caught, cop a serious fine, or be thrown in jail. Maybe all the above?

"Lock your hands," Louie orders.

I cup my hands and do my best to take most of his hefty

weight, while he clambers up the fence, slipping and sliding his feet against the wood with his Italian loafers that have zero grip. Somehow, he manages to get to the top where he straddles one leg on either side of the fence, but he's huffing and puffing from the exertion. He gives me a smile from his flushed, sweaty, red face as he does his best to stay atop the fence that buckles and wobbles under his mass. But it doesn't last because Louie loses his balance and crashes down onto the other side.

Worried, I jump up and peer over the fence. He's not moving. I immediately hurl myself up and onto the fence with a lot more ease and dexterity than him, however, I notice the wood is badly rotted and is barely able to hold my much lighter frame. I'm about to hop off when one of the support posts snaps beneath me and before I know it, I'm sent over the fence, face first, to join him.

Thanks to the plush grass I land on, it's a relatively soft landing. I pick myself up and dust off the leaves and dirt. I then attend to Louie, who's just laughing that familiar smoker's cough laugh of his, only it's much worse in person. In person he openly hocks up the phlegm, spitting it out onto the neatly, manicured lawn.

I look back at the fence that now has a serious 45 degree lean to it, with its posts all bent at odd angles.

"Geez, Dorothy's going to be pissed when she notices that," Louie says with a smirk. "That'll teach that old bird for not returning my calls," he quips.

"Is there anyone you haven't pissed off?"

"Define pissed?" he says.

Perturbed by the answer I'll get, I don't press it.

We're both back on our feet, though I don't think it's a good idea to stick around much longer in case we run into

Graceland's ground security or worse, Dorothy. Louie, however, is nonplussed as he trudges away from the sad looking fence and in through a large, overgrown section of trees and shrubs.

"This is the Meditation garden," Louie asserts. "Only thing is, Elvis never meditated a day in his life," he grumbles before snapping off some of the tree branches to clear us a path.

We creep our way slowly through the garden, well I do. Louie just tramples over the flowers or kicks and displaces the carefully laid out stones with little care for the tranquility of the place. We near what appears to be the way out, when he crouches down and stops. He raises a clenched hand in the air, military style, and gives a signal I assume is for me to kneel and stay quiet, even though all the noise is his.

I look over his shoulder and there, just ahead of us, is the big, white mansion of Graceland. Several people mill out front posing for photos, while a couple of attendants check the wrist bands of others. There's also a security guard patrolling the grounds, with one mean looking German Shepherd ready to savage would be intruders.

Louie seems not to care, which offers little consolation given his tour approach so far. He turns to face me.

"So this is how it's gonna be," Louie pants at me. "We'll wait until a tour group strolls the grounds. Then when no one's looking, we walk out of here as casual as can be and wait for them at the bottom of steps, like we're leading the group. They'll never suspect a thing. Now do your best to act cool and fit in," Louie lectures me.

I want to point out all the holes in this theory–the attendants checking wrist bands, the security guard, the savage looking watchdog–but just as I am about to speak, sure enough, a large group walks up the driveway nearing the steps to the entrance.

"Go!"

Without warning, Louie steps out from behind the covers of the trees and half jogs, half clomps his way towards them. It's now or never, I say to myself. The irony of that being an Elvis song is not lost on me when I exit and follow him.

We get to the bottom of the steps and watch as a large group of Korean tourists saunter up the drive.

"Right this way," he calls out.

"What was that about fitting in?" I joke.

Louie ignores my dig and waits for his moment. When most of the group have gathered around in a big congregation, some snapping photos excitedly, he grabs my sleeve and drags me along. Before I know it, we're in the middle of the group and rather than be inconspicuous like I thought we would be, Louie then offers to take photos of four Korean ladies nearby who are using one of those selfie sticks. Without a chance to say anything, he proceeds to grab the stick, mangles at the phone attached until he somehow figures out the right way to take their picture. Once they get over their confusion and hesitancy, the women all giggle and pose for the camera.

He continues to take photos of the other group members, even though the four original women want their phone and selfie stick back. The group begins to lurch forward en masse, Louie holding the selfie stick aloft for them to follow. While one of the mansion's ticket attendants gives us a puzzled look, we amble past, until just like that, we're inside Graceland.

While he may not have the most conventional of methods, I've got to hand it to Louie, what he lacks in careful planning and organisation of any kind, he more than makes up for with spontaneity, determination, and desperation.

He leads us through into the main entrance hall and it's

every bit as opulent and ostentatious as you can imagine, capturing the late seventies in all its vibrant glory. The place has become both a shrine and a time capsule, representing everything from that period when Elvis was still alive. In short, a place for people to never let go. It's almost morbid. I don't get to dwell on those thoughts too long when a Graceland attendant and guide starts the official tour for "our" group.

"Graceland was once part of a 500 acre farm that was owned by the S.E. Toof family. The land had been part of the family for generations and was named after one of their female relatives, Grace. According to Graceland history, in 1939, Grace's niece, Ruth Brown Moore and her husband, Dr. Thomas Moore, built the mansion. The Moore's daughter, Ruth Marie, was musically accomplished and became a harpist with the Memphis Symphony Orchestra. Classical recitals in the front formal rooms were common, just as rock 'n' roll and gospel jam sessions would be after the next owner moved in," the guide says, in that flat, monotone voice they speak. It's enough to bore even the most avid fan.

"In the spring of 1957, at just 22, Elvis Presley purchased the home and grounds for just over $100,000, after he reached super stardom the year prior," the unanimated guide drones on as my eyelids begin to feel heavy.

A team leader of the group then repeats what the guide just said, but in Korean. This is when Louie seizes the moment to shuffle me through a side door, out of view and ear shot, from the tour guide and group. For the first time since joining his unofficial tour, I'm actually thankful.

"You can have that boring, lifeless tour or you can have the *real* tour," he says with a sly smirk.

Louie then turns his jacket inside out before putting it on again. It takes me a minute to recognise what I'm looking at, but then it dawns on me. It's a replica jacket. One that looks exactly like the official Graceland tour guide's, only Louie's jacket is more stained and frayed.

I long ago gave up on any "official" tour, so nothing surprises me anymore with Louie and his antics. Rather than protest, though I doubt he'd listen anyway, I decide to go with the flow, especially given the alternative, which would only bore the bloody pants off me. I have to trust that I don't come to rue my decision.

Once I decide to embrace it, however, I feel this rapid change almost violently grab hold of me and sweep through my mind and body. That former, fun and carefree guy that I used to be (long before life subdued and beat me down), appears to roar back to life. It cajoles and goads me, telling me to let go, run wild, and enjoy myself for a change. So that's exactly what I plan to do.

With no time to catch my breath with this new assertion taking hold of me, Lou whisks me off to the kitchen, which is not far from where we stand, and opens up the fridge to help himself to whatever is inside it. I'm amazed at his careless attitude. He opens up one of the drawers, grabs what I am sure is a genuine knife Elvis used in the 1970s, and proceeds to make a peanut butter and jelly sandwich for himself.

"If it's good enough for the King, it's good enough for Uncle Louie," he exclaims between mouthfuls of sandwich which he spits out in globules while he talks.

Whatever Louie has in store for me, from here on out, I'm all in. One thing I can almost be certain of after seeing his rudimentary actions and questionable behaviour firsthand, it shapes to be an unpredictable ride, that's for sure. I have to wonder whether I haven't unleashed my own former immature and irresponsible demons, long buried from my past, to now run amok in the process. I grit my teeth knowing only time will tell.

Lou ushers me into another room, which is equally as garish as the last. It's honestly like a bad LSD nightmare, one where you never get to wake up from 1977! We keep moving through the home, past another group dying of boredom, who all watch on in amazement when we walk behind roped off sections, seemingly afforded privileges they didn't know existed or could pay for. If only they knew, I think to myself.

Louie leads me to the game room, which is stacked with classic 1970s memorabilia, key among them, a couple of old-school pinball machines. Despite my hushed protests, and the gasps of several onlookers, he reaches around the back and flicks the switch on one of the machines. It takes a few moments to flicker to life, possibly because it's been decades since it was last played. But soon enough, that familiar sound of a classic pinball game comes to life.

The ding and clink of the old metal ball bearing hitting the bumpers and other zappers is music to my ears, while I watch as the score ticks over. But it soon fades when Louie isn't able to save the ball from disappearing back behind the flippers. In frustration, he bangs the glass top before he gives the machine a kick.

"That game's always had it in for me," he bemoans.

I look at previous high scores and see the initials EAP. I assume they stand for Elvis Aaron Presley.

"Elvis really was the king in more ways than one," Lou confirms with a certain fondness.

During the game, I spot the group from last night. A few of the faces recognise me and look over in bewilderment and wonder why I am getting preferential treatment. I just smile and wave at them as another tour guide enters the room behind them and notices Louie by the pinball machine.

"Sir, no one is allowed up there," he says, almost freaking out that someone dare break house rules.

"It's okay, I'm with the Elvis Aaron Presley estate service team," Louie mumbles, before he reaches into a pocket of his jacket and holds out what I can only presume is a fake ID.

He doesn't wait for a reply, instead, chaperones me away into another room, shoving other patrons out of his way as he goes, before closing the door behind us.

"Such a stuffy bunch," he groans.

But I don't hear him. Instead, I stand incredulous before a floor to ceiling wall of all the gold and platinum records Elvis secured during his reign at the top of the charts. To say it's immense in size, scope, and achievement, is an understatement. Presley had over 20 number one hits on both sides of the Atlantic. Even after he had ceased living, one or two re-mixed versions of his songs, still managed to hit the coveted number one spot! A remarkable feat for a man long dead for over 30 years.

As I stand here in awe, it dawns on me that regardless of the bad taste in furniture and carpet, he was a phenomenon the likes of which we may never ever see again. It's impossible to argue his success, even when his career and health declined. It's fair to say, Elvis truly was the King!

I don't get to savour the moment too long because before I know it, Louie is trying to wrench one of the hit records from the wall with a screwdriver he's concealed on him. There really is no shame to this man. He isn't able to get very far though, because the gold records are screwed into the wall with a different screw head than the type he brought with him. Frustrated, he pockets a nearby ashtray instead and whisks me away before I can say anything.

I am amazed at this man's audacity, even more amazed security hasn't been alerted to his antics. They're not short of CCTV cameras that's for sure. I am certain it is just a matter of time before they notice him and his reckless abandon in the home of none other than Elvis Presley. A man during his peak, some think was more powerful than God, and is still alive.

I can only hazard that maybe the security cameras are more for show than being fully functional. Either that or perhaps the monitor guard slipped out to get a coffee so the cameras aren't being monitored. I don't concern myself with it as we tag onto the tail end of another group, who follow one another into a room off to the side like sheep.

We now stand right at the bottom of the big marble staircase, with its steps that lead upstairs. A sign in front of them reads in big, bold letters, 'No Entry'. Louie brushes the sign aside like it's not even there, and the next thing I know, he heads upstairs without a care in the world. I furtively follow behind but rather than risk any wrath, I play my part and turn the sign around. Little do I know though, that on the other side it says, 'Open'.

I scamper up the stairs to catch up to Louie, who now stands on the top of the landing and waves down for me to join him.

"Hurry up, I've got to take a dump," he says as he rushes off towards a room out of view.

With some caution and much trepidation, I follow behind. Is he really about to take a shit on the King's throne? Now there's a vision I could have done without. I can only pray I'll be spared that indignity.

"Oh crap, no toilet paper," I hear from the nearby bathroom.

Please tell me he hasn't, I mumble to myself.

When I walk in to what is a truly gargantuan bathroom fit for a king, Louie's in the middle of zipping up his fly. There's no flush and I'm not game to peer into the toilet bowl, but the smell. Holy mother of God! It's so pungent, my legs buckle momentarily and I'm forced to grab a nearby towel rail to keep from keeling over. Overcome by the strong, obnoxious odour, I beat a hasty retreat from the room, all the while questioning Lou's level of morality and sanity. I mean, how low one man can go?

When I make my way back out into some much needed fresh air, I just shake my head at this man's impudent conduct. Not even during my wildest, impetuous worst, was I ever this disrespectful, especially in a place as revered as this. Yet as much I am shocked and disgusted by his behaviour, I am also completely captivated by it. I have to profess; I actually admire his nonchalance. While it won't win him many friends, if any, Lou is a man who plays by nobody's rules. You have to give kudos to a man who lives like that in this day and age.

"You just exited the bathroom Elvis died in," Louie says to me on my way out.

If Louie was anywhere near the vicinity when he passed away, I'd wager the toxic fumes emanating from the bathroom were what did the King in, not all those deep fried sandwiches Elvis was rumoured to love.

"Want to see where the King slept and conquered his women?" Louie asks me, before hastily adding, "After Priscilla left him of course. Have to admire a man who on any given night could have had his pick from an endless stream of adoring, beautiful female fans who would throw themselves at him. Of course, that's not to say a handful of us boys didn't take advantage of all those hyper horny women flinging themselves about the place. I mean, how could we resist? Ah, the fun we had."

When I look over at him, he's wearing a smug grin that would put a Cheshire cat to shame. I want to quiz what Lou did or was to Elvis, but because I don't want to interrupt his tale, I hold off on asking him until later.

"But not Elvis, he really loved his wife, and was always faithful. He was devastated when she asked for a divorce. It was the reason he recorded 'Always On My Mind' so soon after the separation. He was crushed. He needed an outlet, that song was it. Its lyrics spoke to him on a deep, personal level. Elvis once told me in private, that despite that song going on to become a worldwide hit, he'd have given it all up if he'd been able to convince Priscilla from leaving him."

The reflective thought from Lou hits its own resonant note with me. Despite his questionable antics and disgraceful behaviour, I am impressed by Louie's knowledge of the layout of the house. For someone who was no doubt banned from here many years ago, he still knows his way around. But it is his personal anecdotes, that make me wonder whether Louie had indeed been much closer to Elvis than I ever gave him credit for.

"Lou? How did you come to know Elvis?"

"You got your question wrong way round, kiddo. The better question is, how did Elvis come to know me?"

Before I can rephrase it, he's already answering for me.

"He was the loner kid at school, a real mollycoddled momma's boy. No joke! I was the popular up and coming guitar wiz. Everybody loved me. Somehow, we both ended up at this country fair music contest. Neither of us won. They awarded it to some Mary-Sue type with curls like Shirley Temple, who sang Good Ship Lollipop. She only won because she was the mayor's daughter. But one thing led to another, and we became good friends, exchanging records, guitar chords, and song ideas as we grew up. Then Elvis got a lucky break when I was laid up in hospital with rickets. While performing at another contest, some bloke who called himself a Colonel despite never fighting in a war, offered to manage him. I thought Elvis was crazy for agreeing to a deal that gave this guy fifty percent of earnings from his first recordings. I offered to shepherd his recording with plans to impress people with my much better talent and secure my own record deal, because let's be honest, I was the better muso, Elvis even said so, you know?"

I give Lou a dubious sideways glance.

"Truth to god, he did. Anyway, Sam 'Shyster' Phillips, the owner of Sun Studios, took one look at me and my bow legs, and locked me out of the session, thinking I was some juvenile delinquent out to steal something. Elvis didn't realise until it was over. Next thing you know, he's an overnight sensation on the back of those recordings, and I'm treated like some no good bozo busking in the street. Elvis felt bad after that, he told me that. So he kept me on as his personal roadie to haul his guitars and bags about the place. I taught him his signature 'rubber legs' dance move, on account of my bowed legs, but when no one would take me seriously, I sank into depression and alcoholism. I was no good to anyone, but Elvis kept me on his team. He used to get a lot of flack for that, but we were buddies. He confided in me so many times when everyone else was out to take, take, take from him because he trusted me. It's crazy to think I was propping him up while I was at my lowest," Lou laments.

As we walk into the lavish bedroom, I can't help but feel

a little remorse, both for Elvis who had surrounded himself with so many vacuous people, most who no doubt leeched off his fame and success, but also for Louie. Despite all his obvious flaws, he really did know plenty about Elvis, which most people seemed to have discredited him for. If things had turned out very different, who knows where both might have ended up.

There's no time to reflect, however, because just when I thought this tour couldn't get any crazier, Louie is now jumping up and down on the bed like a child.

"Come on," he said. "The King wouldn't mind. This is how he used to get ladies to loosen up before he had sex with 'em."

I hesitate a minute, more out of respect for Elvis than anything, before further embracing my inner child. I then let go and join Louie on the bed and bounce right alongside him.

"Elvis would have liked you," Louie says in a moment of sincerity. "You're a risk taker, rabble-rouser, and fun-seeker."

Whether true or not, I am touched by the genuine sentiment. Here I am, jumping on Elvis's bed, in his home, with a guy who clearly knew him, and regardless of a sour deal or not with Sun Studios and Sam Phillips that may never have been, you can't help but like the guy.

We're soon interrupted by a small group of people who've also wandered upstairs. I stop what I'm doing but Louie doesn't, nor does he even apologise.

"The King wanted everyone who came here to have fun," he broadcasts to the dumbstruck onlookers.

Somehow the "official" guide jacket seems to empower a few of the visitors, one or two of who now join us up on the bed and jump alongside us, squealing with delight.

"You!" an angry voice says that stops us cold.

When I turn around, standing there in the bedroom

doorway and blocking our only way out, is a male authority figure who looks like the head of security, and boy is he furious.

"How many times must you be told that not only are you banned for life from here, but prohibited from being within ten miles?" he shouts, his face blowing up like an enraged baboon.

"You've some nerve after the last time," he continues.

Louie knows the jig is up and true to form, rather than take the wrap, he just points at me.

"This is the asshole you want. He's the one who forced me back here," he says before he rips off his fake jacket and tosses it back in the face of the guard, temporarily impairing his vision, before he makes a mad dash past him and back down the flight of stairs.

The guard runs after him, which allows me to escape and make my way to the top of the landing. Down below, I can't help but laugh as I watch this old, fat man, run around Elvis's grand piano making sure to glide his fingers across all the untouched, dusty keys, while the guard gives chase around it.

I'm not sure whether to make a bolt for the mansion's exit or stay, because despite the trouble I might end up in, I'm having a blast watching Lou get chased round and round the piano, much to the delight and amusement of other onlookers, with some cheering him on. While I haven't laughed this hard in ages, in the end I decide the punishment is not worth the risk, so I leg it out of Graceland. I almost run head first into the side of a taxi that's waiting for someone. Rather than face the prospect of being caught, I take Louie's courage with me and dive into the backseat.

"Mississippi River Front Motel and fast," I yell at the driver who stares back in a state of shock at my hurried entrance.

Hesitant, the taxi driver starts to pull away as he eyes me with suspicion in his rearview mirror. I turn around just as Louie exits the building, somehow evading two security guards on the steps. Eventually, he's encircled by five other security guards who now surround him. I watch on as most of the tourists out front hold up their phones to record the event. He may not be Elvis, but he's about to have more hits than the King ever did, thanks to videos that go viral on social media, I chuckle to myself.

I catch the taxi driver avert his stare beyond me.

"Friend of yours?"

I take a minute to think about it, then reply, "Nah, he's just some silly old bugger who thinks he taught Elvis a trick or two."

We both let out a hearty laugh together before the driver relaxes and returns his gaze ahead. I breathe a little easier once I exit the gates of Graceland, bound for the hotel.

I take one last look back over my shoulder, extremely satisfied. That's one tour the many throngs of adoring Elvis fans will never get. While I had a tonne of doubts before taking his tour, that fun, carefree attitude and inner child, which had been missing from me for so long, are truly grateful. Without realising it, Louie was the circuit breaker I needed. As I look back one last time, observing Lou getting bundled into the back of a police car, I smile to myself and mutter, 'Long live King Louie'.

15

Gone, Vanished

Rather than hunker down and hide out in the hotel to let it all die down, I decide to check out. I figure it's better to make for the state line in case Louie implicates me in the debacle and I'm wanted by the authorities.

Because Memphis is right in the bottom hand corner of Tennessee, I've got two choices: Arkansas or Mississippi, both of which have their pros and cons. In the end it all comes down to one simple fact, Arkansas is literally on the other side of the Mississippi River. From where I am, I can walk across the state line. That's all the logic I need.

I pack everything up in a hurry, then rush to pay my bill. Grace asks me how the tour was. I take a moment to think about it. While I have a slew of differing thoughts, I reply with the only word that best sums it all up.

"Memorable!"

I thank her for the recommendation, then make haste for the border. It won't take me any more than about 20 minutes to walk across to Arkansas but that doesn't mean I don't get jittery, especially when a police squad car cruises on by and scopes me out like I'm some kind of vagrant. It takes all my restraint not to break into a run, but I remain cool, calm and collected, at least on the outside. The rapid heart rate and sweat beads that cling all over the inside of my clothes tell another story.

While the I-40 is the fastest, most direct route over the Mississippi, it's also the most dangerous. There's barely any room on the side of the road to walk over the Hernando de Soto Bridge–they didn't think to add a separated pedestrian lane–and given it's a state line, trucks roar past me.

A few of the truckies look to have some fun at my expense, with a couple seeming out to scare me, either by getting as close as they can to me as they rumble past or by honking their loud air horns when they're practically right on top of me. Even though I hear them coming from behind, I jump every single time.

Only once I cross the Mississippi River and get off the bridge as fast as I can, am I able to resume normal breathing to semi-compose myself. My clothes, now covered in sweat, cling to me as a result of the ordeal. It takes me a long time to calm my jangly nerves and get my heart rate back to a slower, more normal rate.

Even though I'm spooked, I'm also angry. Angry that the bridge builders in their infinite wisdom didn't see it fit to install a safe, separate walkway. And spooked because one slip from a distracted driver, and I'm dead.

I can't shake that last thought from my mind. By the time I make my way to the only roadside diner I find, I'm a mess. My hands are shaking and I'm trembling. It takes a good hour and three cups of Earl Grey tea, to finally come down and de-stress. The longer I sit, the more I breathe normally and relax. However, that near terrifying experience has really rattled me.

Soon the dreaded 'What ifs' start in. *What if one of the*

truck drivers got too close and clipped me? What if one knocked me down? What if I wound up lying in a pool of my own blood? What if the life drained out of my body? What if I was dead on impact? What would the news do for Clea? The pregnancy?

Just when I start to become haunted by the impact my death might have on her, an unknown voice replays the arguments, the constant snipes at one another, the cultural differences, the numerous changes I underwent to have to please her, right through to the reasons I left.

Although it's only late afternoon and not even close to dinner, I need something to eat. I'm hoping more than anything the food will calm the knots twisting in my insides and quell the mental anguish within my mind. When it comes (the food, not the calm), I take long, slow deliberate bites. I don't get more than halfway through before I feel my stomach convulse and I have to make a mad dash to the toilet.

I manage to slam the cubicle door shut behind me before I vomit deep and hard into the toilet bowl. The dinner and anything else I had that day gushes out of me. With a few last guttural groans, it seems the worst is over. I rise to my feet and lean on the back of the toilet door to steady myself, just to catch my breath.

It doesn't last long because I hear my bowels gurgle and churn away below again. I undo my pants as quick as I can and squat down over the seat, and not a moment too soon, as projectile excrement explodes out of me.

My body sweats profusely as a result of the discomfort, so I move around atop the toilet seat for a more comfortable position until the violent bowel eruptions have finished. It feels like an eternity but it's all I can do to allow my body to recover, cool down, and relax. I feel weak but I'm at least confident my insides have expunged everything they possibly could.

When I finally get to my feet and exit the cubicle, I feel okay and somewhat human. I wash my hands in the basin and splash water on my face to rinse off the last of the sweat. When I look up, the reflection staring back at me looks gaunt, pale and a mere shadow of itself. While Memphis offered me some much needed respite, it's obvious this journey is taking its toll on me in more ways than one.

"*This is what you wanted,*" a dark, demon voice asserts.

"*Forget feeling sorry for yourself,*" declares one.

"*Don't doubt your decision,*" remarks another.

"*You don't need her,*" one more chimes.

"*Coward,*" the last one bellows.

I pull at my clammy hair as I scream into the mirror, ready to smash it. I begin to curl up my fists to do exactly that, but a sharp pain shoots up from the duke I used to punch the jukebox (and which hasn't fully healed), reminding me it's not a good idea. I unclench my hands and rush to escape the bathroom, even though I know I'm unable to leave the voices behind.

When I make my way back to my table, a cold cup of tea is all that remains. My plate has been removed but so too has my sole possession, my bag. In a mad frenzy, I rush to find the waitress to immediately harangue her and bombard her with questions of its whereabouts.

She shrugs an 'I don't know' before the manager steps over to intercede. I explain to him my predicament and he offers up a feeble apology. I don't accept it. Frustrated and distraught, I shove him. He tells me to calm down, which is not easy given I am now frantic and half crazed. After my bathroom adventure, this breaks me. All my possessions–wallet, bank cards, journal, laptop, phone, iPod, money... everything–have all been swiped. I'm left with nothing, save for the few dollars in my pocket and my cap on the bench seat.

I want to run outside and check inside the small number of cars that sit in the parking lot, but I don't have the energy. Besides, it's a futile exercise because I know the thief will have long since vanished. I demand to see security footage but the tiny, out of the way roadside diner doesn't have any. I sit back down at my table and start to choke up.

"My whole life was in that bag. My clothes, all my writing and music, most I'll never be able to replace, gone," I stutter between sobs to the sympathetic waitress.

The manager brings over a fresh cup of tea.

"On the house," he mumbles in apology.

But it doesn't help, nothing does. Everything I had or held dear, now gone. If there's a rock bottom, surely this is it.

The manager offers to call the police, but I decline. With no security cameras or a way to track a number plate for the vehicle of the perpetrator, it's a waste of everyone's time. I'm at a total loss what to do next, so I just sit here, numb.

It's now after 6pm and while I've only been here for about 3-4 hours, it's closing time. I can't stay here any longer, I need to move on. The manager has decided not to charge me for my meal or the numerous cups of tea I've had, or the muffin the waitress slipped me on the side. He offers me a ride into town to the nearest bus stop. With no alternative, I have to accept.

It's a short, uncomfortable drive and even though it's not his fault, I am sure he feels regretful for my predicament. He pulls up out front of the bus stop and I can tell he wants to say something, offer me some words of hope, but I just stare blankly at the bus terminal ahead. It's an awkward 30 seconds or so before I summon the will to open the car door and climb out. On reflex, I reach around behind my seat to grab my bag, but then realise I no longer have one.

He gives me a feeble wave of good luck, which feels more like one of relief, before he drives away. I take in a deep breath and walk into the main terminal, where the heating inside at least offers some comfort.

In my despondent state, I'm surprised my ears pick out the mellow, sorrowful tune of 'Lost In The Light' by the Bahamas. It's a song that I had only recently added to my iPod, but which now is being filtered through the terminal's in-house speaker system. The song's lyrics seem even more pertinent than ever, because right now, I do feel lost.

With no possessions and little money, I wander the terminal foyer in a confused and disorientated state. Rather than make a rash decision and choose where to go next, I simply find the nearest quiet corner and nestle among the vacant seats. I can only hope that by morning, something or someone, can help me. I curl up, shut my eyes, and try to find rest in an agitated state. Somehow, eventually, sleep comes.

16

Humble Pie

It's an interrupted sleep, constantly broken up by one terminal announcement after another, as a bus is set to leave. It's also not helped by the hard plastic seats, which make it virtually impossible to find a comfortable position. When I open my eyes and stare out through the large windows, rain streams down the surface of the glass. It could always be worse I think to myself, thankful I'm warm and dry inside.

When I sit up, I feel a slight twinge in my back courtesy of the unaccommodating seats. I add it to my other body aches, bruises, cuts and further issues. I notice I'm not the only soul calling the Trailways Transportation bus terminal, home. Several bodies all lay twisted and contorted over seats or spread out on the floor, using their bags or jackets as pillows, while they wait for their bus.

It's still dark out, I figure maybe around 5am, so I decide to get up and see what I can find. With only $24.57 in my pocket, I know I won't be going too far south or too far west. Ultimately any choice will all depend on how far I can go with what little money I have. I also have to eat. With no debit or credit cards on me (they were all safely tucked into my wallet, inside the bag I no longer have), I'm hesitant to buy anything until I know the price of a bus ticket.

I stroll past a few food shops not yet open, wondering what I should do next. I look up at a big clock face high above me that reads 3:26am and groan. This isn't the time to be thinking straight let alone eat, so I wander back to my little corner only to find it's already been filled by someone else hoping for a better chance of sleep.

I slump my back down against the window nearest to me, and feel the heavy rainfall beat hard against the glass behind me. Each splatter of rain like a lash to my back, minus the whip and the pain. With no phone, bank cards or laptop, I feel despondent and helpless. Unsure what to do, I do the only thing I can. I lower my head in the hopes some rest will give me time to figure things out and provide some clearer answers.

I must have fallen into a heavy slumber because when I stir, I find the bus terminal much more active than before. I crane my stiff neck back up towards the big clock and find it's now 7:48am. The rain that was falling behind me has given way to a small break of morning sun, as daylight streams through. I lean my head back against the window a little longer and allow the sun's warm rays to penetrate me. They do more than that, however, brightening my mood and clearing the fog in my mind.

I go to rise to my feet when I notice something is askew. To my amazement, my cap which must have fallen off my head to the floor as I dozed, now has a handful of notes and coins inside. I scratch my head a moment wondering how, when some more coins drop into it. I look up and catch a man walk away. When I turn my head back around, a woman tosses a dollar bill into it when she strolls past.

It takes me a minute or two to realise what is going on

but then it eventually dawns on me. I lift my head skyward and mumble a small 'thank you' out into the universe. After about 15-20 minutes, and with even more coins and notes, including a five-dollar bill lobbed into it, I now feel a lot more hopeful and re-energised.

The generosity of the passersby has not only lifted my spirits but allowed me to formulate a plan. With the unexpected windfall sitting in my cap, I can grab a bite to eat, then find a nearby public library in order to access their free computers. I'll call my bank to put a hold on my cards, something I should have done yesterday but it completely slipped my mind given the frenetic state I was in.

While there wasn't a lot of money in there to begin with, I'll keep my fingers crossed that my accounts haven't been cleaned out. I'll also see whether the banks can expedite new debit and credit cards to me, so I can access my funds.

Buoyed and with my spirits lifted, I pick up my cap and get to my feet. There's about $8 in change, and $17 in one and five dollar notes. It might not be much, but to me it's breakfast and hope.

With overpriced, deep fried food, I leave the bus terminal and look for a cheaper, healthier alternative. I find it in the form of a food vendor on the side of the street. He doesn't have much, but right now a $2 hot dog and small side salad never tasted so good. I forgo any of the soft drinks on offer and opt instead for a complimentary cup of water from the drink flask that rests on his stand to wash it down with.

I give him a smile of thanks and despite my lack of money, I place a dollar into his tip container. To my surprise he retrieves it and places it back in my hand.

"You look like you could use this more than me," he says.

I start to well up from his kind gesture.

"We make a living by what we do, but we make a life by what we give," the man smiles.

Unwashed, unkempt, dirty and desperate, I must look like shit. Other than thanks, I don't know what to say so I go with the only quote that comes to mind.

"The heart that gives, gathers," I reply as I proceed to walk off, but he calls me back.

"I've never heard that before. It's beautiful. Who said it?"

"Not so much who, more they," I add.

He looks at me perplexed.

"No one knows the text's real author or authors, despite debate. All I know is that it comes from 'The Tao Te Ching', a late 4th century BC, classic Chinese text."

The man is fascinated. I can tell he never expected a history lesson from someone who looks like they're a homeless bum. I find out his name is Mesut, and that he's originally from Turkey.

"What the hell is an Australian doing here in Arkansas of all places?"

I wonder the same thing. I don't tell him that, instead I go with the classic line.

"Doing what Australians do best–travelling," I reply.

Mesut lets out a hearty laugh.

"You Aussies sure do love wandering the globe."

He asks me a few more questions. I give him the bare details, skipping the part about walking out on my pregnant girlfriend, and mention I'm on an exploration of the U.S. and of self. It seems to satisfy him because he makes no more enquiries.

I'm about to leave when I remember to ask Mesut if he knows where the nearest library might be. He can't answer me fast enough. I think Mesut believes that despite my dishevelled appearance, I'd like to go to the library to read up and learn. I haven't the heart to tell him it's to use a free computer and cancel my bank cards.

With much excitement, Mesut points the way, giving me directions to make a left here, turn right there, and be careful to avoid the roadworks. When he catches my bewildered look, he pauses, grabs a napkin off the stand and scribbles it all back down again.

I cannot thank him enough. I'm moved by his kindness and generous spirt and while I've nothing to give in return, I nod a sincere thanks of appreciation then wrap both my hands around his as a mark of gratitude. He surprises me one last time when instead of shaking hands, he grabs me with both arms and proceeds to hug me. In typical Turkish fashion, his hug is one full of gusto and strength.

As I walk away, I start to think that despite peoples' differences and perceived views of others' cultures, most of us are really warm and generous. In my experiences and the many travels I've been on, I find most people to be kind and generous, and all very willing to help when and where they can.

I let that thought carry me all the way to public library, which is roughly a short 15-20 minute amble. I even manage to avoid the road works that has closed down the entire road and one side of a footpath, Mesut warned me about.

When I get to the library, I pocket the napkin and walk to its doors to find it's closed. I look for hours of business and see a sign. Thankfully it opens at 9am, so I don't have too long to wait. I find a park bench out front to think about my next move and to bide my time.

It will take some considered planning and frugal use of my resources (less than $50) but I'm confident that after experiencing total strangers' generosity, I can make it work.

I start to also think about Clea and why I haven't heard from her. Is she all right? Is she in denial? Is she relieved? I also think about the baby. Are they being affected by my absence? Might mum's melancholy sadness be filtering into it? Will it be a boy or a girl? I even start considering names. Why? I have no idea but if I had a pen, I'd scribble a few down on the napkin. I do my best to lock away the couple in my memory bank that resonate the most with me.

I also find myself thinking about Brianna. I wonder how she is getting on in her quest. I'm hopeful she's faring much better than I am. I wonder whether she's given me any thought since we left one another that day. It's probably a pointless exercise to think about, so instead, all I do is sit and wait.

17

Park Bench Plan

You'd be excused for walking past The West Memphis Public Library, which sits on the corner of North Avalon and Oliver. It must be one of the smallest, quaintest libraries I've ever seen. I think my tiny primary school library was bigger. If not for Mesut's detailed directions, I would have easily missed it given that it's nestled among the residential houses that surround it. I only hope they have a computer with free internet access, though I admit, if its size is anything to go by, it looks bleak.

Off to the side, there's a small driveway that doubles as the car park, where two cars, both with drivers who seem content to wait it out like it's part of their regular routine.

While I've had time to sit and wait on the bench and warm up in the sun, I've also had time to formulate an idea. My plan of attack is to call my bank back in Canada, then the bank I have in the States. I'll do this through my Gmail account, where I can make free calls. God bless the digital age. Next, I'll see if I can find homeless shelters between where I am and where I think I'll be for the next few days. From there I'll just have to play it by ear.

I'll keep my fingers crossed that the remainder of my

money is still in these accounts and hasn't been drained. However, if they have, then I hope that the banks can replace the money and expedite my new cards. While I don't have a fixed address for them to be sent, I'm hoping the customer service rep and I can figure out a destination.

It's early Friday morning, and there's still a few minutes to wait before the library opens. I'm not anticipating a long wait time on the phone calling the banks. Normally I'd reach for my iPod to play out the remaining minutes but with it long gone, I allow my mind to drift back to my earlier thoughts where it wanders to Canada and Clea.

She'd be at work now, probably working her little butt off to hit yet another impossible architectural deadline. Those were always stressful times. There wasn't much I could do during those periods other than listen and do my best to empathise. I felt useless to be honest, though often a hug would make all the difference she would say. I wonder if she'd like a hug now.

I had also been talking to her belly in an attempt to connect more with the growing baby inside. Sometimes I would read a children's book. 'Guess How Much I Love You' was a go-to fave. In it, the two main characters, Little Nutbrown Hare and Big Nutbrown Hare, would say to each other, "I love you this much," and then tried to show how much love they had for each other as they each stretched their arms out wide, or reached up tall with their hands high, or turned upside down, etc. It was an easy read and a beautiful story. I miss it.

Then in the evenings I would play a soothing song from my iPod, carefully placing my headphones over her belly. I'd lay up close and listen at the same time. They were the moments when I felt most close and connected. There were too few of those.

More often than not though, we'd end up in arguments over petty things. Things that no one should get worked up about in my opinion. Leaving one unwashed tea mug in the kitchen for example. She was concerned it would leave a stain, then repeat it ad nauseam every time. It got to the point that if I didn't get up and do it right then and there to appease her, she'd never let up. Even now, I can feel my eardrums pulsate at the verbal onslaught I would regularly cop.

I worked out of home so it was usually me who would have to break up my day to carry out the many chores she'd command of me. The place was already hospital grade clean, so it wasn't like I wasn't doing my fair share. Laundry, vacuuming, dusting, mopping, whatever it was, I did it but it was never good enough to meet her exceptionally high standards. She'd come home and rather than be happy it was one less thing for her to think about or do, she would pick out the tiniest dust mote I inadvertently missed or point out clothes that weren't folded to her exacting standards. On a couple of occasions, she'd even thrown the clothes at my face for me to refold, then stand over my shoulder critiquing me until I got it just so. It not only drove me insane but often started heated arguments that quickly escalated and spiralled out of control. It probably most explains my sudden exit and this road trip. I couldn't cope. Something had to give. In the end, it was me.

It's not like I didn't love her, I did. I mean, didn't I? But you don't leave a warm city you live in and love (Los Angeles), to travel all the way across to the other side of the country and go north of the border, where it's bitterly cold. You don't do that on a whim. And now, here I was in bloody Arkansas… Arkansas! Who saw that coming?

Had the love faded? Was I blinded at the possibility of what could be and didn't see what was? So many questions that percolated around inside my head, all of which I had no answer for, though not for lack of trying.

I was hoping this journey would give me some answers and the space in which to get them. Maybe even rethink my decision or see things differently. While I had the space, no answers were forth coming. Instead, I seemed to get more questions or to my surprise, revelations, that I could never have anticipated. Revelations which often set me back on my heels.

Before I could delve too deeply into why that was, I heard the jangle of keys to signal the library was about to open. In my daze, I'd missed my chance to wait by the door and be first in, however, given there were just two people, the 30-something, female librarian who had unlocked the door, and an older woman who chatted to her like an old friend, I wasn't concerned.

The thoughts I'd had, while mixed, were still useful, nonetheless. A couple even bringing up some recent happier memories for me. I hadn't really done much soul-searching or self-reflection so far, in part, because I felt plagued by the inner voices and demons in my head. Although I had wanted to "find myself" on this journey and had so far fallen short, I was still grateful for the small chance to do a little introspection whenever, and wherever, I could.

I strolled through the swinging door and into the main library. While on the outside it appeared small, on the inside it was a different story. The former home had been gutted and completely remodelled. It gave the appearance of being much larger than it was. I was impressed. Whoever had done the renovation had done a great, innovative job with the limited space. There were numerous shelves of course, and many more than I would have expected, but there was also strategically placed tables and chairs that didn't clutter up the space. There were also some lounge chairs further back, which made for a very inviting reading area, plus a kid's play area that had been partitioned off by glass, and finally an area for the internet, which was tucked away from full view. It had been designed to fit the necessity of having one yet not interfere with the overall aesthetic. The former home now looked more like a modern, architectural design with its many angles and multipurpose functional areas.

I immediately made my way over to the internet area, where to my surprise, they did have a computer. Unlike the rest of the library, the lone, solitary, sad looking relic from the past was out of kilter with the rest of the modern feel of the place. Much to my chagrin, however, when I got to it, it was already in use by the old lady. I just stood slack-jawed as I watched her type one slow letter after another. E, F, L, O, W. I wanted to scream but this was a library, so couldn't.

I went back to the main desk to speak with the only other person in the place, the 30-something librarian. I was hoping maybe she'd have a spare computer I could use in the office. She explained in a strict, condescending manner, that they did indeed have an *office* computer but it was for <u>employees only.</u> She made sure to articulate the last two words. She didn't express any sympathy for my predicament, merely adding I would have to wait until Gertrude had finished.

"How long will that take?" I asked.

"As long as she needs. Now if you'll excuse me, I have work to do," she said in a dismissive tone before she turned away to a pile of books.

"Don't you have a 30 or 60 minute limit," I interjected?

The librarian stopped what she was doing, and I could tell she saw me as a nuisance, because she turned back around with a look that could only be described as disgruntled.

"During weekdays and after school hours yes, but on weekends when it is much quieter, it's first come, first served, for as long as they need," she declared.

"Seriously? Bloody hell," I vent a little too loudly.

"Sir, if you can't keep your voice down, I will have to ask you to leave. Now either wait your turn or find the nearest internet cafe."

"Can I at least make a call to my bank to cancel my cards?"

She points to a well placed, handmade sign next to the phone. 'Employee use only'.

"I suppose borrowing a pen is forbidden, too?"

Without mouthing a word, she points at a blue pen in front of me, taps the sticker attached, and just like that, goes back to the pile of books on the desk.

Stuck to the side of the pen is a small note which reads, 'Employees only. Do not move.'

"Great," I grumble.

That zen like state I seemed to be in outside, dispersed in seconds. I'd allowed my frustrations to bubble to the surface and boil over. It was a continual work in progress for me. Something that had also contributed to, and inflamed, my relationship with Clea. I'd never been able to gain control over that side of my personality for very long.

I thought about approaching the old woman, what was her name again... Gertrude? I'd then explain why I urgently needed the computer but then I was concerned I'd be too blunt and she'd take it the wrong way, so I decided against it.

With nothing to do other than bide my time, I silently fumed. As I seethed, however, a new option popped into my head. Rather than sit and wait it out again, I headed over to the reference section and pulled out an atlas. I flicked through the pages until I found what I was looking for, a map of the United States. It had occurred to me that I'd not only been travelling without one but that I didn't really know where I was, what distance I'd travelled, or how far there was left to go. I thumbed past several pages until I found what I was looking for, a road map of the southern half of the United States.

I peered down and found West Memphis, Arkansas. I then flicked back a page or two to look at the greater map of the U.S. To my amazement, I'd come almost halfway already. I then looked at the rest of the journey and noticed that it would be possible to head south into Mexico from Texas, if I didn't go on to L.A. That would mean bypassing the ex-flame altogether, and the thought of seeing her and welcoming me with open arms, seemed more and more ridiculous by the day. But that had been the plan from the beginning. It had given me a destination to aim for. Now, well now I was unsure where to go and what to do. For reasons unknown, dropping down into Mexico from Texas, also felt too soon. I felt compelled, for whatever purpose, to take the longer, slower route through New Mexico, Arizona, and onto California and Los Angeles, before then possibly going south. Whether I saw my former lover or not, it all seemed to sit much better with me, even given my precarious predicament.

I then get to thinking about Tyson or as she was more commonly referred to by most people, Ty. Her name, Tyson, meant 'Firebrand' and like the very essence of her name, I questioned why was I even going to see her. Despite the fact the heat and sexual tension never dissipated between us, as a couple, we had crashed and burned years before. She had, unsuccessfully, tried to keep her distance, scared we'd end up in bed together again, regardless of whether I was single or not. I know where I stood on the situation and knew she was right. However, when you have something that intense, passionate and all consuming, where it not only rocks your body but your mind, and where we'd both hit a sexual tantric high, the likes of which neither of us had experienced before, well, I wanted to see if we could revive and relive it again.

Of course, the demons never let up on that. Always telling me what I once had even though I needed to let go of it by the end, though I didn't have full say in that matter. I mean, how do you convince someone to fall right along with you and go all-in? Someone with their own personal demons to exorcise, along with an undiagnosed bipolar disorder they didn't recognise? The answer is you don't. Despite Ty knowing she had everything she wanted in a partner, standing right there in front of her, she always held something back. I had enough awareness to recognise it, but even more dignity to step aside and allow her the time to process her unresolved issues.

Yet through desire (or desperation), I now convinced myself things would be *different* this time, that she'd be in a better place, mentally and emotionally, to receive the love I had so willingly laid out at her feet last time around. It just involved me exiting my current situation, fleeing to the other side of the country on impulse, and having it, her… us again. But when you're in a loveless, unaffectionate, unhealthy relationship, and you've tasted something as intoxicating as what Ty and I had, where it feels like your whole being is electrified, then what did I have to lose?

HA!

However, it wasn't all about a heightened sexual connection either. There were also the numerous, open and vulnerable conversations we'd had just sitting on her comfy green couch. Most of them made us feel so raw and exposed, that it wasn't uncommon for either of us to feel aroused as a result. It was something neither of us had ever been able to explain or figure out. It was as if laying yourself so bare in front of someone you fully trusted, just flicked a switch internally on a deeper soul level. Those discussions, no matter the subject matter or the depth of the dialogue, where tears could be shed in a moment of unadulterated vulnerability, I'd find myself rock hard and she'd be sopping wet. Before we knew it, we'd be making love more deeply connected than either of us ever thought possible. It took a lot of energy, however, and often would take us into dark, unexposed places within the recesses of our subconscious, that frankly, were never easy to handle, let alone deal with. If I could hazard a guess, it was this more than anything else, that had stopped Ty from falling over the edge and crashing headlong into a deeper, more powerful love than she'd ever known possible.

Me on the other hand, I took the leap of faith knowing love would protect me. It didn't. It was tough to look back up at her, not having made the full jump into love with me. I endured for a few more months, but something had shifted between us. The tighter I gripped, the more she slipped through my fingers, until eventually I just had to let go to preserve my self-esteem. The friendship then floundered, stumbled and spluttered along until it felt like it was on life support.

How had two best friends, in what I thought was a lifelong love, walk away from each other? It had befuddled me in the proceeding years. How had I let something that powerful slip to step blindly into something as serious and demanding as fatherhood, which was a whole other lifelong commitment? That thought had always plagued me, causing me many sleepless nights.

Deep down I knew the answer, fear. While a love had been

there on her end, I knew she felt scared by what we had and discovered in one another's presence. The depth and connection, through to the exposed, raw emotions and the possibility to see out the rest of her years with me. It scared her. Had it been too much for her to handle or accept? Did she not think she was worthy enough? Had I underestimated what we had? I couldn't force her to be in one hundred percent, totally in love and feel what I was feeling, day in, day out, moment to moment. I also couldn't allow myself to sit and wait on a change of heart, one that may never come.

While it had hurt and left me a damaged, untethered man for a couple of years afterwards, sooner or later I had to pick myself up, dust myself off, and move on. No heady, tantric high is worth the mental, emotional and spiritual distress waiting for someone to fall in love with you, knowing they may never do so, no matter how painful that is to accept.

Yet here I was, ready to possibly step back into that unpredictability again on nothing more than a whim, all to escape my current predicament. Maybe time had shown and given her reason to change her mind. I'm reminded of the simple quote, *"Love isn't complicated, people are."* Perhaps Ty had mellowed in the time since and is now a lot less complicated than she had been then, while also being much more aware of what we'd had. And who knows, quite possibly much more willing and open to exploring what she knew was rare. I wouldn't or couldn't know the answer to that unless I went to find out. Only now it was a lot more complicated, less clear for me.

In desperation, and to escape the thoughts that had now ransacked my brain, igniting old memories and exploding hope within my mind again, I grab the atlas and walk over to the photocopier. Figure I might as well use my time wisely while I wait for 'Gerty' to take her sweet time. I lift the lid, place the map face side down, then close the flap back on top. I'm about to hit copy but there's a coin box. It reads:

'50c per B&W copy. $2.00 for color.'

Fifty cents? That's highway robbery, I mutter to myself. When I weigh up the fact I want to print several pages of the maps I'll need to guide me, including Mexico, it'll be well over six dollars. Six dollars I can't spare at present.

I flip the lid up in frustration, snatch at the atlas and head back to my table. What now? I wonder. I tap on the page with my fingers as I mull over my choices. I can either not worry about it and keep winging it like I have. It's been working so far or... There doesn't seem to be any other option. I keep tapping my fingers on the page a little louder and louder each time, considering, pondering, questioning another choice.

"Shhhh," the librarian calls out in my direction.

And just like that, my decision is made. I grab at the corner of the page, wait, then pretend to cough, ripping the page out from the spine, coughing loudly as I do.

I then fold the page in on itself and tuck it into my back pocket. I repeat the coughing 'fit' four more times. Twice for Arizona, and a third and fourth time for New Mexico. I fold the pages up and also slip them into my pocket. I can tell my cough is getting to the librarian, but with her back turned she's none the wiser. All that's left is Mexico, which covers four pages. I stare at it a while and decide I can't rip more pages out without alerting the librarian who will discover my ruse. I close the cover, slip the book back into the shelf where it came from, out of index order of course just to mess with her. When she ends up in this aisle to restock the shelves with books, she'll discover the anomaly. It's the stupid, little things that have always made me smile. While it's immature, my inner child is happy at least.

I move across to a water fountain, slurp on the cool water and make sure to overemphasise my sigh of satisfaction when I see her look over at me. When I'm done, I point at my throat indicating I was parched and needed water. She frowns before she carries on about her business. Talk about a staunch bitch. There's no getting through her tough exterior.

When I finish sucking down some water, I wipe my mouth and look over at where Gerty is or was supposed to be. I say supposed to be because she's now no longer sitting at the computer. I swear this old woman was a ninja in a former life. First, she beat me in the door, now she's disappeared. Talk about stealth. I do a quick scan and find she's now at the main desk in conversation with the librarian, who's stopped what she was doing to fully engage with her. I shake my head, incredulous.

Without waiting to find out whether Gerty's finished, I hustle to the computer and sit myself down. In automatic operator mode, I open a new browser window and log into my email account. I enter my details and wait for the super slow Internet Explorer browser to open. It really is the laughing stock of the world wide web. Eventually the archaic egg timer stops flipping and opens up.

I don't bother looking at my emails, of which there are many, but go straight to the Gmail Google Talk phone option. It occurs to me that I don't actually know the Royal Bank of Canada customer service phone number, so I have to open another window and search for it. When I eventually find it, I copy and paste it into my G-talk and click the call button. I look for the volume buttons on this ancient computer when the phone is answered by the tele-prompter.

"Welcome to the Royal Bank of Canada," it screams out.

I scurry to turn it down as it keeps spouting out, "A customer service representative will be with you shortly," but I'm not having any luck finding it. Just when I think it can't get any worse, the librarian charges over towards me, her face flushed with anger.

I hold my hands up in protest begging for mercy when she's almost on top of me, but rather than lash out at me, she reaches around the back of the machine and turns it down before she drops a pair of earbuds on the desk. 'Library use only. Return when done', written on a small label attached to the earbuds. I don't even get to thank her before she storms straight back to the desk to re-engage in her conversation with Gerty.

I shove the lead into the computer, which I find much easier than the volume knobs, and listen to the message being repeated again. How I pine for the old days when customer service meant you actually spoke to someone, not listen to a robotic computer voice spruik the company's latest offers.

Eventually after pressing too many options, I'm connected to a voice on the other end who sounds like they're half asleep as they prattle through their welcome speech. I cut them off in the middle of it, which you should never do if you want them to help but I've become impatient.

I bang on at a rapid rate of knots recalling my story to the detached operator, who feigns interest. By the time I'm done they politely say they're terribly sorry for my loss–I can hear the insincerity from here. With a short explanation, they then transfer me to another department. I go to interject but before I'm heard, I'm drowned out by the muzak these big conglomerates all think will soothe us but only enrages us further. I do my best to breathe through the wait.

By the time the second representative answers, I'm doing

my best not to lash out. I'm greeted by the much livelier, Shanice, who listens intently as I explain my plight.

Shanice tells me, in a very calm, understated manner, that because it's a debit card and not a credit card, I will have to wait 5-7 business days before they can assess my case and determine if my money has in fact been stolen? She goes on to say that it would be different if it were a credit card, because that's the bank's money and not mine, which they happily refund inside 1-2 days. It doesn't help cool my mood any.

I take a deep breath as I take all this in. I could let my anger and frustration boil over but it's not Shanice's fault. She's just a company puppet. I ask her if there is any money in my account.

She takes a moment to tap a few buttons before glumly saying, "Your account balance is negative $100."

"Negative $100?" I stammer.

"Yes, you have an automatic overdraft feature which kicks in when any unavailable funds don't reach above $100."

Great, I think to myself. Not only has my account been cleaned out, of which there was about $800-$900 left, but now it's in overdraft.

"The good news," Shanice goes on, "Is that because we've now logged the incident, you won't be charged the $5.50 late overdraft fee."

"Ha!" I laugh in disbelief.

"I'm truly sorry, sir," she adds.

We talk a little longer and I find out the only way to get a new card sent to me, is to have a fixed address for me to sign upon registered delivery, though there doesn't seem any point with no money in the account. Regardless, I explain that I'm currently on the road and in the U.S and not likely to have a fixed address any time soon. I'm told that if I can't provide one, then my only alternative is for my new replacement card to be sent to my currently listed Canadian address.

I think about it a moment but know that it's not a viable option. Instead, I provide her with the only address I know in the US, my old apartment in Studio City, L.A. Thankfully, I arranged some friends to take over my lease before I left. I'll have to get in touch with them and explain why I'm getting a card sent there, avoiding the reasons why where possible.

Once Shanice is satisfied that I will be there to sign off to receive my new card, she adds. "Is there anything else I can help you with?"

I want to yell, fix the system, replace your elevator muzak with something more modern, and screw the Royal Canadian Bank for being so rigid in their policies. But I don't. Instead, I utter a small thanks and end the call.

I do the same thing with my US Chase account. While there was less money in it, maybe $350 at a pinch, like my Canadian bank account, it too has been drained. The saving grace is that that I can order a card and pick one up from any branch within the US. It'll just take a few days to be delivered.

I don't even bother calling my Australian bank, in part because there was no money in it. I do email customer support, however, letting them know what has happened. A replacement card will no doubt get sent to my mum's address back in Australia. I'll figure out the logistics of her posting it to me later, for now I have to figure out how to generate extra money to see me through these next 5-7 business days. I can only hope my banks are able to quickly and easily resolve the fraud and refund my money.

The thought comes up to contact Clea, ask for something to tide me over, though she was already stretched. I'm also not ready to speak to her and starting with a financial favour is the worst way to begin any conversation when you've left someone. I could ask a friend, though he recently went through a bitter divorce, so I know his funds have been tied up in that. He had been strapped the last time we spoke anyway. That leaves my mum, but she's bailed me out more than enough during my overseas dreams and the last time I spoke to her, she told me she wouldn't do it anymore.

Despondent, I troll through the many messages which flood my inbox looking for inspiration. It's all I can do to distract myself. There's the usual promotions, subscriptions, junk and other non-urgent emails, but then I freeze. Right there, buried half way down, is an email from Clea.

I hover over the message for a long time, pausing to open it, unsure if now is the right time given my current mood. My finger twitches and pulses nervously fighting the many mixed emotions I feel. I'll admit, I'm scared by what it might contain. My curiosity eventually gets the better of me, and I click it open.

'I miss you', is all it says.

Short, simple, to the point.

The more I sit and stare at it, the more it packs a strong, emotional punch. Had I not left, I wouldn't be in this situation in the first place. It's little consolation.

I log out of my email, not ready or equipped to reply. I close the browser windows, clear my history and am about to shut down the computer, when I notice an open document right there on the screen, which I'd missed in my haste to open my Gmail and phone up my banks. The headline draws me in.

PARENTING: THE DARK TRUTH BEHIND
THE FAUX SMILES

'Any experienced couple who have had children will tell you the road to parental bliss is far from smooth. Often arguments and disagreements ruin the harmony created and can damage the very product of love the two people created – their baby.

[Insert arguing couple image]

If not properly taken care of, a relationship no matter how strong, can become a battleground in between a baby's cries.

[Insert some facts and figures]

But it doesn't have to be this way. A baby can also bring a couple, even those who have problems, closer.

[Insert supporting infographic]

As a five time mother, eight time grandmother, I can help clear the obstacles so that the adjustments of a new baby strengthen the relationship, not destroy it.

[Insert a couple in a hug photo]

The hardships of life with a newborn baby are real. Don't become a statistic.

[Insert final graph or stats in support]

Let the love flow, not slow.

[Insert third/final image: a happy couple & baby]

For more information, call Gertrude on: 818.BUB.BLISS.'

I sit there a moment, stunned. I turn to look over at the little old lady I had dismissed as nothing more than a nuisance but she's no longer gabbing to the librarian. I look around the library to see where she has disappeared to when from out of nowhere, she appears. I jump in fright.

"Can I help you with something," she says in a terse tone, peering over my shoulder at her open word document.

"Sorry, I just… I didn't mean to. I needed," but she dismisses my stumbles.

"If you don't mind, I'd like to finish my advertisement."

"Sure, sure," I say getting up out of the seat and offering it to her.

She plonks herself down into the seat, gets annoyed by something, then realises I readjusted the chair. She lowers it into the position she had before, then goes to continue but sees me linger nearby. She knows something is up.

"Can I help you?"

I'm tempted to explain my situation and maybe seek her counsel, but I don't. I just leave.

18

Lost & Found?

After that email, I couldn't stay in the library any longer. I had to get out and grab some fresh air. I'm also not ready to talk to a relationship expert, even though I am sure Gerty would have been able to impart her wisdom and share what she knows to at least give me a little clarity. Of everything Clea could have written, that was the single most beautiful, eloquent, and painful thing for me to read.

If I'm honest, it's thrown me for a loop and affected me more than I would have ever imagined. Up until now, while I had given her some passing thoughts, I'd never truly given it much more than that. I knew she might not be surprised at my leaving Toronto, given I despised that city, but she would be shocked and devastated by my sudden exit. While I believed it was for the best because if her past criticisms were anything to go by, it felt like I was only going to stuff up my unborn child's life in her eyes. However, by not sticking around, I was no longer sure if I may have made a reasonable difference or left a more lasting impact upon them.

This was not a question I was ready to answer, let alone deal with. I was in an uncomfortable, compromised position, and I hated it. All I wanted when I found out she was pregnant was to be a better father than my own dad ever was. I only had to stay to do that. But I couldn't even last six months, and that was before they were even born. What chance of me staying when they arrived? Dad of the year I was not.

Yet here I was, over 1600 kilometres away, and all I can think of are those beautiful moments that were all ours. From the memorable, ethereal 'Bloor/Yonge street hug' as we dubbed it. A hug that was so much more. It was one where we stayed in a comforting embrace for a full 10 minutes as people rushed about us to catch trains during peak hour, and of how my body sighed when it sunk into her clutch while she held me. Or the 'Airport shuttle cuddle' that moved a shuttle employee to tears who had witnessed us do something similar when I left Toronto to head back to Los Angeles after a short visit. Or more recently, thinking about our little one and the things I was looking forward to, such as teaching them to swim, ride a bike, or kick a footy. These were the moments where time melted away, the world disappeared, and I thought we would last forever.

In my efforts to escape the library, and my own head, I'd wandered far and now I was lost. Then again, you could argue I had been lost since undertaking this journey. Perhaps I'd been lost long before that. Born out of frustration and a desire for something more, it was a selfish move and I knew it.

Our relationship hadn't been a total fraud. I still felt something for her, but what, and on what level, even I didn't know anymore. We still enjoyed some good times and travel together, the happier memories as I liked to call them. One that stood out, included a fun visit to the Dominican Republic that we took together, where I think I left a tiny piece of my heart in its 500+ year old town of Santo Domingo.

We'd made a huge commitment to each other that trip,

little did we know then that our escape would also be the beginning of a new life–one where two become three. When we found out about the pregnancy, however, it seemed to also spell the demise of us. The beautiful moments that had brought us close, soon become too few and far between. Every day new concerns and issues would arise. Trust me when I say this had been the hardest decision I have ever made. Being on the road hadn't made it any easier to accept, let alone deal with.

I knew I needed help. I'd never been comfortable asking for it, even when they were placed right in front of me.

While I should have headed back to the library to see if Gertrude would be open to hearing a torn drifter, I now find myself on the corner of a busy intersection. At first I'm surprised by the rush of traffic, but then it becomes a welcome distraction from the clatter inside my mind. I press the pedestrian signal and wait, head down.

"Remember, look up, so the sun can shine its smile on you," a little voice tells me.

I look over and see a small child holding the hand of its mother, who's preoccupied on her phone. With innocence in its eyes, the beautiful remark throws me for a loop. I knew I had been glum since taking those first steps, and while I'd had a few moments of fun to distract me with Brianna, and then at Graceland with Louie, I'd forgotten to appreciate what I had in my life. A solid and loving relationship, a stable and safe home, my writing, and my health (mental and physical), along with all the travel I'd been able to undertake. There was a lot to be grateful for, yet here I was moping around like some sad sack always lost inside his own head.

If my travels and meditations had taught me anything, it was that I should be thankful for everything. Every breath I took, every new day I received, every moment big or small...

being alive.

When the lights change for us to cross, I stay behind to ponder where I drifted so far from that course. The child looks back at me with a puzzled expression when I stay put. I must look pretty silly waiting at the lights while they walk across to the other side. For some reason I feel compelled to wave as I stand there. When they get to the other side, the child waves back with extra enthusiasm before its mother drags it away down the street, all while still on her phone.

The lights change to red before I get a chance to move off and cross, but in that moment, that fleeting exchange, I can feel something grow inside me. I don't know what it is, but it feels like a glimmer of hope.

While I knew I didn't like my current situation and loathed the city I was living in, often pining for home after being overseas for eight long years (though every time I brought this up it generated a whole new set of arguments), something had to change. It wasn't my living arrangements. It was me!

19

Tune Of Hope

Filled with a sense of renewed hope, I walk to a nearby diner, which also doubles as a truck stop. It's filled with an assortment of drivers, most of whom sport oversized bellies, shaggy beards, and a weariness that comes from long haul driving. I'm about to ask a few of them if it's possible to bum a lift, when a song I have not heard in over 20 years, plays on the radio tucked up in the corner.

The Manhattan Transfer's, sweet 'Chanson d'Amour', which translates as 'song of love', stops me in my tracks. It casts me back to a gentler, easier time, when I had that wide-eyed wonder and was more of a free spirit. One where anything was possible, and where I didn't have a care or the weight of the world on my shoulders. Even though I got nicknamed 'The Thinker' at high school, in so much as I'd unknowingly and unintentionally, strike the pose of Rodin's famous bronze sculpture that made it look like I was deep in thought, I rarely had anything deep to think about.

My mind drifts back to that devil-may-care time while I stand and listen, allowing the French words to seep through me. The waitress and one or two customers give me weird looks when I remain rooted to the spot while it plays out. I don't know if it's a sign or just a silly coincidence, but when the song's finished, I retreat outside with a sadness in my heart longing for that easier, carefree past I can no longer attain.

What's wrong with me, when a song can conjure up faded memories from over twenty years ago, and allude to a better version of me? I was far from a decent guy back then, being more arrogant, selfish, reckless and just plain stupid. One who didn't really care for much or for anyone. I know that I've changed for the better in the years since, and while I am a far cry from that immature guy, some self-doubts remain.

I must cut a forlorn figure as I wait by the exit that leads onto the main road. With no more than about $40, taking the bus further south is out of the question. I've no idea what I'll do for money between here and Los Angeles either, given it will take me about the same amount of time to get there as it will for any funds to return to my account, if they actually do. I'll have to figure it out. If I have to work an odd job here and there, washing dishes or cleaning toilets just to get a feed, then so be it.

As I'm contemplating my dilemma, a truck drives up slowly, then with a puff of its airbrakes, stops beside me.

"Where ya headed," a gruff voice inside asks.

"South West."

"Near enuff. Get in."

Although I didn't have my thumb out to hitch, I don't turn down the offer of a free ride. I grab the side rail and clamber up onto the passenger side step. With no bags, I open the door and climb into the passenger seat. I close the door behind me and introduce myself.

"Roy," the driver says matter of factly, before he shifts his big rig into first gear, and we set off.

20

An Uncomfortable Gaze

Roy isn't much of a talker, which is perfectly fine with me. Other than he's "not from 'ere" and "been drivin' for 30 years", there's very little exchange between us. All I know is we're heading west and that's good enough for me.

There's bugger all to see along the way, it's just flat farmland and little else. I doze on and off a couple of times to the truck's sway and hum of the engine, but it's more fitful than a solid sleep. It also doesn't help that my mind is a hive of activity, thinking about Clea's email, as well as the little child's interaction at the stoplight, and Gertrude's advert. They've all given me something to ponder.

I'm absent in thought so I don't hear Roy ask the first time. It's not until he speaks louder that I hear him.

"Hungry?"

Yes, I nod.

"There's half a grinder behind ya," he mentions.

I've no idea what a grinder is let alone what it even looks like, but I unclip my seatbelt and climb into the cabin behind me. I look around, notice a couple of playboy posters stuck to the walls, a small shelf with a carton of Marlboro cigarettes on it, a half empty bottle of whiskey and a stained glass beside it, along with an unmade bed but no food. I'm about to say something when I catch Roy's eyes in the rearview mirror.

"Doggie bag."

Right, the doggie bag. It's easy to miss first time around because it's a crumpled up paper bag hidden in the unmade bed. I pluck it up and return to my seat.

"Thanks mate," I chime as I dive into the bag.

When I do, that's when I learn that a grinder is just another term for a sandwich. This one is a meatball sanga, that's half eaten and looks a day old but I'm not going to quibble about it.

I scoff it down a little too fast, spilling some of the tomato sauce down my chin, with a few drops spilling onto my t-shirt. Rather than grab the napkin inside the bag and wipe it away, I simply rub it in to the other stains that have amassed.

"Coke?" Roy enquires.

"Sure."

With eyes on the road, one hand on the wheel, he opens a small bar fridge, hidden from view under the wide arm rests in the middle, and tosses me a can. He closes the fridge door and continues to focus on the road ahead.

I lift the metal tab and press it into the can opening. Bad mistake because it fizzes up and over the rim. I do my best to suck it up or catch it in my hand, but some of it inevitably spills down into my lap. Great! Now it looks like I've peed myself. I reach back into the doggie bag and snatch at the napkin inside, pulling it out to then pad at the wet patch to dry it off.

When I turn to face Roy to say thanks for the food and drink, he's already looking at me or more to the point, my crotch, with a look that lingers way more than is comfortable. I shift uneasily in my seat, trying to get into a less susceptible position, then drop the doggie bag into my lap. I notice the look of disappointment on his face before he returns his attention back on the road ahead.

Grateful I'm no longer being leered at, I let out a small, silent sigh. I make a mental note of where the door handle is, making sure it's unlocked, however the six-foot jump could be a problem. I then scan about me, hoping to spy some kind of makeshift weapon, just in case I might need one.

I spot a medium sized Maglite down by my feet, though it's clipped in tight to the side of the passenger console. I look at its unfamiliar clip, unsure how to unclip it, however, at least I know it's close at hand. This could all be in my head but it's the first time, however, I've ever felt so vulnerable, so I'm trusting my gut.

While the Maglite offers me little peace of mind somewhat, knowing its hard, metal exterior will come in handy if required, I honestly feel uneasy. Even though Roy may turn out to be completely harmless, and regardless of whether he's headed in the direction I need to go, I decide then and there that the next time he stops for gas or food, I'll politely thank him for the lift and seek out another ride.

I go back to eating the grinder, but now it has an unsavoury taste to it, so it makes it hard to swallow. That ill at ease feeling only grows. There was something about his long, lecherous look, that made my skin crawl.

21

Despoliation

Little Rock, Arkansas, now there's a place I thought I'd never wind up. But here I am, smack bang in a small town with a population of 197,357 according to the sign we passed.

"Here's a fun fact for you," Roy announces out of the blue. "It's not only the state capital but also very near the geographic centre of the state."

"Okay," I mutter not wanting to engage.

Oblivious to my disinterest, he carries on.

"And did you also know that the city derives its name from a rock formation along the river, named 'La Petite Roche', so called by the French back in 1799?"

"No," I reply adding, "I'm not here to play tourist."

He gives me a puzzled look, one that's mixed with bewilderment and irritation before he shuts his mouth and goes quiet, ending his little impromptu factoid tour.

Good! The less I have to hear from him, the better. Right now, I'm hoping that any one of La Petite Roche's citizens will be heading south, because I don't plan to stay long. The longer I've been sitting in Roy's cab, the longer I've felt more perturbed. At one point on the drive, he suggested I remove my pants "to let them fully dry". Err, no thanks! I'd much

146

rather a wet, coke-stained ball sack than his unwelcome, leering eyes.

There were also some crude attempts to joke about my wet situation, enquiries apropos to my sexual preferences, and more. I barely uttered a word, keeping my replies as short as possible to cut dead the conversation.

I hear the truck slow as he switches down gears, ready to pull into the nearest truck stop to fill up. Once stopped, I thank him as quick as I can before I'm straight out the door. I make my way to the nearest toilet, which sits a good deal away from the main truck stop diner, close the stall door and lock the latch behind me. I feel on edge, knowing that the large, bear-sized frame of Roy, would have easily overpowered me had he wanted. I'm not sure if he's one of those predatory type of guys who preys on people he can easily overpower or if he's simply a harmless trucker with a penchant for cock. Either way, I wasn't going to hang around to find out.

When I feel my heart rate return to a more regular pace, I venture out of the stall and face the mirror. There's an obvious dark patch right across my front. It'll dry but it really does look like I've peed myself. The chances of hitching a ride further south looking like this will diminish, so I take my pants off to run them under some warm water. I knead some soap from the hand dispenser into them with my hands rubbing it back and forth. When I'm satisfied the stain is gone, I proceed to dry them as best I can with one of those stupid hand dryers that requires you to place your hands down, fingers first, before it turns on. Oh for the old days when all you had to do was simply push a button for hot air and place your hands underneath.

Because the hand dryer is super loud and on the far wall facing away from the entrance, I fail to hear or see a figure enter the bathroom. A strong hand covers my mouth from behind as their other hand reaches lower and forces my boxer briefs down. They then tug and loosen the belt around their jeans.

I struggle, fight and push back as best I can but the physical strength of the man behind me only makes him grip harder. He shoves me up against the wall, where I smack the side of my head on the tiled surface. It leaves me dazed. Before I know it, I'm being penetrated, receiving his hard, painful thrusts over and over.

Whoever stands behind me is rough, forceful, and doesn't hesitate to rape me, giving it everything they've got. It hurts like hell, and I feel utterly powerless, pinned to the wall, as the hand dryer crushes into my abdomen, forcing me to breathe in shallow, laboured breaths.

At one point it feels like I am about to pass out as my legs buckle underneath me. My body begins to slip down the wall but this just angers the man behind me, who tightens his grasp on me as he's forced to prop me up. This only makes him angrier and his thrusts more urgent. I'm sure I can feel more than just a trickle of blood running down my inner thigh.

With a final flurry and a last thrust, the attacker rams himself even harder inside me before he lets out a guttural groan and ejaculates. He then retracts himself, which is a different kind of agony again, before he hurriedly does up his belt and then with heavy footsteps, makes a quick exit out the bathroom. When he's gone, my body slumps to the floor.

The pain I feel is excruciating as I lay here. I do my best to slip my boxers up my thighs and over my blood-soaked rear. If I thought I had hit rock bottom before, I was wrong. Dead wrong.

Unable to move from my crumpled position on the floor to reach up and grab my jeans, I curl into a ball and sob. I then go into a complete state of shock, and before I know it, my eyes glaze over and I black out.

When I come to, it takes me a while to register a voice, which shouts and calls out above me while they attempt to rock me awake. I push them away and recoil back in fear, unsure who it is or what they want. They realise my concern and take a few steps back to allow me to get my bearings.

Once I realise where I am, I gingerly prop myself up and lean against the wall. While I can't make out the face of the gentle voice, embarrassed by my state of semi-undress, and the incident, I place my head in my arms and cry.

The male voice speaks to me in a calm, soft, soothing tone, and I can tell they're not a threat, but in my frantic, irrational state, all I think is to protect myself so I squirm into the corner. After what must be several long, silent minutes save for my sobs, the male bends down with my jeans in his hands. He gives a calm, reassuring smile, indicating I am safe in his presence, then hands me my jeans. He stands up, backs away, then turns around, allowing me some privacy.

I rise painfully to my feet and grimace when I attempt to lift one of my legs up to slide my leg through the jeans. Once I have both legs in and zip myself up, the man turns back around to face me.

He extends his hand, and in a kind voice says, "Mitchell."

I'm not in the right mindset to return the gesture, which he picks up on, so he retracts his hand.

"It's okay," he says in a soft, soothing tone. "I'm a youth counsel worker. While I deal in mostly teen issues like drug and alcohol abuse, teen pregnancies, that kind of thing, I have also dealt with sexual assault."

I instantly retch vomit upon hearing the last two words. How does he know?

"Before you came to," He takes a considerate pause before he responds with an answer. "Your boxer shorts, they're stained dark red."

My face flushes a shame of red.

"I can take you to a nearby local hospital if you like, one I use for the teens, have them check you over, make sure everything's all right," he explains.

I've just been raped and am far from all right, but I nod okay and follow him out of the bathroom.

As we get nearer towards his car, I stop. Mitchell turns around, studies me a moment. He's seen this before.

"You're perfectly safe now," he reassures me.

But it's not that I feel unsafe in Mitchell's presence, it's something else. My eyes scan all around the truck stop as I look for something or namely someone, but he's not here. The brute and his rig have vanished. I'm not sure whether I'm relieved or irritated, because neither offers any comfort.

Given what just happened to me, I make a mental note of Mitchell's licence plate number as we approach his car, a white, late '90s Honda Civic. However, as a sign of good faith, he hands over his driver's licence for me to hold on the drive to the hospital. I cling to it with everything I have because right now, it is all I have.

It takes all my effort to bend down into the car and get into a seated position to sit down. As soon as I plant my full weight down on the car seat, I feel the tear from the attack, start to open up and trickle blood once more. I grimace again. Staring out the window, I feel beaten, battered and bruised, but more than that, I feel ashamed, embarrassed… dirty.

22

The Test

It's a silent drive and I'm grateful for not having to force a conversation I don't want to have, though I am sure it'll come when we get to the hospital. Mitch turns into the hospital entrance and rather than use the carpark, he drives straight up to the emergency entrance, puts his car in park, hits the hazard lights, then gets out of the car. My eyes follow him until he disappears into the building.

He returns with a wheelchair and a hospital staff member.

"Elise here will take care of you while I go park the car. I'll be back as quick as I can," Mitch says.

I watch him get back into his car, unsure if he really will return or not.

Elise ushers me into the hospital waiting room, where I find a bunch of other patients who look a lot worse off than me.

"Thank goodness for people like Mitchell. He fights a good fight," she says before she passes a clipboard with a form attached for me to complete.

"Just fill in the details as best you can. We'll take care of the rest," she smiles.

I look down at the form and it's your usual information. Name, address, emergency contact, etcetera. I start to fill it in as best I can, skipping over the emergency contact for now. When I'm satisfied I've completed as much as possible, I lay it in my lap and wait.

I look around the waiting room where I see a mix of people. I spot a young white couple, the woman clearly in pain with her bulging belly, while her young, tattooed boyfriend does his best to calm her, holding and stroking her head. There's an older, early 60's black guy, who cradles his bloodied, bandaged hand, while his wife sits lovingly beside him. There's a mid-30-something, interracial couple who look severely distressed with a wailing baby in their arms. All look like they need much more urgent attention than me.

If I could easily get up and walk out, I would. Before the thought takes root though, Mitchell returns back into the waiting room. He takes the clipboard from my hands, scans over the form, checking to make sure it's filled out correctly.

"No one you can contact?" he enquires.

I shake my head.

"No insurance either?"

I shake again.

I see a small look of concern creep over his face before he gives me a reassuring smile, saying he'll take care of it. I've no idea what that means but I utter a quiet thanks.

It's almost an hour before I'm finally called. Mitchell offers to come along but I politely decline. I'm wheeled away into a curtained partition, where I have to wait some more. From my vantage point behind the closed green curtain, I hear a few shrieks from another partition, and muffled voices from several others. For the first time since stepping foot out of the door back in Toronto, I feel helpless and truly alone.

While I wait, I work through my head what I remember. I feel stupid and ashamed that I allowed something like that to happen. Even though I know it wasn't my fault, I still blame myself. I can't help but work through how I could have better handled my exit from Roy's truck to avoid the attack altogether. I run a whole gamut of emotions, from anger and spite, to shame and guilt. I want to scream out and cry all at the same time.

Before I can, I'm greeted by Dr. Zieliński or at least that's what I think it is, it's hard to understand his thick, Eastern European accent. He helps me to my feet, where I'm told to remove my jeans and lower my bloody boxer briefs. He tries to be as gentle as he can, but I flinch as soon he places a rubber-gloved hand on me, with the horror of the assault visible for him to see.

In words I can't fully make out, he speaks to the nurse on hand, who exits only to return with some medical apparatus.

The nurse dabs away the dried blood with a warm washcloth, while Dr. Z, speaks to me about what he has to do next. He keeps calmly talking as he gently inserts a long, cold, metallic instrument inside my anus to take some swabs. It's over as quick as it began but I already feel sick.

"I'll be back soon," he tells me before he disappears through the curtain.

I'm told to lie down on the hospital bed, where the nurse begins to stitch me up. *Only three stitches,* she tells me. Though, I'm not sure if that's a good or bad thing.

When she's done, she gets me to sit up, albeit with a little bit of assistance from her. She takes my blood pressure, assuring me that it's really good and healthy, before in a quiet whisper she says, "This next part we have to do. It will give you peace of mind."

I've no idea what she is alluding to until she places a rubber tourniquet around my right arm and waits for my vein to appear. She then softly inserts a needle into my arm to take a blood sample, and then it dawns on me–STD's!

"I'm sure you'll be fine but this is just a routine check we have to do," she says but the warmth is missing, replaced instead with that of consternation.

Once she's drawn the blood and labelled it, she too leaves the partition, where I'm left to sit and ruminate the ramifications of the violation. If the assault was not already bad enough on me physically and emotionally, I can only imagine the mental side of being told even worse news.

I do my best to dismiss it, hoping the results will come back all clear. I've no idea what to do if an HIV test were to come back positive.

The howls from a nearby cubicle soar in intensity, which only heightens my own mind's concerns. They race deep into some dark, unwanted place.

"Serves you right," an inner voice says.

"Got what you deserved," chides another one.

"It's not too late to ask forgiveness," offers one more.

I do my best to banish the demon's mean-spirited voices, by saying everything will be all right. Somehow, they, and I, are not convinced.

When the nurse returns some time later, I look at her face to gauge what she knows. She can't bring herself to look me directly in the eyes, I take that as a bad sign. When Dr. Z re-enters the cubicle soon after, my mind, body, and emotions, tighten up as they all collide into a nervous pool of agitation and genuine worry. My pulse quickens, the sweat glands extrude, and the hairs on the back of my neck stand with the anticipation of what's to come.

With no time to pray, the Doctor takes my hand in his.

"So, Mr. Walker," he begins. "We have some good news,

and we have some bad news."

I feel my oesophagus constrict, and the beads of sweat that pooled at the back of my neck trickle their way down my spine.

"The good news, you are not HIV positive."

My throat widens and a huge gush of air that was suppressed down in my abdomen as I held my breath, surges up my windpipe and escapes my body. I have never felt and been more relieved in my entire life.

"However, I must warn you, that it can take a full year after possible exposure to determine a negative result. I strongly recommend and urge you to do some follow-up tests in the months to come, okay?"

"Tests. Follow up?" I mumble, letting his words float and swirl around my mind where they immediately reside in that dark 'what if?' place.

I take a further deep breath as he continues.

"The bad news is the tissue inside the anus is a very thin membrane and not as well protected as the skin outside the anus. The external tissue has layers of dead cells that serve as a protective barrier against possible infection. The tissue inside the anus though, does not have this natural protection. What that means is, it leaves it vulnerable to tearing and the spread of a possible infection," Dr Z says.

I brace myself for what's next.

"Even though serious injury from anal trauma is not common, it can occur. Bleeding can be due to a haemorrhoid or possible tear, or something much more serious such as a perforation (or hole) in the colon. This can be a dangerous problem that requires immediate medical attention. Treatment involves a hospital stay, surgery, and antibiotics to prevent any infection."

And here it comes.

"Though thankfully, you narrowly avoided this, however, it is traumatised as a result of your ordeal. I'm going to pre-scribe both a cream and an antibiotic to help it heal faster. If for whatever reason you experience any bleeding after-wards or you notice any sores or lumps around the anus or a discharge coming from it, I strongly advise you to see your doctor as soon as possible. You may also find taking a warm bath once a day with Epsom salts, will help any tears heal and reduce the risk of infection."

By now I'm in tears. On one hand, I'm grateful for not con-tracting HIV, which can go on to become AIDS, or any other sexual disease or infection, but also concerned at how close I came to something far worse, both physically and mental-ly, as well as financially. For someone without any medical insurance whatsoever, the thought of having to spend a few nights in a U.S hospital is the stuff of nightmares, though that's nothing compared to facing a lifetime with a disease that can kill you.

He gives me a sincere smile and hands me a prescription, then leaves to tend to other patients. The nurse hangs back a moment. I'm not sure what else she can add.

"Your briefs and jeans, Mr. Walker," she says. "They're heavily stained with blood. I'm not sure if you have a spare pair on hand but the hospital has a small lost and found area. For a nominal donation, we can find you something for you to leave in until you wash yours. We can also throw them out if you wish. We find some people prefer not to be… reminded."

Her last comment catches me off guard and makes me re-think keeping them at all. I know the examination was cov-ered or paid for by Mitchell, and I really couldn't have done this on my own, so as much as I can't really spare what little I have, I cannot begrudge her request.

I reach into a pocket of my jeans and pull out my money. I stare down at it, all crumpled and crushed. She reaches out her hand to receive a donation and for the slightest moment I hesitate, before placing the very last of my money into her waiting hand.

She looks at the money then back at me, knowing this is probably all I have.

"Are you sure you can spare this?" she probes.

I take off my t-shirt and hoodie and hand them both to her to take as well.

With an apprehensive smile, the nurse closes her hands around the money, then walks back out through the curtain, pulling it tightly behind her. I sit on the bed, naked, exposed, and now more vulnerable than ever before.

To have no money left feels like the least of my worries, especially as it dawns on me how close I really came to a fate far worse. I can only imagine the mental and emotional anguish that comes with receiving that news.

While I don't smile, I do allow myself a mini moment to relax, thankful the test was favourable.

Surely, this is the moment I come to my senses and seek relief and comfort and return to Clea.

The nurse returns and offers me three pairs of jeans to try on, as well some other clothing options. I take the only pair that fits along with a brand new pair of boxer shorts, still in its original packaging. It's a small win. The tops, however, are either a green and mustard yellow checkered shirt or a bright white sweater with 'Hillary For President' splashed in blue and red across the front.

Even with my mind where it's at, the irony of the country & western look that I now unfortunately sport is not lost on me. But walking around with that ugly sweater was destined for far more ridicule.

I get dressed and thank her before I finally exit the cubicle. Despite the pain and torment surrounding me, I hobble back to the waiting room, where Mitchell still remains. I give him an embarrassed nod to say everything is all right, before we exit the hospital and step into the late afternoon sunlight.

Knowing that things could have been very different, for the first time today, I allow the sun to bathe me in its warm, soothing glow.

23

Josie The Wonder-dog

It didn't take much persuading for me to agree to stay with Mitchell. With no money, feeling sore, still feeling guilty about what occurred, as well as dirty and ashamed, a warm bed for the night is exactly what I need. He'd already shown his intentions were pure by freely offering genuine care to me, besides the alternative had zero appeal given my physical and emotional state.

The drive to his house is mostly done in silence, save from a few questions from Mitchell, who despite my lack of input does his best to wheedle some information out of me. I know it's just the caring counsellor in him, and while I would normally have obliged, I feel it best to remain quiet for now.

Through experience, he knows not to push further, instead, he just flicks on the car radio where I recognise The Cardigans, 'Couldn't Care Less'. It occupies the space not only around me, but in my mind. The song's poignant lyrics strike a chord.

I definitely feel like my heart can't carry any more, I'm in pain, it's aching, I'm sore, and if I'm honest, I'm not sure I can bear any more. While the physical assault may be over, I know from former rape and assault victims (good friends, an ex-girlfriend), that all who suffered some kind of sexual abuse, that the mental and emotional anguish headed my way is far worse. Once it arrives, it never leaves, no matter how hard you try.

Mitchell lives on the outlying districts of town, in a leafy, outer-city suburb. His house is nothing special, neither big nor grand. All that matters is that it's a warm, safe place to stay the night. As we walk up the paved path to his front door, I hear the small yaps of an excited dog. Once he turns the key and opens the door, an animated Jack Russell, jumps up and down to greet him.

"Josie, meet Raiden," Mitchell says.

After a few pats from him, Josie then pays me attention. At first, she sniffs my feet and legs, like all dogs do, before she stands on her two hind legs and softly paws at my pants. No matter what state you're in, there's something intrinsically beautiful about animals who stare at you with wide-eyed wonder. Whatever it is, I give her a small smile.

I bend down and lay my hand out flat in an attempt to give her a pat, but Josie's got other ideas and licks my hand before she scarpers back inside. Mitchell then steps into his home and I follow them both in. While I proceed to take off my shoes, Josie races back towards me, a mangy, rubber ball in her mouth before she drops it at my feet. I give it a quick kick with my foot and she scurries off after it, her tiny legs and paws working double time on the slippery tiled floor.

I've barely taken off my second shoe when Josie returns lightning fast, ball in mouth, dropping it back down at my feet.

"Looks like you've made a new friend," Mitch quips.

I kick the ball away once more and like before, Josie scampers as fast as she can back after it. When she returns,

Mitchell picks up the ball.

"That's enough for now, Josie, let's give Raiden some time to settle in first."

She cocks her head sideways as if to ask, *'but why?'* and when she sees Mitchell is serious, she looks disappointed that she can't play anymore. Like all well trained dogs though, she lets it go and trots off to some other room.

Mitchell leads me down the hall past the charming old-fashioned kitchen, showing me each section of the house as we go, until we get to a small bedroom at the end. It's quaint and sparse, just a single bed, one side table, a chest of drawers with a small, old fashioned alarm clock on top, a wicker chair off to one side, plus a selection of other things to make it feel more homely. Things such as generic, scenic pictures on the walls, a mirror, and a pile of books.

"It's not much," Mitchell interjects.

While that may be true, to me it's everything. It's more than I've had in days. I give him a smile of gratitude.

"There's a bathroom on the opposite side of the hall, and if you feel so inclined, a small study/library in the back of the house. You're free to use it," he adds. "My wife will be home around six. We usually eat around seven. For now, I'll let you rest. If you need anything else, just holler."

When Mitchell exits the room, Josie, who followed him down the hall, stays a moment to watch me, curious at the interloper. I muster a thumbs up reassurance.

"I'm okay," I say, even though I am not.

Satisfied, she turns and heads off after Mitchell. I turn my attention back to the room and walk its small confines. My fingers run over the dresser and up onto the books, which are piled six or seven high.

I pick them up and peruse their covers. They're mostly

self-help books for suicide or drug dependent teens but one title catches my eye. 'Me and Daddy's First Big Adventure', which looks totally out of place among the other books in the stack.

I flip it over in my hands and read the short synopsis on the back. It's a book about a relationship between a father and a young child who go on one big outdoor adventure together, as told through the eyes of a child. It looks like it tells a compelling, captivating tale and has attracted enough of my attention for me to read the opening page. I lie down on the bed and start to read more.

Somewhere between lying down and reading, I must have dozed off because I'm greeted by the sounds of a dog panting nearby. When I open my eyes, I spot Josie on the floor, studying me. There's a ball by her feet and as soon as she sees my open eyes, she wags her tail in anticipation.

I rise up from the bed and look at the clock, it's almost 7pm. There's a gentle knock on the door frame before Mitchell peers his head around the corner.

"I see you've been woken by our little four-legged alarm clock," he laughs as he looks down at Josie. "We've got some hot food on the table if you'd care to join us?"

I nod a yes.

"Oh, and I've laid out a clean towel and face cloth in the bathroom, if you want to freshen up. Otherwise, see you down in the kitchen? Come on Josie, let's give Raiden privacy to get ready, you can play ball later."

They exit the room and pad back down the hallway. I step off the bed and am about to place the book on the side table but before I do, I notice the next chapter, 'Daddy Disappears'. The title sends a small shiver down my spine. While I'd made it as far as page 20 before I drifted off to sleep, I take that as a good sign I was enjoying the book, however, the bold heading hangs heavy inside my mind. I gently fold the corner of the page over to mark my place, then close the book.

I cross the hallway to the bathroom opposite and find the freshly laid out dark blue towel and matching face cloth waiting for me, along with a beautiful pale pink and white hibiscus flower, which is sitting on top of them. It's a nice touch.

I splash my face with water in the basin and dab the hand cloth on my face. I drop the moist cloth back on the bench and look at my reflection. It's the first time I've looked at myself since this morning's assault. While my eyes are bloodshot and look weary, there's a vacant, coldness that stares back at me. I can't place it, but it unnerves me.

I decide to skip the shower for now because I don't think I can handle the stinging hot water on my exposed, raw skin, so I exit as quick as I can and make my way towards the kitchen.

Even before I get there, I can already smell the delectable home-cooked food waft down the hall. There's a familiarity about what I can smell and I find my body relaxes. I feel a small smile form across my face, while there's an excitement and purpose to my walk I've not felt since… I turn the corner half expecting to see Clea and her protruding belly. Instead, when I enter the kitchen, I'm greeted by Mitchell's wife.

"You must be Raiden," she proclaims as she comes in to greet me with a hug.

I feel awkward as I stand there, arms by my side, being hugged by a total stranger, but I also feel deflated. She senses something is off and backs off from the hug.

"Sorry, excuse my manners. I'm Ilene. I probably should have asked if it was okay, just a default mechanism of mine."

I stand there in silence.

"Come, come, we've got a seat with your name written on it."

I follow her to the table where Mitchell is already seated, Josie by his feet, and sure enough, there is a place reserved for me. Ilene's even gone to the trouble of printing my name on a card and putting it on the place mat.

"It's a thing," Mitchell says to me when he notices me look at the name card. "An Ilene thing," he jests.

I take my seat, which I notice has an extra cushion, and since I'm still sore down below, I'm grateful for the extra care. She clearly knows what's happened or Mitchell has at least filled her in on the basics. I feel a little let down as it's not something I had planned to share with anyone, though I'm sure Mitchell had to explain why he was bringing home a complete stranger, so I can't begrudge him too much.

To their credit, neither of them brings up the incident over dinner. I find out they met when he was teaching a health and awareness course to teens–she was handling the administration side of a refuge centre–and while he was packing up, she asked if he'd like to get a coffee. The rest is history. While it's both their second marriage, they've been inseparable ever since.

To keep the conversation going, I ask if they ever wanted kids, where it stops dead before Mitch picks it up.

"We had one..." he trails off.

"Our son passed away when he was three," Ilene intercedes.

"Heart complications," Mitchell chimes in.

"Nathan just had too many hurdles to overcome," Ilene says, with a tear in her eye.

"I'm sorry," I add, now feeling bad for having brought up what is obviously still a very fresh wound.

"You weren't to know. You'd think ten years would be more than enough time to get over it and move on, but no amount of time will ever replace the void left behind," Mitchell says as he comforts his wife.

"We wanted to try for another one but we both got so caught up in our work as a way to cope with the grief, that it just never happened. To deal with the loss, I now counsel teens and young people in trouble, while Ilene handles the appointments and logistics of the small centre we both manage," Mitch adds.

"It's a modest way to make a living," Ilene chimes in.

"In some ways, Nathan's spirit lives on. Each person we have stay in his old room, is a way to fill the emptiness. The book you are reading for example, was one Ilene bought. After he passed away, I couldn't bear to let it go. I'm glad it's getting some use again," Mitchell reminisces.

To change topics and lighten the mood, they ask where in Australia I am from, a country they both would love to visit one day. Ilene then asks what brought me to North America, and whether I miss home. I know the questions are geared to finding out more about me, help them paint a picture, maybe fill in some gaps as well as get me talking, though I can't help but think it's also to avoid their own pain.

I oblige, however, given I have no problems talking up Melbourne or why I went to Los Angeles, and then onto Toronto.

I can tell Mitchell is the more observant, analysing one, while Ilene is the more talkative, inquisitive of the two. Maybe it's because she's a woman and likes to play the nurturer, using her motherly instincts and warm nature in the hopes to get me to open up. To some degree it works.

Though the topic never comes up, and I know they both want to help, I don't mention anything about this morning. To be honest, I'm doing my best to forget it.

We end up talking for a couple of hours about my travels, my writing, life in the US, even families. Well, theirs and how her father didn't approve of Mitchell the first time he met him. 'The long haired hippie with zero ambitions' he dubbed him. They assure me as time went on, he came to love Mitch like the son he never had before he passed away many years later.

Whether they intentionally know it or not, they've got me thinking about how I miss Clea, my family, and one I am about to have, as well as thinking about home to maybe reach out.

I haven't contacted either my mother or brother, since I up and left from Toronto. My mum in particular, had emailed me many times to find out any more news in terms of Clea's pregnancy, about how the baby was growing, and more. She'd taken a keen interest. I know she was also really looking forward to becoming a grandmother. She had expressed so much excitement when I told her the news over the phone almost two months ago.

Eventually Ilene decides to call it a night, something about a "big admin day" tomorrow at the office. I know it's designed to allow Mitchell and me privacy to talk. I thank her for dinner before she asks if it's okay to hug. This time I indulge her. She clings on to me tight like I'm a long, lost family member. In some ways, I feel like I am.

In fairness, I need the hug just as much as she does. Ilene eventually releases me from her arms. Once she leaves, Mitchell suggests moving into the much more comfortable lounge.

We leave the warmth of the kitchen and the lingering smells of leftover food, to take up two new places in his study come lounge come library. The smells are now replaced with those of musty books.

Like the rest of the house, it's modest but it also has a small gas fireplace, which Mitchell duly turns on given it's much chillier in this room than the kitchen. Josie takes up a position on the rug, then curls up and falls asleep in front of the warm fire. I wish I could do the same.

24

The Tough Talk

"I know you won't want to talk about what happened, which is perfectly understandable, but in my experience it's always better to discuss it sooner than keep it bottled up forever," Mitchell says directly.

My mouth opens, I go to speak, to say something, but no words come out. It's not that I don't want to, in part I do because I know it will help me better deal with it somewhat, but it's a touchy topic that I'd prefer to avoid right now. It happened; I can't change that. That's not me being stoic or pig-headed, but as a man, I feel emasculated because of it, not to mention embarrassed, ashamed, even guilty for what happened. In truth, as traumatic as that experience was, it all seems secondary to the more pressing topic that would be better to discuss–leaving a pregnant girlfriend. If not for that, then this incident would never have happened in the first place.

When I don't open up and close my mouth again, he offers me a Scotch to calm the many emotions I can sense building inside, which I am sure he can see rising up in me.

It relaxes my body somewhat, but not my mind, at least not with the topic he wants me to discuss.

"I left my pregnant girlfriend," I burst out. "Because of that, this monster raped me."

I see his eyes widen at the revelation, before they return to normal. He's also processing the remark, ready to respond.

"You know, what happened is not as a resul–"

"Yes it is. If not for my callous behaviour, the despicable act that occurred to me would never have happened."

"Blaming yourself is-"

"The only answer!"

Mitchell tries a different tack to guide me back in the direction he's hoping to take the conversation before I get too riled up.

"For arguments sake, let's say that it is. With that said, what's your greatest concern now after the attack?"

Hmmm, I hadn't thought of that. I take a moment to mull the question over in my mind.

"That I make a shitty father and shoddy partner. That I might contract AIDS and never able to have unprotected sex again with a partner. That no matter what I do, I am unable to reconcile my past indiscretions, all the time taunted by inner demons that keep wanting to steer me down the path of least resistance, one where I'll fuck around and ruin yet another relationship because of the poor choices I make. That I'll end up like my own dad–abusive, absent, and ultimately, irrelevant from my own child's existence. But in general, that I'm a deplorable person and make a lousy excuse for a man."

Frankly, I'm surprised by my admissions. Even though I can see he is doing his best to process it all, it's a lot for Mitch to take in. It's a lot for me to reveal all in one go.

Mitchell sips on his Scotch, rolling the lone ice cube around in his glass as he ponders what to say next.

"Did your dad ever sexually abuse you?" he says.

"No, never," I reply, startled by the question.

"So, no inappropriate touching or anything similar?"

"Slapped, punched, kicked, smacked by a leather belt, hardcover books thrown at my head or other heavy objects on hand. Verbally abused, put down and made to feel worthless many times, yes, but no, never anything *inappropriate*."

The barrage of the types of abuse I respond with are probably nothing Mitchell hasn't heard before. But to me, as I recount them, I recoil at the man I had once looked up to and called my dad. How could a man do such terrible things to a child? His own flesh and blood.

"Is he the reason why you left your partner, do you think?"

"I haven't spoken to him in years, so no."

"I don't mean because of him. I mean because you were worried you'd become him?"

Now it's my turn to take a swig of whisky, mulling the idea around in my mind, over and over.

"In my many years of counselling, there's usually always a root cause as to why we do the things we do, whether rational to us or not, no matter what others or society deem normal or appropriate behaviour," Mitch says.

I look down at my feet then back up at Mitchell.

"Yes!"

"Yes what?" he asks.

"Yes, I ran away because I feared turning into the very man I despised."

"Even though you are clearly not him?"

"But capable of becoming him," I retort.

"That's not true. In my experience and studies, while the chances to repeat certain behaviours or actions could happen, we rarely re-enact our most severe childhood traumas. More often than not, most people choose to go in the completely opposite direction, even if it means those horrific moments get buried down deep, or they feel ashamed or guilt riddled that it happened to them, despite it never being ever their fault. While we cannot excuse the despicable actions undertaken by those in authority, especially parents, more often than not, it builds a steely resolve in us to never be like them," Mitch expresses.

I slink back into my chair to allow Mitch's words to sink in. I knew I was nothing like my own father. In many ways, despite my struggles, I am a far better man than he.

"Look, it's a lot to take in I know, and while I had hoped to deal with the trauma of today, I can also see you're hurt from something far greater. It may not mean much in the scheme of things, however, I believe that by starting here, from way back in your own past, you'll be much better equipped to cope with that of the present. Does that make sense?"

I nod a yes.

"In talking to you, if there's one thing I do know, it's that you are not your own abusive father. You have a chance to do things different. To create your own amazing legacy. A chance to reset and be remembered for something far greater. I only wish I could have experienced it for longer than the three years I did."

His last comment rocks me. Here is a man, also clearly hurt by his past for very different reasons, and perhaps envious of my situation, even if I hadn't made a great beginning at it.

"All I can pass onto you is this, Raiden. We get one chance to make an impression and leave a lasting effect on someone's life. A life that not only depends on us for survival, but one we can shape and guide, bypassing our own miseries. Seize it as best you can."

It's close to midnight by the time we decide to call it a night. I'm truly grateful for the conversation and his words have resonated, that much I know.

"Thank you, Mitch," I say before standing up to give, and receive a man-hug. But it's not just a thanks for the conversation. It's thanks for all that he has done so far.

Mitchell wishes me goodnight and heads off to his bedroom. When I get to my room, despite the late hour, there's a renewed vitality about me. I lay down on the bed and grab the copy of 'Me and Daddy's First Big Adventure' and pick up from where I had left off.

25

Unrecognisable Face

I've no idea what time I fell asleep but despite going to bed with a semi-soothed mind after my talk with Mitch, part way through the night I woke up in a cold sweat, disrupted by a disturbing vision. In it, I saw Roy's smug face, his belt unbuckled, jeans partially unzipped, pointing and laughing at me as I lay on the bathroom floor in a molested mess.

I was unable to settle after the nightmare, so I opted to read the book by the bedside table to calm myself down. Although I reconciled with the fact that it was only a dream, I was also reminded that the assault happened! However, reading must have helped, because when I look over at it, I see I made it about a third of the way through.

For once, I ignore the chattering voices in my head and instead do the unthinkable, bask in the recognition that I am warm, cosy, semi-relaxed, and don't have to be anywhere... well, not yet anyway.

As I lie here, my ears become attuned to the fact it's dead quiet. I don't hear any sounds from inside the house, save for a chiming clock. I can only assume both Mitchell and Ilene headed to work hours ago.

Eventually I drag myself out of bed and open the bedroom

door. I make my way across the hall and into the bathroom where I take a leak. While I pee, I recall Dr. Z's advice to take a warm salt bath as often as I can, when and wherever I am able. While I am definitely sore, it's less painful than it was yesterday... well, physically so.

I'm still somewhat angry at myself for putting myself in such a vulnerable, stupid position and not being more aware. I keep thinking I could have easily avoided it all had I been more conscious of my surroundings and my decisions. I think back to how I should have just sat it out in the diner, used the toilet they would have had inside for customers. How I could have waited to wash out a coke stain or not even bothered. In my haste to get away from the uncomfortableness I felt in Roy's truck, I simply compounded and inflamed the situation further. The more I ruminate on it, the more I believe it's all my fault.

After I flush the toilet, I turn on the taps of the bath to wash away some of the shame and guilt. I open up the bathroom cupboard and dig around among a mix of shampoo bottles and various cleaning products. It takes a moment but then I spot what I'm looking for, Epsom salts, tucked way up in the back and partially hidden by a disused shower cap. I grab for the container and pour it into the warm bath water. I swish my hand around the water to help stir it in.

When the bath is full, I switch the taps off and just stare at the water until it settles. I undress and then dip my foot into the warm water. It's a little hot at first but then my skin adjusts to the change in temperature. I place my other foot inside the tub and allow the warm tingle to dissipate, before I slowly sink my body into the tub. It's only when my butt hits the surface of the water, that I have to proceed with a lot more caution. I use my hands and arms to steady myself as I submerge myself even further. At the point when my abused anus touches the heat, I instantly tense up. It's still painful and I'm not sure if it's the hot temperature adjustment on my skin or whether it's just my body's reaction to protect itself. It takes me a good minute before I'm able to fully submerge myself into the water.

Once I've lowered my full bodyweight and allow my arms to slip down into the water beside me, do I feel the first of the sharp, saltwater stings. At first, it's just a small tingle but it soon spirals into something more intolerable. I know it's the familiar sensation of salt on raw, exposed skin. I do my best to close my eyes and rest my head on my arms, which now drape over my knees. I grimace as I lay there, trying my hardest to ignore the stinging irritation, knowing that despite my obvious discomfort, it will help my body heal. My mind, however, will require much more than a simple salt bath.

When I reopen my eyes, I notice a tiny string of blood that seeps from down below. Aware I've split and reopened a micro-tear, I can't help but feel dejected. I watch the small trickle of blood swirl around my legs in a tiny red cloud before it disperses into the salty water. Eventually the blood slows then clots, which I know is a good sign, even though it doesn't give me any extra comfort.

I spend the rest of the time in the bath mulling over what I can do next, and how to do it with no money. While I'd love to jump on a bus and make my way south into Texas as quickly as I can, hoping to see a distant friend who lives out of Dallas, with no cash, I can't see how it's feasible. As much as I want to avoid hitch hiking for now to play it safe, it's my only free, viable option. However, it's food and making sure I eat, that has me worried most. I can't simply lay out a cap and hope people drop money into it like they did in West Memphis.

Despondent, I recast my mind back to the nightmare. While I understand the part Roy played in it, with his smugness and arrogance to belittle and mock me as if in victory. Even though it was nothing more than a bad dream, I'm having a tough time accepting how unwilling I was to retaliate and fight back, or by how compliant I was. It's the frozen state I found myself in, that now makes me feel weak, wimpy... a lesser man.

Why? I am not fully sure at this stage, but I don't get too long to think about it because the bath temperature changes from lukewarm to cool. While I'd like to just top it up with more hot water and stay here for another hour or two, if I want to make my way to Texas before nightfall, I need to get a wriggle on.

I step out of the bath and onto the mat to dry myself, I'm careful to pad at my anus and pat dry the sensitive area. I'm grateful that Mitch and Ilene have given me a dark coloured towel, which hides any blood streaks. After I'm done, I drop the towel into a nearby laundry basket and reopen the bathroom cupboard. I'm hoping to find an old razor and shaving cream. To my surprise, there's a brand new one in an unopened packet, as well as a fresh can of shaving cream. I fill the small basin with hot water and rub some shaving lotion into my hand and slather it into my face.

The first glide of the razor removes the scruffy part of my beard. The second one cleans up the loose hairs. The third reveals a smooth face I've not seen in two years. Once I'm done, I wash off any excess shaving cream with cold water.

When I look up, I barely recognise my own self. Staring back at me is a wretched version of myself. My face more gaunt, I look like a beaten, shattered man. A mere shadow of my former self. Before I started this journey, I was in good physical shape. My face was fuller, healthier, so too my body. To now see myself look like this is hard to take. I know I've been doing it tough, but nothing could have prepared for me what I now see.

I do my best to replace the hopelessness and despair I feel with the tiniest amount of optimism. If I can get to Dallas today, then there's a good chance a friend might be able to put me up. I say friend loosely, because we have never actually met–she's someone I'd flirted with, exchanging racy pics and dirty messages here and there online a few years back, mixed with deeper, more personal emails along the way. To go there and take a chance, however slim, is better than to stay here and dive further into my past with Mitch, because I'm just not ready to go there. I know it's a long shot, but it's all I've got.

26

A Lasting Impression

I get dressed and walk into the kitchen to get myself one last decent feed before I hit the road. There's a small envelope on the kitchen table with the name 'Raiden' written on it, which rests against a brown paper bag. I pick it up and pull out the note inside.

Raiden, it's not much but it's all we can spare. We hope you stay (you're most welcome to) but if not, then we didn't want you to leave empty handed or go hungry. ps: Feel free to take the book for the journey ahead. Mitchell, Ilene, and Josie.

I'm about to put the envelope aside when I notice something else tucked inside. I tip it upside down and watch, as first a printed bus schedule slides out, falling onto the table, before a $50 bill flutters down to join it. I'm gobsmacked. The generosity of these two people amazes me.

When I unfold the lunch bag, I find it's filled with food. Two tightly packed sandwiches, some fruit, a couple of granola bars, a mini packet of trail mix, two small juice boxes, and wrapped in cling wrap, some of the roast potatoes and pumpkin from last night's dinner. It's a veritable bounty, and more food than I deserve after all they've done for me.

Both Mitchell and Ilene have gone to so much trouble, that I feel terrible leaving without saying goodbye. I'm sure they're used to it if they house troubled teens, but still, it leaves an impression, not to mention a lump in my throat.

Grateful, I rewrap the lunch bag and open a kitchen cupboard to grab a bowl then go to the pantry where I find some cereal. I figure it's best to save the food I was just given until I need it. I make myself a cup of loose-leaf Earl Grey tea, oh how I have missed thee, to accompany my breakfast before I dig in.

While I munch down on my cereal, I flick through the bus schedule which advertises CHEAPEST RATES ANYWHERE. I don't expect to find anything under $50 but to my surprise there's a fare to Dallas/Fort Worth for $39. I scan down the page and find there are only two buses that do the trip daily. One that departs at 11:45pm, the other at 12:30pm, both doing the trip in just over six hours.

I sip my tea so as not to make any rash decisions, and to weigh up the pros and cons. Take the bus and spend almost all the money I received. Or hitch and keep the $50 in my pocket for when I'll need it later. Take the bus, get all the way to Dallas. Hitch and wait for a ride, with possible more waiting and hitching in between to make it all the way to Dallas. Take the bus, and not have to worry about a thing. Hitch and worry about everything.

I take one last sip of my tea, replace the cup on the saucer and make my decision. Sold! Megabus it is. The hell with the money, besides, I'm in no mood to make small talk, jump from vehicle to vehicle… or worse, when I can go direct. Thanks, Earl Grey!

Once up out of my seat, I wash the dishes and place them in the rack to dry. I clean my teeth courtesy of the new toothbrush I found, and once I'm done, I pocket it. I snatch up the book and by the time I'm done, it's almost midday. I've got about 30 minutes to make it to the bus terminal.

I scribble a thank you note, saying how grateful I am for everything they've done. I contemplate giving them my email address but decide against it for reasons I am unsure of. I place the note on the kitchen table and take one last look around. After the assault, I couldn't have asked for a nicer couple to take me in. They've not only made a difference to my mental state, leaving a lasting impression, but also given me plenty to ponder, too.

Once I exit, I take one last look back at the house that offered me respite and salvation right when I needed it. I couldn't be any more appreciative. I pull a pen from my jeans pocket and write down the address on the side of the paper lunch bag. I'd like to be able to post the book when I'm done at the very least. I then make my way to the terminal ready to board a bus, bound for what I hope will be welcome arms and a fold out bed for the night.

27

Megabus

With barely any time to spare, I make it to the Megabus station on East Roosevelt Road, but when I get there, I think I'm either at the wrong location, or worse, missed the bus all together, because it's nothing more than an Exxon service station. I kick away a few pebbles in frustration and curse myself for taking too long to leave. Before I can beat myself up too much though, a big, blue bus with a bright yellow capped cartoon figure adorning its side and advertising 'Fares from $1', pulls into the station's apron and parks up. I breathe a sigh of relief and fist pump the air to rejoice.

A few people emerge from parked cars that I hadn't noticed before and start to gather outside, ready to board. When the doors retract open, despite only a handful of people and more than enough empty seats, they all rush forward. The driver is almost bowled over on his way out when he steps onto the asphalt. He just shakes his head before he looks at the waiting bags left in a jumbled mess by the side of the bus. Before he can slide them under the bus, he starts scanning bar codes or taking fare money. I'm the last to join the line, and when he sees I don't have any bags, he gives me a smile. I hand him the $50 bill courtesy of Mitchell and Ilene, before he dips into his pocket to give me back some change.

"Anywhere you like," he says.

I'm tempted to say Australia, but not sure he'll get my joke. I then watch him as he opens up a side compartment of the coach and begins to hurl the bags recklessly underneath with incredible force for a guy his size. Quick lesson, never piss off a bus driver.

I step up into the bus and move along the cramped aisle to take a seat in the middle. I place my lunch bag and book on the spare seat beside me and ease myself into what I know will be an uncomfortable and long, six hour ride ahead. I look back over my shoulder and notice a toilet towards the back. I'm thankful at least, that should I need it, there's one close at hand. For now, I just stare out the window hoping my rear end will endure the distance and discomfort.

With a loud thud, the driver closes the side panel and re-appears on the bus's top step. He does a quick head count, jots down the number onto a clipboard nearby, then looks at his watch. The clock above his head reads 12:29pm. He steps out and lights up a cigarette, where the smoke swirls like a serpent rising upward.

When the clock clicks over to 12:30pm, he stubs out the cigarette, re-enters the bus to take up his seat. With the flick of a lever, the front door hisses to a close and we pull out of the Exxon service station bound for Dallas. As we do, I work on pulling out all my best, *"Hi, remember me?"* approach lines I can think of for my unannounced visit. Even if Araceli remembers me, the off chance she'll put me up seems slim to none. In six hours, I'll find out.

28

Grapevine

Other than passing through a tiny outer section of the Ouachita National Forest, or what's left of it from the freeway, it's an uneventful journey from Little Rock, Arkansas to Dallas, Texas. It is, however, a long time to be sitting. I'm not sure if my rear being this numb is a good thing or not.

When Lake Ray Hubbard appears on the fringes of Dallas's outer rim, I know there's not much further to go, thankfully not a moment too soon. There's only so much I can do to get into comfortable positions inside a bus for six hours.

I've not the faintest idea how I'll go about finding Araceli, or how I will be received if I do. With Texas being the gun-toting state it is, I'm hopeful to be met by a smile rather than the end of a shotgun should I find her. Last time we interacted we got into a squabble on Tumblr and haven't spoken since. In that time since, I deleted my account. Prior to that, it was on Pinterest, the social media platform where we originally 'e-met' some eight years ago and hit it off. We subsequently created our own private board to share a mix of posts, quotes, and erotic and x-rated material we liked, along with personal photos, before then messaging each other through that platform's messenger service to continue our online relationship.

However, it's been at least four years since we've both been on it and used it. We chose to boycott Pinterest after they began censoring erotic or sexually artistic images, which explains why we moved over to Tumblr, who had a much more neutral policy.

Unfortunately, we never exchanged surnames, phone numbers, addresses, let alone friend requested one another on Facebook–it was just easier, cleaner, more discreet that way. What I do know, however, is that she lives in Dallas-Fort Worth. I know she's half Texan, half Mexican. I know she looks a lot like Eva Mendes. I know she works in a bar. I know she's spicy and hot as hell. And I know if circumstances had been different, one where we would have found ourselves in the same place at the same time, we would've wound up in bed. That was assured, given our stated and oft repeated desires for one another. However, it's a moot point, it didn't go that way. It's also no longer something I crave. I'm merely looking for an old friend and a place to rest my weary body.

The coach driver disrupts my train of thought and speaks into a microphone to announce that we can either get off at North Olive Street, which is nearer to the downtown district of Dallas, or go a little further on to Davis Street in Grand Prairie, near Arlington, another 30 minutes more. I've no idea which is the better destination to get off at but it's clear my backside has had enough of squirming in the seat.

When the bus pulls away from the East Transfer Center, I'm faced with the decision–what next?

I've honestly got no way of knowing where Araceli works, what neighbourhood of Dallas she lives in, or even if she would welcome an unexpected visitor. I keep rattling my brain, hoping to shake out a skerrick of information from it, but other than a bar possibly called Longhorn or Big Horn or Big Longhorn or maybe Little Bighorn, something bloody horn, I haven't the faintest clue how to locate her.

I take a deep breath and look around me. Across the road lies the Sheraton Hotel and while I'd love nothing more than to stay, I figure they may have free computer and wifi access. I'm hoping like crazy that even though I don't have the foggiest idea of the name of the bar, that maybe a quick internet search will reveal the name to me. At this point, it's all I've got.

I march across the road and do what I've always done when entering an upscale venue, look confident like I belong there, regardless of whether my hand-me-down, country yokel get up and brown paper lunch bag say otherwise. I walk into the Sheraton determined to find an answer one way or the other.

Like all big hotels, it's a labyrinth of sectioned off areas and enclaves so it takes me a little longer than I'd like, but I eventually find the stylish computer area tucked off behind some plants. It's fairly secluded and from my vantage point, I can't be easily seen. As I had hoped, there's free wifi and when I look over the expanse that is the hotel's main foyer, almost everyone is taking advantage of it, which is probably why there's no one at the computer.

I pull up a plush seat, enter the computer login access, which is conveniently laminated on a card atop it, and wait. Before I get too far, I'm interrupted by a hotel staff member who creeps up behind me and almost makes me jump.

"Drink, sir?" the waitress says.

I do my best to act nonchalant but come across like I'm thinking hard about it and taking a dump.

"They're complimentary for hotel guests," she adds.

"Maybe a ginger ale?"

She leaves and I go back to my search. I type in variations of Longhorn, Big Horn, Big LittleHorn and anything else

I can think of. I think I strike it lucky when the Longhorn Bar comes up but when I click through I find out it's in another state. There's one place here in Dallas with the word horn in it but it's a micro brewing company. I wonder if that's it but a deeper dig reveals it's just part of restaurant called, Humperdinck's.

If there's one thing I know, she never worked in a restaurant. One of the regular photos she did add to our Pinterest board was of her smiling in a small bar, so I know this isn't it.

My drink comes and I smile gratefully at the waitress. When no tip comes, she turns to walk away before I call her back.

"Hi... (I peer at her name badge) Sasha. I'm wondering if you can help me. I'm looking for a bar here in Dallas that might have the name 'horn' in its title AND isn't the Big Horn Brewing Company," I say cutting her off when she goes to answer.

She closes her mouth and thinks a moment. When her mind draws a blank, she just shrugs her shoulders in defeat. I thank her anyway, then peel off one of my remaining dollars. Grateful, she leaves me to my search.

Because I've come up blank, I'm not sure what to do. I decide to ditch the fruitless bar name search and try another tactic. I enter Pinterest into the browser window and provide my email address. I try a number of password combinations and come up short every time. It's not surprising given it's been so long since I last logged in. I click the 'forgot password' option and re-enter my email address. I then open a new browser tab and wait on the inbox to refresh with a new link so I can reset it.

I don't bother reading any of the emails, which now fill my inbox since the last time I checked, including many from my mum asking, Where am I? Do I want to Skype? Is everything all right? I can't help but glance at that one solitary message from Clea again. The 'I Miss You', still seared across my heart.

Thankfully I don't have to linger in it too long, when a new message lands from Pinterest admin. 'To reset your password, please click this link'. It opens up another tab and I'm prompted to enter a new password, then re-enter it directly below. I take a sip of my ginger ale and a few moments later, I'm finally logged in.

I go to my old boards in the desperate hopes the private board remains. I'm not surprised to find it isn't. I can't remember if I deleted it when I got into a relationship or she did. It doesn't matter, knowing why is of little consolation. But it now leaves me exacerbated.

It's starting to get dark outside. I know I won't be able to stay here at the Sheraton too much longer, but then again, it's not like anyone is about to say otherwise, so maybe I can. It sure beats a bus shelter. I'm about to give up when a notification pops up on my screen. I instinctively hover over it. It's just a note letting me know someone has liked one of my pins and repined it. It joins the other thousand plus notifications I have, including a couple of messages that are years old.

I click on the private messages and am instantly filled with hope when I find an old message thread between Araceli and me. I skim through it hoping that maybe there was a mention of a name or place but other than a lot of hot, dirty talk about what we both wanted to do to each other, there's nothing concrete or anything resembling a clue for me to find. I'm not sure if she is still using this account anymore but I decide to write a small message anyway. I can only hope that maybe she'll see it in her email inbox.

I type a short, friendly message. 'Hola bella. Never guess

where I am?', then hit send. It's a desperate move but it's the only one I have left given I have no idea of her last name, while a quick internet search of her first name, revealed over 100 other Araceli's living in Dallas, so that was pointless.

After I'm done re-reading our exchanges, which I have to admit, manage to turn me back on (they really were explicit), I go across to her Pinterest account, which looks like it hasn't been touched in a long while. I skim over her board titles, of which there some 50+ to look over, and select the one that catches my eye the most, 'Me-Araceli'. Not sure why but that's one I think I did follow back in the day.

I don't expect to find anything, so I'm not really paying attention as I scroll and scroll and scroll. This girl sure loved to pin. Then it hits me like a bolt of lightning. There's the photo she sent me of her smiling at the bar she worked at. All I can do is stare in disbelief.

While there's no recognisable bar name anywhere to be seen, I notice she's wearing a black tank top, which has a small logo or insignia on it right there over her ample left breast. There appears to what looks a lot like a bar name underneath it. I look for the computer's zoom button in the hopes that if I can enlarge it, I might be able to see the name more clearly.

It's fuzzy and hard to read, but I can just make out the faintest of letters. 'G' or possibly a 'C', an 'R' I think, something, something, it's hard to tell as the two letters almost overlap, then an 'F', though it could also be an 'E'. Other than a distinct 'I', the rest of the remaining letters are impossible to decipher.

With renewed energy, I go back to the search engine and type in the first two letters starting with the C and the R, and add the word bar, and Dallas, into the search box. CrowBros Automotive comes up and very little else. I then replace the C with the G and boom! There it is, the Grapevine Bar. When I peer closer at the insignia, I start to believe the missing letters are the rest of the word Grapevine. At least I convince myself they are. I hurriedly jot down the address on the courtesy notepad provided and add it to my lunch bag.

I enter the address into Maps. Thankfully it's only about 40 minutes up the road. Knowing I'll have to walk there, I want to print it out with all its many directions, but there's a print surcharge. Instead, I write it down, one direction at a time, on another piece of paper and slip it into my pocket.

I log out of my email and Pinterest, down the rest of my drink and exit the hotel with purpose. Before I left the business centre, I took one last look at the venue's website, where its homepage read: 'A place for those in search of adventure'. Say no more. Long shot or not, 'Grapevine' here I come.

29

Surprise!

On my way up towards The Grapevine, it occurs to me, what if Araceli isn't working tonight? What if she's not even at the bar anymore? What if she doesn't want to see me? What if she doesn't even remember me? I shake off the worries and lingering doubts by pretending she'll be excited to see me, while also trusting that even though it's been a while since we last had any contact, we cared enough about each other beyond our lustful feelings. Hopefully she'll be really happy to finally meet in person. It's those thoughts which spur me on and carry me onto the bar.

'The drinks are stiff but the crowd is always strange,' reads the bright coloured neon sign overhead The Grapevine's door. I think it's a good omen, but I cross my fingers all the same. I take a deep breath before I enter the bar. It's small, quaint and cosy, with just my kind of low key, laid-back vibe. It's easy to see why Araceli once described it to me as her *home away from home*. When you factor in the eclectic furniture, the hip jukebox, pool table, ambient lighting, and assortment of cool memorabilia, I can see why.

I'm greeted routinely upon walking inside by its sole bartender, a late-twenties male with a well groomed beard, a sleeve of mixed tattoos on a muscular arm, adorned with wrist jewellery, and one of those trendy man buns.

It's already past 9pm, and with only a handful of patrons, any hope I had that she may be working this evening deflates me. For now, something tells me to just sit it out here a while and have a drink because where else can I go?

While there was no real plan, and with me already ruling out during the walk over saying, "Hi, remember me?", among a few options if she happened to be working behind the bar, it's back to square one. For now, I opt to take up a seat on a corner table–I figure I can kind of hide in the corner so I'm less conspicuous, though my brown paper lunch bag might let on differently, but first I have to order a drink. While a double Scotch feels right about now, the $10 in my pocket says otherwise. I opt for the cheapest drink they have, a lemonade. I also request a water so I can sip on it in between to make both stretch so as not to be hassled to order more.

At $2.75, I let out a suppressed, manic chuckle when I get back my change, not because it's expensive but because I'm now down to $6.25, once you factor in the dollar tip. Thank Christ for the contents in the lunch bag to make me feel rich.

I thank the bartender, and for a brief moment I toy with the idea of asking him if Araceli still works here, but decide against it. I don't want him to think I'm some kind of freak or stalker. Besides, these tiny watering holes are usually protective of their own. I slide over a dollar bill for a tip, grab my two drinks, and head back to the corner table tucked out of the way.

From my vantage point I can see the entrance, the bar, plus I'm also right by the pool table, so I can at least watch a game to blend in, yet still remain fairly inconspicuous. In the meantime, I'll hope like crazy that Araceli simply works a much later shift. If not, I've no idea what I'll do.

I'd love to play a few games of pool but at $2 a pop, I'm forced to sit it out and watch on with envy. The jukebox cranks out great tune after great tune. I'm tempted to throw a dollar or two into it myself to contribute to the amazing mix that's playing, however, my lack of money dictates otherwise. I've always loved and respected a fantastic jukebox. I might forget some important dates, but I can always remember venues I frequented solely from their jukebox alone.

Rather than allow myself to get too nostalgic, I get carried away with the music instead. I see how many songs and artists I know or can recognise (or that I had on my stolen iPod) versus those I don't know or are unfamiliar with.

Currently the War On Drugs, 'Under The Pressure' plays and while the place isn't too busy or loud, it provides the perfect background soundtrack. Prior to them, I identify The Avalanches, Ben Harper, Beatles, Stones, Inxs, Midnight Oil, Zeppelin, Fleetwood Mac, and Elvis of course, which I will now always relate back to Uncle Louie. There's also a handful of acts and songs that I don't recognise but equally enjoy. If I had my phone, I'd be Shazam'ing their arses in an instant. Either way, I find myself tapping my foot, bopping my head, and silently mouthing the words.

I'm something of a serious melomaniac, but then I start to reminiscence about the music I had on my iPod, which had a tonne of cool music on it, much like what I am currently listening to at present. It also looked bloody awesome, with a supernova Gelaskin protecting it. I'm not sure I'll ever be able to replace all the music I had managed to add and upload onto it–some 1500 albums or 25,000+ songs–because it was the best part of thirty plus years of buying and collecting music. I sigh.

The place starts to fill up, while several of the newcomers say hello to the other punters who've been here a few hours. I always thought I'd love a local pub, that no matter whether if you came in alone, you'd always be able to recognise and talk to someone you know. I've never had a regular bar. Watching all these people mingle and interact, makes me pine to have one.

I hear snippets of conversation from the usual sports banter to the always juicy, *"Did you hear such and such hooked up with such and such last weekend?"*. Got to love small gossip. Maybe that's where The Grapevine got its name. I bet they even have Marvin Gaye's 'I Heard It Through The Grapevine' on their jukebox just for shits & giggles.

It must be close to midnight, and although I filled up on the free water using the jug on the bar, somehow managing to nurse my lemonade through the evening, eventually mother nature calls. I get up out of my chair, leave my lunch bag on the table to save my spot, and go off in search of the toilet. I walk through a small corridor and out through another door that I think will lead me to the restroom. Instead it opens up out into an outdoor patio, or beer garden as we Aussies call it, and it's packed! Almost every table is crammed full of people and small groups. The music that is playing on the jukebox inside, roars outside, and it feels more like a party.

I'm left flummoxed. All this time I've been inside, there was a whole other bar outside. It never dawned on me that when a few people entered the front bar to then disappear out the back and never return, I just figured the front bar wasn't to their liking, so they left out the back exit to a carpark.

I feel like an idiot for not looking around when I first got here. But I've no time to beat myself up, I need a loo and now. I wade my way through the crowd to seek out the toilet and find it. It's a relief when I unzip my fly to pee. Once I'm done, I re-enter the throng of people and that's when I see her– Araceli. She's working the back bar and looks run off her feet. All this time she's been right outside, not more than about 30 metres away from me.

She looks up and catches me staring. I smile sheepishly. She returns with her own smile, only much more perfunctory than mine, although it's still a warm, courteous smile nonetheless, more so than one of recognition. She then goes back to taking peoples' orders and pouring more drinks. Rather than standing here gawking like a halfwit as I watch her work, I'm in a state of shock that she's here. She's actually here! Rather than going up to say gidday, I force my way back through the crowd and go inside to the front bar. Once inside, I stand in the corridor between the two bars, taking a moment to think.

I can't believe it's her. And I can't believe I'm behaving like some dumbstruck teenager. A man of 45 years of age, who's never struggled to hold a conversation, is now tongue-tied and flustered. I'm not sure if it's the surprise of seeing her, even though I came here hoping to do exactly that, or if it's my confidence being shaken because she didn't recognise me. I walk back to my table where I discover a small group have taken up residence at it. My lunch bag still sits on top, though it's now open. I step up and snatch it off the table.

"Man, what is this? It's good shit," one of the guys says through a mouthful of one my sandwiches.

I've no idea what's inside and while I'd like to give him a knuckle sandwich instead, I'm not looking to cause any commotion or get kicked out before I've had a chance to say hello.

"Enjoy," I say through gritted teeth.

One of the other group members is reading 'Me and

Daddy's First Big Adventure' book. When he sees me, he just gives me a knowing nod before he hands it over. Somehow in that little exchange, I feel calmer by the time I get back outside. My eyes search for Araceli again, where things seem to have quietened down. I seize the moment and use it to my advantage and walk straight up to the bar.

"Surprise!"

30

Warm Conversation

The night passes by in a blur during the next couple of hours. As people leave, the crowd thins, until eventually, save for the bus boy, it's just Araceli and I who sit outside alone talking. At first she was a little freaked out that I just rocked up unannounced. I can't say I blame her. If someone I only had contact with online visited me out of the blue, I'd be questioning their modus operandi (and their sanity). But the longer we talk the more she eases into the conversation.

"I'm glad you came," Araceli says as she places her hand on my thigh.

My inner demons race ahead but I take the hand gesture for exactly what it is, a genuine show of appreciation.

"It's good to see a familiar face," I reply.

"I have to help clean up and close, but I'd really like to continue the chat. Where are you staying?"

I'm tempted to say I've got a room back at the Sheraton but settle against it. If there's one thing which always kept us connected, it was that we were usually honest with each other, no matter whether either of us was in relationship or not. There were no dark secrets or half-truths here.

"I hear the Dallas bus terminal is good this time of night."

She looks me directly in the eyes to gauge whether I'm joking or not.

"It's either that or try my luck in the Sheraton lounge," I add with a halfhearted chuckle.

She half turns her head away from me for a moment and I watch her as she considers my predicament. I sense her hesitance even before she speaks.

"While we've known each other for a several years, albeit online, know that I never do what I think I'm about to, Raiden, especially not with someone I've only just met for the first time in person. God, I can't believe I am about to say this. If you're truly stuck with no place to go, you can stay at my pad—but on one condition," Araceli says.

"Name it."

"Don't expect anything."

"Of course. Absolutely!"

"Good! I just wanted to make sure that was perfectly clear," she adds.

"I didn't come here with that in mind, Araceli, far from it. I simply came to talk with a friend. Right now, you have no idea how much I need that."

Upon hearing the sincere sentiment behind my words, and knowing I really do mean what I say, her body relaxes.

"While I've always been able to trust you, I also need to be careful. A woman can't be too protective."

"I wouldn't expect it any other way. Believe me, my intentions are pure," I state.

Safe with that knowledge, she gets up off the bar stool and proceeds to tidy up and clean the bar.

"I won't be too long," she says in between placing dirty glasses into the dishwasher.

31

Secrets & Other Matters

It's well after 2am when we finally leave The Grapevine. I stand outside and watch the sign flick off before Araceli emerges from inside, along with the male model bartender from the front bar. He casts a wary glance past her shoulder at me, makes a quick assessment then says in a voice loud enough for me to hear.

"You sure you'll be all right?"

"Relax, Raiden's an old friend. We've got a lot of catching up to do," she says to soothe his concerns as she gives him a comforting smile.

"Okay, well if you need me, just call. I'll come right over," he adds.

"I'll be fine, Eli. Go home. Get some sleep."

She leans in and gives him an appreciative hug.

"See you tomorrow," she calls over her shoulder before she grabs my arm and we disappear into the night.

"Quite the protective one," I say when we're out of earshot from him.

"It comes with the job. In this line of work, you tend to get a lot more suggestive offers and proposals than you can imagine. Most are harmless, drunken flirtations, but every so often one of them doesn't take no so well. Eli has always had my back."

It takes us about 15 minutes to walk to her place. The streets are empty, save for the odd stray cat on the prowl. There's something beautiful and serene about a city at this time of the morning. I've often thought that to truly feel a place and know its energy, it must be felt during this time, when not a living soul is around and it's just you and the city. I never felt that back in Toronto. Lost in a reflective mood, I almost miss Araceli's question.

"Sorry?"

"You look like you're a million miles away. Penny for your thoughts," she enquires.

"I was just thinking how calming a city can be when there's not a constant barrage of noise. These are the times when I feel most at peace."

"Well, I hope you won't mind endless chatter from me then to break the peace? There are so many things I want to ask and find out about you. I hope you weren't planning on an early night," she says with excitement.

"I wasn't planning on it," I say a little too eagerly, conscious there's still an attraction here. I dial it back by adding, "It's not everyday I pass through Texas on my way to someplace else."

"I hope that someplace else can wait," she says with a flatness in her voice.

I'm aware my last comment came off a bit harsh, so I give her a smile in the hopes it will disarm her. She just turns away to enter a key into a door of her apartment. She throws her keys on a side table, waits for me to enter, then locks the door behind me.

Araceli's apartment has a simple homely feel with a charm

all its own. There's an old Texan flag under glass, which resides over the small fireplace, along with a Mexican flag hanging off the corner of one side that dangles downwards. A few ornaments and trinkets decorate the mantlepiece, with a wooden dining table off to the right. On its white table clothed surface, sits a vase with flowers that are slowly wilting, a bunch of letters, bills and paperwork, and on the other end, a ball of thick yarn resting atop a half completed small craftwork of some kind.

"I didn't know you were into macramé."

"There's a lot of things you don't know about me," she says.

Araceli moves across to an old stereo unit, the kind that still has a cassette deck and turntable, and flicks it on. She adjusts the volume, then walks into the kitchen to turn on a kettle.

"Cup of tea or do you want something stronger?"

"Tea's fine for now."

"Chamomile, green tea, or maybe a Rooibos?" she enquires.

"Ooh, Rooibos please."

As she preps the tea, I watch the record spin on the turntable. I recognise the distinctive vocals of Rod Stewart straight away but it takes me a little while to recall the song. When the chorus kicks in, however, I remember it well.

'I Don't Want To Talk About It' rings around the room. I'm not sure if it's intended for me to interpret or not but the more I listen, the more I feel his words penetrate me as he warbles, in this slow, deeply touching song.

"Rod Stewart fan, aye?"

"You can change it if you like," she calls out from further away in what I can only presume is her bedroom.

"On the contrary, I like Rod."

When she re-enters the lounge, she hands me the tea and

takes up a seat on the couch. I look for another place to sit but the small space doesn't allow for another lounge chair. I take my cup and sit down with obvious discomfort, on the opposite end of the couch facing her.

"Everything all right?

"Yeah, fine. Been a long day on the bus," I reply.

There's an initial awkwardness to how we interact but it passes and soon feels like the most natural place to be. I've seen this woman naked in photo form, and now here I am, sitting on her couch, me in donated clothes, her in red sweat pants, a marl grey hoodie and black singlet top that's visible underneath, with nothing but a single cushion seat between us.

Despite her casual appearance, she looks better than any picture she ever sent me. And because there's a familiarity with her, I feel I could lean over and kiss her, but I don't, respecting her one wish. Besides, that's not why I am here, so I look at her watching me, studying her.

"If it's okay with you, Raiden, I'd just like to talk," she says reading my mind.

I blush out of embarrassment and divert my eyes downward at the carpet. She smiles at my obvious bashfulness. She giggles when I jump as she places her warm hand on my forearm, reassuring me that it's okay.

We sit in silence for a while, a mix of old '80s music in the background, one of the finest decades of music in my mind, and sip our teas.

"Why are you here, Raiden?" she asks in a tender manner, breaking the silence.

"I... I don't really know."

And I don't. I know I was on my way to Mexico to escape my current situation because I wasn't coping. I know

I was planning to go via L.A to see a former flame. I know I'm searching for something yet still feel lost. But I've got no real idea why I am here, in Dallas, inside Araceli's home. All I know is that I am, and it was a conscious decision to do so.

"I know you well enough to know that's not true. Why turn up out of the blue? What do you want? What are you hiding?"

Her barrage of fair, direct questions totally catches me off guard. I want to reveal the truth about leaving my pregnant girlfriend... about actually having a girlfriend, but I don't. Forced into a corner like this with no way to talk myself out of it, my mind goes into overdrive and panic sweeps across my brain until I blurt out.

"Because I'm lost. I'm afraid. I'm overwhelmed. I'm not coping. And I was..." but I can't bring myself to say it.

"You were what?"

Araceli's no nonsense Latina questioning is replaced with one of genuine concern.

I look away into the distance then to the floor, unable to bring myself to look at her.

"I was... assaulted," I mumble.

She places her cup of tea on the coffee table and leans in closer to me, her hand on my shoulder.

"What do mean, *assaulted*?"

"Sexually. I was... raped. Violated."

She lets out a low, audible gasp before she places a hand over her mouth to suppress her shock. She then sidles over to my side of the couch and drapes her arms around me in support. Once she does, I lose all self-control and openly cry into my hands. Araceli holds the side of my head to soothe and comfort me, while I weep uncontrollably.

It's calming and reassuring, and it's far from how I wanted

her to see me, as the broken, beaten man I now am. When I get my tears under control and the snivelling eases up, I take a few deep breaths.

"I'm sorry," I say.

"What can you possibly be sorry for?"

"For breaking down on you like this."

"Oh Raiden, please don't ever feel like you have to apologise for what happened. It's not your fault, you realise? Trust me, I should know."

I give her a blank look.

"I have been through a similar experience when I was younger, so you've no need to ever apologise, believe me."

"Oh, I didn't know."

"It's not something I talk about. It happened a long time ago. I've dealt with it as best I can in the years since."

"I am sorry for what happened to you."

"It's okay. I've moved on."

"No, I mean I'm sorry for..." I start to utter before I stop myself short.

Araceli gives me a quizzical look.

What *am* I sorry for?

I suck in a big breath of air, hold it a moment, then expel it outwards.

"For landing on you unannounced, for my appearance, for dumping my troubles on you. Most of all, I'm sorry for not being totally honest with you."

Upon hearing the words leave my mouth, I start to feel somewhat relieved. I know that this is possibly as close as I will come to full disclosure with her, for now.

"It's all okay, Raiden, really. If a friend can't be supportive after a traumatic event, then what use are they? But what haven't you been honest with me about?"

"I feel like I owe you an apology or at least an explanation," I start to say.

"You don't owe me anything."

"I think I do."

I sense her pull away from me, waiting for whatever it is I want to discuss. I also know it's a big reason as to why I have ended up here.

"When we met, we were always open and revealed our truths to each other, even if we knew that sometimes they might be hard to hear. If I was in a relationship, I told you. If you were, you also told me. It kept everything easy, clean, simple, and above board. It also played a key part in us getting closer as a result. We knew we could always be upfront and honest with each other, and respect whatever was discussed."

She nods her head in agreement.

"Then we lost contact and we drifted away from that. Then we'd reconnect again, and it'd all come back like before. But since that last time we conversed, I've not been as upfront as I could be."

"You're married aren't you," she states.

"What? No," I laugh.

"Then what?"

"I have a baby–on the way."

She takes a moment to sit with the news.

"How long has this been going on?"

"Four to five months."

"No, the relationship?"

"Oh. Um, about three years."

"Why didn't you tell me?"

"I didn't know how to."

"You have before."

"I know, but this was different."

"This explains why you disappeared."

"Huh?"

"I'd reach out in the hopes you'd respond, want to reconnect, and then finally come see me, but I'd never hear back. And now you're telling me you're expecting a baby?"

"Look, when I found out she was—"

"Spare me the bullshit, Raiden. I opened up to you like I never have before, and I thought you were just as open and honest, too. I allowed myself to believe, thinking, hoping, you were different. You're just like the rest of them."

"Rest of who?"

"Every man that has ever lied to me."

"Wait, let me explain."

"Save your breath."

An uncomfortable silence.

While I want to fully explain my situation and why I stopped reaching out, I reflect on her revelation. It occurs to me with what I know about Araceli–a single mum of three adult kids–that she's been hurt by past relationships. No doubt, her life has taken her in a different, unexpected direction as a result. She starts to take shorter, faster breathes, and I think she's on the verge of hyperventilating, but somehow she holds it together.

I feel her loneliness and sorrow, all her pain and heartache from years past. I want to hug her and hold her, tell her everything will be all right. Tell her that she's beautiful and worthy of that deep, connective love she longs for and revealed to me. But it won't be from me, so I don't. I sit there to ponder how our lives came to intersect, never fully aligning, and now... well, now they couldn't be headed in more opposite directions if we planned it.

I hear Pink Floyd sing in the background to their epic

song, 'Wish You Were Here'. It really does feel like we are just two lost souls.

"It's funny," I say, breaking the quietude which has swept over us. "I always thought that when I met you, it would be different somehow."

"How do you mean?" Araceli says, keeping her mixed emotions barely in check.

"Given our history, I thought we would not be able to keep our hands off of one another. That we'd be fucking each other's brains out by now."

"Me too," she answers coolly.

There's another long, uncomfortable pause. I fill it with my own inner turmoil wondering why I said that. Before my mind can go too far down that rabbit hole, I follow it up.

"Would you even want to anymore?" I say, not sure if it's a serious question or simply more to satisfy a curiosity than anything else.

"Are you serious? I can't believe you're even asking me that after your admission."

"I was just curious, is all."

"Honestly? No! Wonder no more."

To be truthfully honest, a part of me wants to experience her, feel her the way we had hoped to one day a few years earlier. But now, sitting here with Araceli in her house, I know things are different. Even if things were good between us, somehow, I don't think it would be good for either of us. Not given my mental state, her emotional one, and our mixed feelings. It's a dangerous cocktail that invariably leads to disappointment, resentment, and a hollowness you can never fill, no matter how many times you convince yourself of it. While I genuinely care for her, and I do (and always have), I know it's not a wise move. We're both vulnerable and fragile, and now, thanks to my stupid, unnecessary question, she's curt, hostile, and totally pissed off.

"I don't even know if I want to be your friend anymore," she blurts out.

And now she's also bitter.

"Were you ever?"

As soon as the words leave my mouth, I want to retract them. Before I get a chance to back up and apologise, she slaps my face and then turns her Tex-Mex rage to my legs, lashing out with her feet as she kicks me. I cry out in pain.

I do my best to protect myself, which is not easy when you can't move freely, but each twist and turn I make to avoid her blows, exacerbates the injury and agony I feel at my rear end.

When she sees my face contort in obvious discomfort, her anger immediately subsides, replaced with genuine remorse for her outburst. She reaches her hand out to me in an apology, but scared I'm about to be slapped again, I move back out of reach.

"Oh forgive me, Raiden. I just got so irritated by your comment, my defaul—"

"Forget it," I say, cutting her off.

"I didn't mean to fly off the handle like that and lash out. I should know better. That's a part of me I don't like."

"I shouldn't have said what I did either."

A moment of respite, one where we can both catch ourselves.

"Can you tell me where the bathroom is," I grimace.

"Absolutely. It's down the hall, second door on your left. Is everything okay?"

"I'm not sure," is my response.

When I get to the bathroom and lock the door behind me, I know things are not okay. When I pull down my jeans and sit on the toilet, I see the small pool of blood cling to the inside of the boxers. I think my stitches have split. If not for the discomfort, I'd sit here a while longer. I grab at the toilet paper and dab gently at my rear end. With each dab, I can feel the blood slow down its flow.

It's a relief but I am concerned the stitches may have torn. I do my best to clean out the blotch of damp, sticky blood inside my boxer briefs, but they'll need to dry before I can put them back on.

I hear a knock at the door followed by Araceli's soft voice.

"Is there anything I can help with?"

I flick the lock, let her in. My face tells her everything she needs to know, the dark crimson stain on my boxers do the rest.

"I'm so sorry, Raiden," she says full of regret.

"You don't have any Epsom salts on hand, do you?"

"Err, I don't think so but let me look."

She bends down and peers into the cupboard below the sink but comes up short.

"Can I get you something else? Anything? Name it."

"Some ibuprofen, and maybe a needle and thread?" I jest.

She gives me a weird look.

"Needle and thread?"

I swallow hard, turn my back away from her and as discreetly as I can dab a finger to my anus. When I hold my finger back up at her, her eyes are staring wide in disbelief.

"Raiden, did I do that? Oh shit. I'm so, so sorry. Perhaps we should go to hospital?"

"No, no hospital. I can't bear the thought of waiting around for a few hours for a couple of stitches. Do you have any soothing gels or creams which might alleviate the tenderness instead?"

"Let me go see."

She hurriedly leaves the bathroom, and I hear her rustle around in a drawer in her bedroom before she returns with some kind of medicated cream.

"It's a cortisone cream. It's meant to help reduce any swelling and cool the area."

"Thanks."

I take the cream, read the label and think it will help. I give her an embarrassed smile as I place a small amount on the tip of my finger. To her credit, she exits the bathroom and gives me a little privacy to smear it around.

When I'm done, I pull up my jeans.

"I don't suppose you have stain remover?" I holler, holding up my boxers.

"Of course," she says as she moves down the hall before she stops and comes back to the bathroom. "I know this is none of my business, but have you been tested?

"Yep, results came back negative. I also got stitches but as you can tell, they have split. Thankfully, it's just a case of being gentle to my rear for a while and soaking in a warm bath."

"I'm here for you… if you want to talk about it."

"I know."

"Can I get you anything else?"

"A hug?" I reply.

She steps into the space between us and holds me. We stand and stay silent like this for a moment. I feel on the verge of a few tears and sensing it, Araceli embraces me tighter. I bring my own arms up and cling onto her, not wanting to let go.

After what feels like the longest time, our arms fall down by our sides, where we stand facing each other.

"It's late. Perhaps we should go to bed?" Araceli says.

I say nothing, instead allow myself to be taken by the hand

and led to a bedroom. When I get inside, I look around and realise I am in her room. I drop my hand.

"The fold out sofa sags. It's not the most comfortable thing to lie on. My bed has one of those pillow top mattresses. It makes for a much better sleep."

I'm too tired and sore to argue. I'm also conflicted by where I now find myself, and who I am about to share a bed with. She lets me watch her undress, all walls now have fallen away as a result of the fight and her guilt, and slips into a silk night-ie. Where the hug was welcomed, I feel like anything further would be a mistake. Even though our care is unfeigned and our support of one another is real, our love is based only in admiration. Not that we don't have a love, it's just not a deep love for one another.

I take off my shirt and glide my jeans down before I realise I have nothing on underneath. With no extra clothes, I am fully exposed. I cover myself with my hands, wondering what to do when she sees my uncomfortable predicament.

"I've an old night shirt if you want something to wear? I've just got to rummage through some drawers to find it."

I walk to where she is searching frantically in the bedroom closet and place a hand on her shoulder. She stops what she's doing and turns to face me.

"We're both tired. If you're okay with having me in your bed as is, let's save you the hassle of searching for it this late. All I ask for is maybe a black or dark coloured towel to lay down upon the bed in case I…"

She rests her hand on my shoulder, knowing what I am about to say.

"Of course," Araceli says, hurrying off.

Once the towel is placed down, and we're both in bed, do I start to finally relax a little. It's strange to think that I'm now in the bed of a woman I once desired, and yet there's this imaginary line down the middle of the bed between us, that neither of us will cross.

"Would you like a cuddle?" She tentatively says.

"I'd love one."

Araceli moves up behind me and drapes her arm over me, where it comes to rest across my chest. I push back slightly into her so that we're in the perfect spooning position. For once, no dark, sex starved demonic voices can be heard tonight. I know they feel my agony and trauma of recent events. Thankful that it looks like I'll be able to get a restful night's sleep, I exhale a breath of relief.

We continue to hold each other tight, almost matching the other's breath. Even though this feels like the most natural thing for us to do in the world, where I've no doubt our love-making would be beautiful and intimate, I know I wouldn't be being authentic to myself, to Araceli, or to Clea. I feel my body relax, and I sigh once more with the realisation.

But it's not a sigh of regret, more a breakthrough, halle-lujah moment. I used to wonder what was wrong with me. I used to think I was too broken to ever fix… that I would forever walk the same beaten path I'd tread many times before, sabotaging relationship after relationship, and shattering hearts in the process. That I'd always perpetually make the same fatal mistakes and be destined to wind up a sad, lonely old man forever. I now realise that's false. While I'm just like everyone else trying to figure his way through this crazy thing called life, that very love I have been searching for my whole adult life, is right there in front of me. Despite our cultural differences and language barriers, she is prepared to not only love me with all my faults and flaws, but willing to build a family–with me!

In spite of my loathing for a city I don't care for, perhaps, like this journey, it's only temporary. That somehow, we'll find a happy medium, or at least one where it's warmer and friendly. I know that instead of being scared by what lies ahead of me, by the new responsibilities I must now face up to, that I should instead embrace a love that while not perfect, is one of absolute acceptance.

As good as it might be being snuggled by Araceli, feeling her warm body soothe me, I know I must break from the embrace. I loosen the hold to roll away but as I do, I feel her cling tighter to me before I hear an almost inaudible whimper into her pillow. I'm not sure if she's having her own realisation that this now won't go anywhere, or if she accepts, having once confided to me that the one man she thought was her twin flame (me), is about to walk away and leave her alone.

I release myself from her grip and roll over to let her silently weep on her own.

This moment right now, this is heartbreakingly painful. I know she gets it.

I look over at her glassy eyes in the soft light from the side table lamp, and wipe one of the tears from her face.

"I'm sorry," I say over her snivels.

Araceli doesn't respond, instead looks straight through me, with her deep, dark brown eyes for what feels like the longest time. Her silence is deafening. I can almost see her mind work through all the emotions and permutations. She takes a deep breath, sighs, takes another one.

"I knew something was *off* when you turned up unannounced. I'm not sure if you have ever been fully honest with me…" she breaks down mid sentence. It takes her a moment to gather herself again before she carries on. "If it wasn't so late, I'd ask you to leave, stay somewhere else tonight."

"I didn't know how to tell you," I say cutting in.

"You just say it! I'm a big girl, I can take it."

"Yeah but—"

"I'm of an age where nothing men say shocks me anymore. But what I don't or won't accept, nor ever have, are lies and deceit. I don't know if I can trust what you have said to me in the past or say now. If there's one thing I do trust, it's my intuition. There's obviously something deeper going on, something you're having trouble dealing with. I just wished you'd been honest, opened up, and let me in sooner."

I go to reply but she's not finished.

"I really thought you were authentic, true… different somehow. That we had something special," she adds, choking a little on her words. "I guess I expected more.'

"I wanted, I hoped… It's just that," but before I can finish, she places a finger up to my mouth to quieten my rambling thoughts.

"Save your breath, Raiden. I'm exhausted, I don't want to say something I regret. Night," she says before she turns back over to sleep.

I'm not one to make assumptions but I feel she's as confused by my being here as I am, and now feels more alone than ever. She's just as lost as me. Unlike myself, however, she never left home to go and "find herself".

I'm not sure how I ended up here. Maybe it was loneliness, perhaps it was out of sheer desperation, or possibly I just needed a friend after my ordeal. Either way, something is off. Now it's me who starts to run through so many thoughts and emotions, as I work my way through my actions and inactions, my many chances to say something–my reasons. All of them now eat away at my mind.

Regardless of the chance to lay flat in a warm, cosy bed for the night, grateful Araceli took me in for the evening when I had zero options, I know I've let her down. And now I feel that weight. I won't get much sleep tonight.

32

Kitchen Heat

When I wake the next morning, Araceli's already up. She couldn't hide her disdain by pretending to sleep and stay in bed longer than necessary. Yet despite it, there's a glass of water waiting for me on the side table. I hear muffled sounds from the kitchen from behind the half-closed bedroom door. I lay there a little while longer and listen to her go about her morning.

As I attune my ears to the sounds, I make out a drawer opening and closing, a kettle boiling then flicking off, and the sizzling of something landing into a hot pan. I could easily lay here longer and allow myself to drift back asleep, but it's the smells from the kitchen which waft into the bedroom, that make me stir enough to rise. I can smell eggs and bacon even from here. While it's highly likely we won't see each other again beyond today, the fact she has gone to so much effort makes me feel even worse about last night.

In all honesty though, I am grateful for the chance to reveal what had been plaguing my mind, and which I'd hidden from her, to be able to tell her in person. I know it wasn't easy for her to hear, not when the exchanges we've had with each other, paint this wonderful fairytale picture and give them

215

dreams to cling to. I just hope she'll find someone who loves her far beyond what I ever could, because I know she'll make one hell of a partner.

I finally drag my arse out of bed where I feel a sense of relief. Relief because I knew I needed to clear my conscience and reveal my hidden secret to her. There's also a renewed purpose about me. While I had a lot of doubts coming here to Dallas, I know this was the right choice. My body feels it, my mind does, too.

I'm not sure what I will say to Araceli, maybe she already knows I have to move on–perhaps that's why she wasn't here when I woke up. Either way, with less than $7 in my pocket, it is the best thing to do for the both of us. I've no doubt we would have some amazing and honest conversations after clearing the air, as well as share some truly memorable moments, and who knows, possibly have had great sex, too (that I am convinced of actually). But I also know I'm being pulled, almost propelled, towards something else. To what, I have no clear idea yet but there's a force beyond my control urging me on. Perhaps it's been there all along.

When I enter the kitchen, I notice the amazing spread laid out on the table before me. I spot toast with fresh homemade jam beside it, bacon & eggs, baked beans, grilled tomatoes, even some hash browns. There's a freshly squeezed glass of orange juice, and a pot of tea steeping off to one side. Araceli not only remembered an exchange we'd had a while back about what my favourite breakfast was, but has also gone to the trouble to prepare it all.

I want to scoop her up in my arms, whisper a thanks in her ear, and kiss her neck as a show of appreciation but I know that's all a little too familiar.

"I thought about laying myself out for your pleasure," she

says with a snigger, "but then I knew we'd never eat."

"Well… technically, I would be," I say chuckling, grateful her mood has relaxed and the tension passed.

"It's a shame I won't get to find out just how great you are with that tongue of yours, but I figured this was the least I could do to make up for my overly aggressive manner last night."

"You didn't have to," I offer. "Letting me stay was enough."

"I know but I felt really bad for my violent outburst and what it did to you to your stitches."

"It's really okay."

"Maybe so but as someone who has also been abused, I am ashamed by my actions."

"And me, of mine," I say.

We share an unspoken, real moment. One that in spite of everything, and that no matter the different paths we both are on, we have this knowing that we did what we did for our own self-protective reasons. It's in this moment that I step forward and hold Araceli tight, giving her a hug of… I don't know what, but it's one of genuine warmth and care.

By drawing her to me, I sense her frame of mind change again as she presses into me. She almost clings to me, not out of comfort or hope but one of something else. I can't put my finger on it until she digs her nails into my back and nuzzles her face into my neck, before planting soft kisses on it.

'Danger! Danger!' spring the warning signs in my head.

While I am aware of what could happen if I give myself truly over to this moment, I find my body responds all on its own. As she continues to kiss and nibble at my neck, the more I find myself becoming aroused and falling under Araceli's enchantress like spell.

On instinct, the back of my hand brushes the side of her

cheek. She lets out a soft moan of approval. The same hand continues to snake its way down over her very curvaceous body, running from the top of her neck, down across her side, before it slides over her waist and hips, until it rests on the top of her firm, taut, Latina backside.

She leans into me even harder, pressing her bountiful breasts into my chest and letting me know she'd like me to continue. Holy hell, is all I can think. Talk about a complete mood switch. She's either woken up very horny or she's getting a kick out of pushing my buttons to see whether I will break and surrender to her womanly charms and desires. I can't keep this up, I can't. While I know all too well where it will lead if I take charge and finish what she started, the result on my mind and emotions at the end, will be detrimental.

My sex starved demons on the other hand. They're practically shouting from the bleachers, telling me to swing for the fences and go for the home run.

The more she leans into me, the more I can feel her hunger and heat. Knowing I'm melting before her on the verge of surrender, she turns up the flame. It really was my belief that I'd avoid this kind of compromising position and not put myself into such a make or break decision. But I'm losing the inner war with myself with each kiss and neck bite of hers.

After being on the road with all that's happened, especially recently, and doing my best to remain faithful despite any temptation put in my way, I'm failing right now in this moment.

The more I think about it, the easier it would be to just take her and have my wicked way with her. Even if it was from afar, we have a history. And truth be told, I've always had a penchant for a curvy, sexy-as-fuck Latina. While I was tested by Brianna's exquisite mixed race beauty and frisky attitude, Araceli and I have a real history. I won't fail this test. I can't. I won't allow it. My demons know it and roar louder than ever. There's only one way to shut them up.

"You don't make this easy," I whisper, battling my mind that is doing its best to resist pulling her in close and planting a deep, passionate kiss full on her mouth, versus that of my body that's raging with lust ready to go!

"Easy's for chumps," she says, as her fingers begin to trace up and down my back sending me into mini convulsions.

Before my mind goes into hyperdrive and my body explodes, however, I retreat, pull back, and save face as I release my grip right as an oven timer goes off in the background. She steps back and looks at me, her face one of utter shock and her mind in total confusion.

"Whoa! What the fuck?" she snaps.

I just shrug my shoulders, sensing my hesitance yet emboldened by my decisive action.

"You don't want to take it further, see where it leads?" she pleads, placing both her hands either side of my torso.

"Come on Araceli, we both know what will happen," I retort, as I take charge and remove her hands.

"But you're clearly turned on," she sneers, reaching for a bulge I can't hide.

"I can't," I respond, grabbing her wrists more firmly this time to hold her at bay.

"I failed, didn't I?" she asks, a resignation in her voice.

"We both did," I reply, freeing her hands.

An awkward pause, a chance to reset. The only saving grace for me, if there is one, is that when you leave a pregnant girlfriend to fend on her own, it's not sex you're seeking.

She walks over to the oven, turns off the timer with a sense of frustration and disappointment. I on the other hand...

well, while I breathe a sigh of relief, it's really one of dismay. If not for the oven timer and a split second decision, who knows where it would have gone. While I'd like to think I dodged a bullet, I feel like I took one instead.

I am hoping (and wanting) to remain chaste throughout this journey in case I ever do make it back to Toronto. That way when I look Clea in the eyes, I will have a clear conscience.

"Breakfast's ready," Araceli proclaims frostily.

Even though I sit down to eat a magnificent spread, grateful for the plentiful food on offer, we eat in silence. I'm still not sure what possessed Araceli to take the actions she took. Given it seemed that last night we were both cool with our situation in not wanting to take it further, it eats away at my mind. Why would she change her mind? What was she hoping to gain? And where was her self-respect? I'm not sure what the point was. Had I not taken charge, I'm not sure I want to know either. Her reasoning and actions now swirl around in my mind. I feel angry, surprised... betrayed.

While the bacon and poached eggs slide seamlessly down my throat when I bite into them, each mouthful tastes bitter. Not only did I possibly let Clea and the baby down in a moment of weakness... most of all I have let myself down. That's what disappoints me the most.

"What's on your mind?" Araceli cuts in.

"You!"

"We both know that's not true."

I go quiet.

"Did I do something wrong?" she enquires.

I remain silent, nothing but an icy stare on my face.

"I'm not sure what came over me. Just standing there in your embrace, I felt, how do I say this? Safe, respected. Does that make sense?"

"I'll admit, it wasn't easy to step back from you and not take things further," I reply, breaking my peace. "But I truly felt we both had a breakthrough last night, reached a new level of trust. If we'd had sex just now, it would have been for all the wrong reasons. I feel like I have been compromised, maybe even manipulated."

"Manipulated?"

"Yeah, manipulated. I can't say I wasn't tempted. Fuck, I've been tempted by you ever since we started engaging in our conversations a few years back, but things are very different now. But given my fragile emotional, mental and physical state after what's happened to me, honestly, sex is the last thing I want. I would have thought you of all people, would understand that," I declare.

Araceli appears to absorb every word I say.

"I feel like we make better friends than lovers. And right now I think that's much more important for both of us, or at least me anyway."

"I thought about you all night long, Raiden, imagining what it would be like to finally have your body pressed to mine, your hands and mouth on me, what it would feel like to have you inside me, especially as you lay right there next to me in my bed. But I know we're both broken. While I've no doubt you'd make one hell of a generous lover, I know our timing is off. Not to mention all that you are dealing with."

"So why do what you just did then?"

There's a long pause. To calm myself down while I wait for her to reply, I eat some more food and sip on the freshly brewed, loose leaf Lapsang Souchong tea.

"You know I was only playing with you this morning, right?" she finally answers.

"And see, that's the problem, Araceli. You know my state

of mind, you know my situation, and yet you still felt like you could walk all over them just to *play*."

"Do you have any idea how many times I've been walked over, Raiden? Do you?" she counters. "As a single mother of three, as an abused teen… as someone who's not had any form of decent physical touch, let alone genuine love and affection from anyone, in God knows how long, or as a woman working two jobs just to make ends meet, all the time being hassled, groped, put down, and seen as nothing more than just a pussy on legs by men with wives and girlfriends who don't give a fuck about me or my feelings. No one does, not even you! We've always had a strong attraction to one another, hell maybe even genuine care, so forgive me for getting a little frisky and carried away in the moment."

A tension that wasn't there before, boils to the surface. As a peacekeeping Libran, I do my best to simmer it down.

"You're a wonderful woman, Araceli, that's a given, but while I may rue not seizing this opportunity down the line, I believe it is the best thing moving forward. I feel that we'll both be better for it, for you and all you are coping with, and for me and all I am trying to cope with, too. Friends?"

I reach out and place my hand over hers. The vexation and fury that was there only a moment before, now replaced with a calmer, more benign energy.

"Friends," she mutters, putting her other hand atop of mine.

We eat the rest of the meal in relative comfort and silence. When we're done, I help clean up by rinsing and placing the dishes in the dishwasher.

"Thank you," I tell her.

"For what?"

"Everything! For not freaking out when I came to your

bar, for allowing me to stay, for the food, our conversations, but most of all for helping me figure some things out. It's meant a lot to me, so gracias amiga."

"You're leaving today, aren't you?" she asks.

"I have to."

That's not an answer she wanted to hear.

"I had hoped you'd stay a little longer," she says with a defeated tone in her voice.

"We both know what would happen if I did."

She knows it too, and so has a hard time looking me in the eye.

"I'm a fractured, defective man, Araceli, with many things on my mind, and they're all playing havoc with my mental and emotional capacity. You saw the physical state I am in last night. I don't have anything left."

She just shrugs her shoulders in agreement. I can tell she's hurt by my remark. I'm hoping she won't dwell on it.

"Raiden," she says in a hushed tone.

"Yes?"

"You're the first man in a very long time who sees me more than just something he'd like to fuck. I care about you, always have, and I know you care about me, but whoever she is, she must be special."

I don't reply. I'm not even sure what to say.

"I can take you wherever you need to go," she adds.

"But you've already done so much for me. You don't have to do anything else."

"I want to, it's the least I can do to say thanks to you."

"What for?"

"For showing me what I am worth and what I deserve. You're a good man. I've always known that about you. I also know you were never in it for the sex. You took your time to get to know me, which I admit, I don't make easy. I don't let many people in, but somehow you not only found a way in, you penetrated my heart and soul."

I'm floored by her response. I wasn't anticipating such a big statement. I don't know what to say but I don't have to. She grabs my hand and places it over her heart.

"I'll always remember you and smile," she says.

I'm deeply touched. This is a genuine woman who's just trying to find her way and her place in the world like all of us. I know she wants to be loved, find a true connection. All I can do is wrap her up in my arms once more and hold her. It seems the only thing worth saying.

When we're done, there's just one thing left for me to do now–leave.

"I'll drive you," Araceli says.

"I can't let you do that. I don't even know where I'm going," I protest.

"I wasn't asking," she replies.

While her warmth dims, her kind, generous spirit remains. I know she's fighting it. I know this is hard for her.

"Thank you," I say, gratefully. I offer her a sincere smile, relieved. She forces a slight half smile, lips pursed tight together before she gets up and walks away.

When we leave her house sometime later, the drive is done in a resigned hush. She drives me to the nearest bus stop, but with the sun shining, it actually feels like a good day to hitch, so I politely request to be dropped off at the nearest truck stop on the outskirts of town, if it's not too much trouble. She doesn't speak, instead redirects the car back onto the road. I don't mention I've only got a few bucks in my pocket, from which I want to give her some for petrol money.

When we reach a truck stop, she pulls off to the side and

parks up the car. We sit there in silence for some time, nothing but the sound of birds and the odd rumble of a truck driving past. I offer the last of my money but she refuses to take it. I want to tell her everything will be okay but I don't. Instead, we just sit in this uneasy space for a moment, where I hope like crazy the tension will thaw, so that we'll part on a semi pleasant note.

As nuts as she might be, I know there are things she'd like to hear from me but nothing comes out. Instead, we just inhale and exhale separately. After a little while, I place my hand gently over hers, which rests on the steering wheel.

Araceli turns to me and I can see she's on the verge of tears, fighting so many emotions, thoughts and questions, each clashing in her mind. I'm tempted to place my hand on the side of her face, let her know I feel her anguish, but I don't. It's different now. While I came to the realisation earlier, it makes it no less difficult. No actions come, no words either.

We sit in this heaviness and wallow together a while longer, neither of us yet willing to part goodbye for the final time. I summon up the courage to turn the door handle. As soon it clicks upward, I hear the sobs she'd been so valiantly holding back. I admit, this is harder than I thought it would be, feeling my own shame and guilt knowing she expected more from me than I was able to give.

I wish there were more I could do, say, or be for her, but the only thing that comes to mind is to exit the car. I hope she finds solace in knowing that I reached a far deeper level with her through our interactions, while getting to know ourselves better in the process, and that in time, she will come to see this was something special even if it didn't play out the way we both once thought it might. I know I will always hold her dear to me wherever these crazy lives of ours take us.

I place one foot on the gravel outside the car but before I shift my weight to exit, I turn around to face her. It's an awkward moment and I know I can't linger any longer, but I don't want to leave like this. I wipe the small tears away from her cheeks and lean in to stroke the side of her face with affection when in an almost involuntary fashion, I kiss her. Just a soft, gentle kiss of sincere care upon her lips. When I look back into her eyes, I see a small, faint smile appear on her face. A much better memory to leave on.

Satisfied, I get up out of her car and walk a few steps to go sit on a guardrail to wait for a lift. At first Araceli doesn't move, she just stays parked a few feet away from me. With the morning sun reflecting off the windscreen, it's hard to see so I shield my eyes to get a better view. Once I'm able to better focus and see in, I wish I hadn't. That strong, no nonsense persona of hers has shifted, replaced with one of sorrow and regret. Her face is slumped into her hands, her wails all too visible. I feel like a bastard (again). She deserved better. I'm tempted to walk over, climb back into her car and comfort her, but I figured out long ago I can't fake something when it's not there.

Before I've time to think or act, a small, beat up pick-up truck with a sleep cabin plonked on top, pulls up between us.

"Necesita transporte... A ride?" the clipped Spanish voice calls out.

Feeling the enormity of either choice yet forced to make a decision, I get up off the guardrail, take one last look at Araceli riding her emotional rollercoaster, and open the door. I don't ask where he's headed, I just step inside the pick-up.

As we pull away, I look back in the side mirror, the tears, screams, frustrations and more, all pouring out of her. I feel a certain sadness creep up from inside me as well. I swallow down hard to keep my own emotions from running away with me.

I know that while we will never interact with each other again, however, she'll always hold a special place in my mind and that means more to me than she'll ever know. When she eventually disappears from view, I turn my eyes forward to sit with my own bittersweet sadness.

A tune I know but can't recall the name of, starts to seep out of the old AM cassette radio. It's a mellow, jangly guitar tune at first before it slowly builds up in pace and rhythm. Even though I don't remember the name of the song off the top of my head, I find myself quietly mouthing along to the words. And then bam, once the chorus drops, it hits me. James' 'Getting Away With It (All Messed Up)' crackles outward.

Life is messy. People are messier. And we really are all getting away with it all messed up. With nothing to do, I reach into my lunch bag, where I find some of the food from this morning that I wasn't able to fully eat. There's also a small yellow sticky note tucked inside the 'Me and Daddy's First Big Adventure' book, which attracts my attention. I slide the book out and open it to the page.

Go to her.
Be the man I always saw you as.
Become the amazing dad I know you will be.
Stay true. Stay You.
Love, A xo

I shake my head in disbelief. As wild, crazy and unpredictable as she might be, whoever lands and wholly gives themselves over to Araceli, will have a partner for life. That thought brings me joy, along with a small smile that threads its way onto my face.

I'm about to close my eyes, happy with that thought but a strong breeze picks up and buffets and rocks the pick-up from side to side. I look over at the late-50s, Mexican driver trying to gain control of his car. He gives me an unreassuring, thumbs up smile.

"Es buenos, amigo, si. Tranquilo."

My Spanish is mas o menos at best, and so while I understand what he means, he looks far from tranquil, especially when he crosses one hand quickly across his chest. With an exertion and sweat creased forehead, he grips the steering wheel tight to battle the strong winds. Once we cross the long, open bridge and get refuge from the hillside, does his forehead relax.

"Todo bueno," he beams at me with a missing tooth grin.

"Todo bueno," I smile, "todo bueno."

As the last chorus closes out, much like that unexpected, hairy moment we just had, I realise that when things do get messy, calmness is also never too far away.

33

The Uncertain Drive

It turns out I would have a lot of time to think. I know enough Spanish to ask his name, where he's headed, and in the end that proves enough. Pedro, my Mexican driver, is headed to El Paso, an eight to nine hour solid drive away, and that's if we don't stop for petrol and food. His English is clipped, and he only knows a few basic phrases, though I do my best to add a 'Gidday mate' to his lexicon, but for the most part he didn't want to say anything. Perfecto!

The only thing that breaks the silence (and the language barrier), is his crappy AM radio. Every so often a tune appeals to my senses and I'd ask him:

"¿Qué es esta música?" (What's this music?).

"¿Quién es esta banda?" (Who is this band?).

One song in particular really strikes a chord with me.

"De Usuahia a la Quiaca," Pedro replies when I ask him.

I give him a blank stare.

"Gustavo Santaolalla," Pedro says, tilting his head to the side wondering if I'm stupid.

Still means nothing to me.

"Diarios de motocicleta. Diarios de motocicleta," he adds with fervent animation.

I knew I recognised it. It's the music soundtrack from 'The Motorcycle Diaries'. It had been on my iPod. That movie chronicles a motorcycle journey across South America, undertaken by a then unknown young man, Ernesto Guevara, who would later go on to become the revolutionary, 'Che' Guevara.

I remember the film's premise. *"Before he changed the world, the world changed him."* From memory, when this beautiful, haunting tune begins to play is nearer the end, around the time the film shows a touching recollection of all the ordinary, everyday people Che came into contact with on his travels–the poor, hungry, diseased–the very people who would alter the course of his life forever. It was hard not to be moved by such a powerful cinematic scene. Granted, I am in a very different era and continent, I'm moved again by the song with my own journey, and the people I meet, altering and shifting my perspective.

Despite heading south west with what I thought was an air of certainty, I found I started to do my own reminiscing. While not doing it anywhere near as tough as Che had done it back in the '50s, it had still been arduous and life changing for me all the same.

Brianna, "Uncle" Louie, Mitchell and his wife Ilene, and their little dog, Josie, of course, and Araceli. While I've done my best to bury the memory of Roy, those scars will take longer to fade. In a dark, twisted way, he too shaped my odyssey. I even think right back through to the more *random* folk I had contact with, the bitter café waitress, Mesut, Gertrude, the strict librarian, the child at the traffic lights, plus the other drivers I hitched and interacted with, even the U.S. border guard all the way back at the Canada-U.S. border.

Each, in their own way, has shaped my journey. Whether

willingly or not, they've played their part and guided me to this exact moment, a moment where it now feels that I am on the precipice. The precipice of changing the direction of my life–forever! Everything feels different now from when I first began. I find myself more hesitant to want to continue onwards anymore.

The one thing that stood out as I reflect, each had their own flaws, imperfections and life scars they all carried. All of them were doing their best to make a fist of this thing called life. Their struggles were real, their journeys just as difficult to navigate as mine, yet their hearts still beat on.

I was no different of course, only rather than tackle my issues head on, I had run away from them.

It took me a long time to figure out why I never did anything with Brianna, believing we were possibly on the cusp of doing so. I tried to argue with myself that I was in charge, and she nothing more than a prostitute, but I knew that not to be true. I wasn't able to let my thoughts settle with the fact I "resisted" her either. While I did my best to put it down to being my weakened emotional state, making me more vulnerable than usual, in the end I knew my own reasons were misguided. The harsh truth was that she had been in control since the beginning. Ultimately, she drove whether we did anything or not, not that I was some helpless passenger mind you, but I knew better. I consoled myself with the fact that nothing had happened. Should the time ever come where I found myself face to face with Clea, at least I knew I would be free of guilt. However, what mattered to me even more, was that perhaps one day I may be staring into the eyes of my child. I wanted them to know that while I had left, I hadn't strayed. It might be a small consolation, but it made me feel better. Still, not being the one calling the shots with Brianna,

I won't lie, that was hard for me to take no matter what else I may have told myself.

Araceli on the other hand was a lot easier to explain, she was plain batshit crazy. Not to mention it also backed on from my... my, violation. I also no longer desired her the way I once had, regardless of her best efforts to convince me otherwise that morning. But mostly, I had been in charge. I made the conscious choice not to do anything. I set boundaries from the beginning. I did that.

And I also did my best to wrestle with my many demons and swirling thoughts I had, doing what I could to keep them all at bay, no matter how loud their howls or noise inside my mind. I know that counts for something.

But why even put myself in those positions in the first place because that's not why I left. Did I enjoy the game? The hunt? The flirting? Did I like knowing I still had "it"? That no matter what, women still found me attractive enough to want to sleep with me? Did I do things, whether intentionally or unintentionally, so I could possibly damage or sabotage what I had just so I could absolve myself of any guilt? Did I not think I was good enough to deserve true love? Or was I just a selfish, inconsiderate fuckwit? I suspect the last two reasons overlapped and much closer to the mark.

What really churned inside though, the longer I continued this journey, was that deep down, I knew I'd make a great dad!

Only when the car slowed and eventually pulled off the road, did that thought drift away for another time. Pedro indicated he needed to get gas by pointing to the fuel gauge, which was almost on empty. According to the dashboard clock, we'd been driving for about three hours. I'd forgotten just how big Texas was, which was still dwarfed by two of

Australia's biggest states. At least here in the U.S, they had small towns that gave you something to look at. In Western Australia, you had nothing but desert, desert, and more desert.

While I was thankful to see a new town appear up out of the horizon every so often, I wasn't enjoying the long drive. It was a combination of my thoughts and conclusions, but also because whenever I am not behind the wheel driving, I always found it hard to focus or let my mind relax enough to enjoy the scenery. I either became bored and listless or my thoughts would drift to a place where they would wander down some deep, dark path. One that would torment me, which is exactly what they were now currently doing.

As Pedro filled up the tank, I realised maybe I was being too hard on myself. I distracted myself by pondering whether I should offer him the $6.25 I had to contribute to the drive, even though it was a pitiful contribution considering he was driving almost the entire way across the state. But then I hadn't asked him to take me this far, I just lucked out when he picked me up. I then wondered why he was driving across state. Other than the decrepit cabin, he didn't have anything in the back of the pick-up besides a toolbox, some blankets, and a tarpaulin.

When he got back inside the cab, rather than hand over the last of my money, I offer him the choice between a meatloaf and sun-dried tomato sandwich or a tuna salad. He gave me that appreciative, tooth gapped grin of his, before snaffling the meatloaf option from my hands and began to devour it.

We keep up the drive in silence, where even the radio had long been switched off after several gaps of bad reception. As the distance between each small town increases, other than a lot of dry, dusty paddocks and farms, where the places feel like they are operating within an inch of their life expectancy, there really is bugger all to see. It feels like there is this never-ending cloud of doom that lingers overhead, ready to swallow and take back the state of Texas at any time. There are so many foreclosure signs nailed to fences, along with a lot of trucks, tractors and other heavy machinery, all for sale on the side of the road.

Once considered the wild west of the United States, large swathes of Texas now feel like ghost towns ready to crumble in on themselves. The setting matches my mood... or maybe my mood matches the setting. I find myself sinking into self analysing and loathing what I discover. I now also wonder what the hell I am doing.

Why had I run away from my partner, a woman I loved and cared for, during the time of her greatest need, to hit the road to "sort myself out"? One bound for who knows where. What was I honestly hoping to achieve? Some father I turned out to be. I couldn't even stick around for a few more months to see my own child being born. Unforgivable!

The more I thought about it, the more I speculated whether I was of sound, stable mind. All this time, I felt like I was a decent person. I cared about people, her, friends. I was considerate, attentive, loyal and loving. I thought I was a good man. Maybe I'd just been fooling myself all this time. That it's all just a mirage, like the heat haze over the dry dusty roads I now find myself on. One where I stare into the distance yet never reach my destination... or anywhere for that matter.

I had not only moved across the country from a city I really loved, to a city I now loathed, but into a different country. From a warm, relaxed, fun place to a cold, dull and fickle one. Surely, that proves I was serious about this relationship. That I wanted the one thing I'd never really achieved in all my years of hoping, searching–despite the endless string of re-lationships I'd had–that of a deep, all-in kind of love. A nev-er-ending happiness for the rest of my life with a partner I not only cared for, adored, admired, cherished and loved with ev-erything I had in me, but one where we both could open up, be truly raw, vulnerable, and always be able to express and communicate. And never being short of stimulating conver-sation, yet also enjoying those comfortable silences that those deep in love seem to have.

One that was full of passion and desire and could not only light the world on fire... or at least ours, but one that would sustain us for the rest of our lives.

In truth, that was the only thing I had ever wanted.

I felt like I had gotten close once or twice, but through one reason or another, or my waning interest and indiscretions, they all crashed and burned and fell over, like almost every-thing I had ever put my hand or mind to. Something of a common theme, the more I reflected. Something has to give.

Yet I have hope after Clea wrote, 'I Miss You'.

I can't keep running away from my demons or fighting them, hoping to slay them for good, or pretending I was hunky dory when I wasn't. I had to face up to my own harsh truths and confront my reality. As the thoughts keep coming and my mind goes darker, I know I am about to come face to face with something greater. I've been pulled in so many directions over the years, where I chased the next shiny thing that captured my attention only to end up down yet anoth-er dead end. Or where I have been stretched beyond break-ing point, where I can no longer bounce back to what I was. Though in actuality, all roads have led me to this exact point.

I wonder if I am on the verge of a severe nervous breakdown or if I am about to sink into a deep, manic depression... one that I'll never be able to climb out of. Maybe it's worse, maybe it's insanity because it sure doesn't feel like a breakthrough.

So many thoughts swirl around my head that I can barely latch onto one long enough to think straight. Everything I thought I had ever wanted is right there in front of me, even gifting me the very thing I thought had escaped me as I'd gotten older–a baby. Yet I am unable to clasp onto what I have, grip tight and hold it close. Instead, I ran towards something from the past, which although it had once contained a heightened mental and physical pairing, now feels more like a disingenuous friendship given I've not heard from her in almost 12 months, despite me being the one to constantly reach out.

I knew I was heading back down that tired, well-worn path I'd been so many times before. Not appreciating what I was in and sabotaging it for what I thought would be fun, and above all else, freedom. In actual fact, it was the opposite. Always feeling shackled but wanting to break free and delve into something much deeper than just heightened sex.

Why? WHY? My head screams.

I look at the analog dashboard clock click over to 6:13pm. It's getting dark. I feel like we've been on this road forever, while it feels like I've been on my endless road for far longer. Though Pedro does his best to focus on the road ahead, his eyes look weary. I should suggest taking over, give him a break but I've no idea where he's headed. Perhaps he's running away from all his problems too. At least he has a ready made home with him.

I volunteer to give him a rest from driving, however, he waves me away like I'm loco. I guess you don't get between a man and his pickup truck. But now I am curious what drives him on, what keeps him going when he's clearly tired.

"Where are you going, Pedro?"

"Familia," his reply.

There goes that theory. Instead of running away he's running to them, driving across the biggest state in the U.S to reach his family. Now that's dedication, I think to myself. Maybe his mother is sick and he has to hurry home.

"Mi hija esta embarazada. El bebé vendrá pronto," he says with a proud glint in his eye.

While my Spanish is patchy, and I'm not really sure what hija means, I understand enough to think he's saying, my daughter is pregnant. A baby is coming, and soon!

"Felicitaciones," I say, congratulating him, and I really mean it. I admire his dedication to reach them at any cost, though it casts a long shadow over my decision. He's driving more than twelve hours to be with his expectant daughter and see his grandchild, and I'm getting as far away as possible from my own child. I sit in silence, conflicted, desolate... thinking.

Pedro asks me if everything is okay. I say it is but we both know that's a lie.

"Teléfono?" Pedro mumbles.

"No, I'm okay. I've got no one to call," I express.

But he either misunderstands me or just dismisses my words, because when we near a tiny, indistinct town, which is long closed for the night, he begins to slow to a crawl. His eyes, however, are now alert and wide awake, desperate to find something as he frantically searches the small, single lane road scanning from side to side. Only when he finds what he's looking for do I fully understand what he's trying to do.

Again, I reiterate I am okay, I don't need to phone anyone but he ignores me. He pulls up out front of a disused service station, where a lone phone booth is lit by a single overheard light from the telegraph pole behind it. He hurriedly exits the car. I then realise it's not me but him, who wants the phone. He races toward it, picks up the receiver and starts dialing. Clearly something has him agitated.

I take advantage of the unforced stop to get out and stretch my legs. I walk away from both him and the car to give him some privacy, and to look for a spot to pee.

I find a semi-secluded spot away from earshot, at the side of the station's apron, next to what was the old shop front. From my vantage point, I am able to make out Pedro's anxious, hunched figure, the phone pressed into his ear. Save for the hushed tones of his voice, there's a deep, quiet silence that fills the night sky. It's so peaceful and calming. It's soon broken though, with the unmistakable, familiar yell of excited glee from Pedro.

"Es un niño!" he hollers. "Es un niño!"

He then proceeds to dance in the dirt, kicking up plumes of dust in the celebration. As I relieve myself, I burst into a smile, getting caught up in his enthusiasm. While I wished I had shared the same kind of exuberance and excitement that he now is, it never came. It *happened* rather than was planned, so I never really had time to bask in the joy. I'm not even sure there was any because we were either too busy arguing about what we should do or how best to plan for it, rather than actually revel in the joy of our unexpected news.

As I pee, I make out a long faded poster advertising food and drink specials, which is stuck to the inside of the station's shop windows. While I would kill for a coke and chocolate at the crazy price of $1, something else catches my eye, a simple, handwritten quote on a piece of paper discoloured by the sun:

"BEWARE OF DESTINATION ADDICTION..."

A preoccupation with the idea that happiness
is in the next place,
the next job,
...the next partner.
Until you give up the idea that happiness is somewhere else,
it will never be where you are."

~ UNKNOWN

Like an arrow through the heart, I stand rooted to the spot, transfixed. I read it again. Then reread it two more times until the words permeate my mind then penetrate deep into my soul. To say it has a profound and powerful impact on me would be an understatement. It rocks me to my core.

I look back at Pedro, just as animated as before while he carries on talking and wanting to know more details, oblivious to my own little magical moment.

When I'm done, I zip myself back up and stay a moment longer. I don't hear Pedro anymore, he seems to just be listening to the caller on the other end. All I hear now is stillness. It's perfect. I take one last look at the quote and soak in its message, touched by its significance before making my way back towards the car.

When I get back to the pick-up, rather than climb in, I wait until Pedro finishes his call. With one last 'hasta pronto', he hangs up the phone and heads my way, nothing but a big, wide, toothy grin across his overjoyed face. The next thing I know, he hurls his arms around me in a jubilant man hug. For a small Mexican man who's on the wrong side of 50, he sure is strong.

"¡Un niño! Es un niño," he exclaims again after he releases me and taps the bonnet of his car in jubilation. Pedro decides this is the perfect time to also relieve himself so he moves away from the light and trips and stumbles his way in the dark to do so.

I look at the phone in the hollow of the pale lamplight, and in an almost uncontrollable motion, I feel compelled to step up and make my own phone call. I'm conscious I am taking all the actions but the decision to do so seems deep rooted from far behind my own comprehension.

Even though it's only about 7pm here, it's late back up there, well past 10pm. But it doesn't stop me from picking up the receiver, holding it up to my ear to hear the dial tone, then on impulse, reaching into my pocket and grabbing the few coins I have. I slide them one after the after into the coin slot, I push each number with my fingers.

I wait for what feels like an eternity until the phone rings once, rings twice, three, then four times. I'm about to hang up when I hear a faint voice from the other end.

"Hola! You have called Clea," the soft, familiar, Spanish female voice says through voicemail.

Despite knowing the rest of the message by heart, when the phone beeps to record my own voice, it catches me off guard. For a moment I don't say anything. I'm not even sure what I can say. I take some deep breaths readying myself to say something when the loud shrill sound of a car horn rings out.

"Vámonos amigo," Pedro calls out from behind the windscreen before he toots the horn again with impatience.

It's enough to make me lose my nerve, so I hang up the phone fast. I stand there a moment frozen, before Pedro honks the horn again. I wait a few seconds more for the unused coins to drop but like my nerves, they've also become swallowed up.

Toot, the horn blares again. I turn away from the phone and walk slowly back to the car, and when I get back inside, Pedro can tell that I'm flat, almost distraught. He offers his hand up in apology, not realising the importance of my call. I do my best to smile and say it's okay, but he doesn't believe me. I don't believe me either.

He looks at me conflicted, wondering if he should go or stay to allow me more time to make the call again. I wave him on. I know he's keen to get home as soon as he can to see his newborn grandson, and I don't want to hold him up any longer. He gives me one last concerned glance before he reluctantly turns over the ignition, flicks on the headlights, and pulls out from the side of the road.

There's no doubt, however, that I'm affected with this gnawing feeling that I'd like to hear her voice. Mixed with Pedro's news, seeing his unbridled happiness while sitting in the cab with him, where every so often he lets out a small holler of delight, his mind on one thing and one thing only. But even his high soon gives way for reflection, aware there's still much distance to travel before he can see and hold his newborn grandson. I, too, go within to reflect where for the next hour we drive along in silence, nothing but the black darkness and a few glittering stars overhead for company.

With the lonely darkness that engulfs us, save for the odd headlights of an oncoming vehicle passing by the other way, there's nothing to look at. While I roll that quote over and over in my mind, contemplating everything it and my own journey represents, I begin to fidget. To distract myself, I flick on the AM car radio which crackles to life.

A light, somewhat familiar but yet unplaceable piano tinkles back out at me before a soft, delicate, almost quavering voice starts to warble. The song continues to build and build, and I do my best to recognise it but it's slow, it's faint, and I really have to attune my ears to listen in. It's not until the repeating chorus eventually kicks in over and over, some three minutes into what I now know, is an epic eight minute track, that I recall it.

Death Cab For Cutie's, eerily poignant love song, 'Transatlanticism'–an ode to long distance love if ever there was one–is a haunting, sublime track, where its lyrics are so evocative, they cut straight to my core as they ring out repeatedly in my ears again and again.

Its simple words continue to echo for over a minute as the song tempo increases to advocate its calling, then builds up further still and takes it to a whole other level, spurring, challenging, almost pleading with the lover to go to her. It's such a raw, heartfelt song. So powerful in its simplicity, that right now, combined with the quote and hearing her voice (if only in an audio message), it's all I can think about. It's obvious I'm shaken by the deep desire of needing to be so much closer than I am. I'm visibly affected.

When the song's finished, I turn the radio straight back off. I don't need any further accidental reminders of the heartache, the sorrow, and the torment, I now feel within myself. Unable to concentrate any longer, I allow my mind to fall into a hypnotic slumber, the motion of the car and the road's white lines dividing the middle, make my eyelids heavy.

When I wake some time later, I notice the distinctive glow of a town up ahead, its lights arcing up into the night sky. Only when we pass under a sign on an overpass which says, 'Welcome to El Paso', do I realise where we are.

El Paso is situated in the far western corner of Texas, and it stands on the Rio Grande River, otherwise known as Río Bravo del Norte in Mexico. Across the border, a border which now looms large, is Ciudad Juárez. Juárez is the largest city in the Mexican state of Chihuahua, though these days it's known more for being the "deadliest city in the world".

Pointing and smiling, it seems Pedro is about to go south and cross the border, where I assume his daughter and just born grandson reside somewhere on the other side. He quizzes me to see if I am continuing south, even offering me a place to stay but I know this is the end of the line for our drive together. I've now got a choice to make. Stay here in El Paso for the night and find somewhere to sleep, or I can keep hitching my way across states to go through New Mexico, Arizona, and even further onto Los Angeles, California.

Neither option is what I fancy anymore to be honest, not now, not at night on little to no sleep. And crossing the US/Mexican border earlier than I'd anticipated to fight my way through Juárez, a city notorious for crime with the two biggest drug cartels waging a daily war, is even less appealing. I need a moment to sit and plot my next move.

I wave Pedro goodbye, grateful for having come this far. Despite our language barrier, through his elation and dogged determination, he gave me more to think about than he'll ever know. He can barely contain his excitement when he gives me one last smile, and despite the dreaded border crossing, he's happy to join the long queue. How can he not be? An amazing bundle of joy awaits him on the other side.

I stand there and watch him join the congested traffic as it barely crawls along. I've no idea where I'm meant to go if I am to find my way to New Mexico. I'm tired, I can't think, I'm a mix of emotions… I'm so many bloody things.

As I stand alone on the side of the road, a concrete barrier for a seat, I recall the past few hours, the days, even weeks. From a seeming calling to beckon me, through to Pedro and his news, the unnerving assault, all the way back to the beginning of this journey, along with everything that's happened in between, everything has changed. I watch the cars creep along, while on the other side of the road divider, they speed away to freedom.

And that's all it takes to make my mind up. I place the book under my arm, clasp the paper lunch bag tight in my hand, and cross the road to the other side. I've no idea if I'll get a lift, not this close to such a dangerous border, but something inside urges me on.

To my surprise, a car pulls up a little ahead of me on the side of the road. It takes me a moment to register before the driver gives me a friendly toot. I trot up to the side of the car and wait for the driver's electric window to go down.

"Where ya headed," a voice hidden by the darkness inside the car's interior enquires.

"Canada!"

Before they can work out if I am serious or not, I jog to the other side and jump in. As we merge back into the traffic to head back in the direction I just came from, an old familiar tune starts up via the car's CD player. Without even asking, I lean forward and reach for the volume dial and turn it up just as David Bowie's commanding voice begins to resonate from his fiercely intense song, 'Heroes'.

I allow his inspiring, soul-stirring words, to wash over me and give me the endurance and belief I need, for what I know will be the long trek back towards home. I may not go on to become the world's greatest dad, nor be the best partner a woman could ever ask for, but I can be an idol to my own unborn child, and just maybe, a champion for Clea–and a hero for me.

As I settle in, for the first time since undertaking this epic journey, I cannot wait to reach my destination.

Epilogue

The post office bell clangs when I enter. I grab an appropriate padded envelope, slip out a small piece of crumpled brown paper from my pocket and write an address on the front. I turn it over, place a book inside before I pause. I look at a small photo of me and my newborn son and smile. I then slip the image into the envelope and write:

"A little something I think you both will appreciate. Thanks again for everything you did. It made all the difference. Please give Josie a rub under the chin from me.

Sincerely,
Raiden."

THE END

ACKNOWLEDGEMENTS

First in line, the crew and organisation at non-profit, NaNoW-riMo. While you've a terrible acronym, it was your National Novel Writing Month challenge, way back in November 2016, that is the reason for this book's existence in the first place. Write 50,000 words in a month. Sounds easy enough I thought. Ha! But little did I know that when I initially started, by month's end, I would indeed have over 50,000 words of a first draft for my very first adult fiction novel. Six years later, my book is now seeing the light of day. What a ride.

Starr and her stable of adept Quiethouse Editing beta-readers, who were among the first readers to read an early version, and whose thoughtful notes, gave me a greater overall clarity, thank you.

Cheers to former colleague, Sandra Rostirolla, for being open to read my little story on the long flight back to Australia from L.A., and then sharing your opinions not long after landing. Your blunt, no nonsense feedback, was both welcome and valuable.

To my last-minute proofreader, Lauran Doverspike, who ensured there were no typos, errors or silly mistakes. You went over and above to guarantee the best, cleanest, most correct version possible right before print. Muchas gracias, amiga.

My first unofficial editor, Juliette Powell. Your early notes were super beneficial and on point. I only wished you could have stayed through until the book's end. Nevertheless, merci madam T.I.

Huge thanks, firstly to my cover designer, Richard Ljoenes, for tracking down the stunning image I had long given up on finding. Your tireless dedication paid off handsomely mate, with a cover design that's not only receiving a tonne of love, but drawing people in. I couldn't ask for any more than that. Secondly, a big holler to my interior formatter, Mr. Stewart A. Williams. Your keen eye, expertise (and patience with last minute changes), are exactly what I needed. You turned my humble little manuscript into a beautiful looking book. Can't thank you enough, Stew. And thirdly, Noémi Zillmann, for your amazing ebook skills (you saved me so much time), but also for making those last minute changes before it launched. What a gem you are. Long may you shine!

To Fran Lebowitz, my official editor. Oh Fran, what can I say? You tore me a new one in the best way possible. Your honest, precise, cut-through-the-bullshit approach, made ALL the difference. You made me question some of my choices, to even getting me to ditch an entire chapter, but as an unequivocal result, my novel is far better for it. The mark of a truly great editor, is one who doesn't only suggest some edits here and there, but one who enhances your story and writing, elevating it above anything you could ever imagine. Fran, you did that in spades. A big hearted, thank you. You're also funny as fuck. Please keep sharing your hilarious stories.

Fellow bike-hasher and music nut, Mr. Norm Countryman, for resurrecting the story back to life for me. Mate, if not for your persistence, this book would have sat unread. Your insistence and pestering of me to want to read it after a couple of years where it did nothing more than collect digital dust, is the sole reason why this book is now out in the world. The speed in which you read it (and the high praise you gave), humbled me. Honestly mate, a million thank yous!

Finally, the incomparable, sublime and divine, Jennifer Juvenelle. The friend that became a best friend that became my wife. What a trip, aye? Your guidance, support, and unwavering belief in me, both in my writing and my life, have meant so much throughout my own journey. Your unconditional and infinite love, means more to me than anything in the entire universe. You are the most phenomenal woman I have ever known. You're everything! I love you... forever always.

ABOUT THE AUTHOR

MARK T. RASMUSSEN is an Australian author born by the sea, cultivated in the city, formed via the world. Previously a professional journalist and editor, Mark now writes evocative, thought provoking subject matter for his adult novels and screenplays, and fun, captivating, thoughtful books for children. An avid adventurer, he currently lives in a remote Mexican seaside-jungle village with his beautiful & brilliant, author wife, and youngest son, finding it an idyllic piece of paradise to read, write, and love.

(photo by Jennifer Juvenelle)

For more info visit:
WWW.MARKTRASMUSSEN.COM

YOUR VOICE MATTERS!

With book buying happening more and more online, leaving a review and a star rating, is not only one of the best ways to help an indie author you like be discovered, but it also assists other readers in finding books and stories that they can also enjoy.

Sincere reviews help other readers find the right book for their needs, too. So did this book satisfy or delight you in some way? If so, then let others know all about it.

I truly welcome and value your genuine feedback and would greatly appreciate it if you could take a couple of a minutes to leave a review on Amazon, Goodreads, Barnes & Noble, or on your favourite book review platform. Your review is your own, and it can be short, medium, or long! What matters the most is your honest opinion.

LIKE. SHARE. FOLLOW.

Promoting a book you liked across your social media platforms eg: Facebook, Twitter, Linkedin, Instagram, etc, can be a great and helpful experience for everyone. You can aid friends, family, colleagues, and other indie writers & authors, to discover it. If you liked this book, then feel free to promote it across your social media to help spread the word. Lastly, if you enjoyed this book, then subscribe on my website to hear the latest news and updates on new or upcoming books, or follow me via the links below. Thank You!

Sincerely,

Mark T. Rasmussen

ps: Keep reading for a special bonus preview of my latest book, *The Last.*

WEBSITE
www.MarkTRasmussen.com

AMAZON:
www.amazon.com/Mark-T-Rasmussen/e/B0B95QPLTZ/

GOODREADS
www.goodreads.com/user/show/145123343-mark-t-rasmussen

LINKEDIN
www.linkedin.com/in/marktrasmussen/

THE MUSIC

Below is *The Journey's* full, 22-song playlist from within the book. This playlist is also available to listen to on Spotify (see link below):

1. Memory Gospel, by Moby
2. Grain Of Sand, by Oliver Tank
3. Jealous Guy, by Roxy Music
4. Kickstart My Heart, by Mötley Crüe
5. Hold On To Me, by Mondo Cozmo
6. 2 Cent Girl, by The Whiskey Go Gos
7. Last Goodbye, by Jeff Buckley
8. My Love, by Until The Ribbon Breaks
9. The Beast, by Jóhann Jóhannsson
10. River, by Leon Bridges
11. Mystery Train, by Elvis Presley
12. Always On My Mind, by Elvis Presley
13. Lost In The Light, by Bahamas
14. Chanson d'Amour, by The Manhattan Transfer
15. Couldn't Care Less, by The Cardigans
16. Under The Pressure, by The War On Drugs
17. I Don't Want To Talk, by Rod Stewart
18. Wish You Were Here, by Pink Floyd
19. Getting Away With It (All Messed Up), by James
20. De Usuahia A La Quiaca, by Gustavo Santaolalla
21. Transatlanticism, by Death Cab For Cutie
22. Heroes, by David Bowie

THE JOURNEY PLAYLIST (on Spotify):
https://open.spotify.com/
playlist/4OiA1V7r0G3pqZYhvsWeCi

THE LAST*
(Preview)

*The Last is the newest adult fiction novel by
Mark T. Rasmussen, due late 2023/early 2024

Chapter 1

A lone, rare drop of water hangs poised ready to separate
from a long dried vein. Its path now nothing more than a
dusty, dark rust stain, as if etching its final resting place for
all eternity. The droplet lingers a moment as it clings to the
musty cave roof in a desperate bid to stay attached. In its
translucent reflection, a distorted, indistinguishable hand
waits underneath it in a supine, open position.

Gravity's pull is irrefragable, its desire too immense, and
the pear-shaped, aqueous liquid is surrendered helpless.
Defeated, it releases its last tenuous hold to face its destiny.
In a slow motion fall, the last drop of water floats downward
into a cupped, gnarled hand.

The withered hand is not that of a human. More elongat-
ed in appearance, with only three fingers and a longer than
usual thumb, that are mercury grey to speckled chalk white
in colour. Out of focus, a head leans closer to study the water
that now rests in its upturned, desiccated palm. The image

reflecting back on the droplet reveals a larger than normal head, and two big, opaque cold eyes that stare solemnly back at it in wonder.

A tiny, solitary tear slips out from the corner of one eye before a sedate, dehydrated tongue extends out and laps the water away to its finality.

In the muted darkness, the figure rises sluggishly to its feet. It's only now, once upright, that the size of this sentient creature is evident. While rangy and malnourished, it's a good 7ft tall.

A red dawn begins to seep through the darkness. The dreary light breaking through reveals another giant figure by the being's feet, albeit more petite in size. Draped in a tattered and filthy red dust covered shroud, they're long dead. Nothing but skeletal remains are all that exist now.

The extraterrestrial form looks downward at his inamorata with a pensive sadness. A moment of private reflection, which gives way to resignation. It then bends down, places a thoughtful hand upon the dead figure's forehead and savours one last, enduring moment.

He moves away from the recumbent body, forever stilled and tilts his head up to the cave roof. He studies a hand drawn map etched into the russet rock face. The rudimentary map shows constellations, two planets, a rock like object, and a single white line, which streaks across the top.

Its long, slender hand rises up to the cave roof where it pauses uneasy over the sketch. A myriad of thoughts swirl in around the being's considered mind before resting on its final, difficult decision. The hand draws down and over the cave surface and with one agonising stroke, smudges the image from its mind. Tiny red and white dust particles drift through the air.

The figure gathers a small textile sack and strides for the cave entrance. When it nears the opening, it stops, pivots its head back inwards toward the cave and the lone figure that is forever inhumed inside. It lets out a strangled yowl of anguish.

Affected, it takes a moment to recompose. Without looking back, he ducks his head to exit the cave and looks up into the tenebrous early morning sky above, where the gloomy red dawn has not yet fully broken.

A comet or asteroid can be seen blazing a trail across it some distance away. The line from the cave map? Taking one last deep breath, the being crouches down, waits.

As the rock mass scorches across the inky black firmament directly above, the Martian springs up and out of sight, as red dust sprays outward in a plume of rocket launch mania.

The dust soon settles but the figure has long vanished, swallowed up by the stellar empyrean high above.

Visit

WWW.MARKTRASMUSSEN.COM

for more information, news & updates.

Manufactured by Amazon.ca
Bolton, ON

34799669R00157